Sweet Solace

The Seattle Sound Series
Book 1

Alexa Padgett

This is a work of fiction. Names, characters, places and incidents are the product of the author's imagination or are used fictitiously. Any resemblance to persons, living or dead, business establishments, events or locales is entirely coincidental.

The opinions expressed in this manuscript are solely the opinions of thoughts of the publisher. The author has represented and warranted full ownership and/or legal right to publish all the material in this book.

ISBN-13: 978-1945090097

Edited by Nancy Cassidy and Nicole Pomeroy
Cover Art by Sarah Hansen of Okay Creations

To Jeffe. You know all the reasons.

CHAPTER ONE
Dahlia

My wineglass slid down my stiff fingers, dropping the last few inches to the scarred wooden table. No way. Peeking up from under my lashes, I drew a shaky breath. I'd wanted to listen to Simon play music, lose myself in a melody. I hadn't planned on reliving this much of my past.

And I really wasn't prepared to deal with Tristan Asher Smith.

My cheeks flamed as I slammed my mouth shut, hoping he hadn't noticed me still acting like the lovesick girl I'd been all those years ago. His brown hair was longer than I remembered. Even from my vantage point across the bar, I could make out the cleft in his chin. Each time I'd seen his picture—or better, him in person—I wanted to lick that spot. I'd never had the chance.

Asher slid his aviators from his nose as the sunset shone through the glass doors behind him, hazing him in a soft glow like those old saint paintings.

Ignoring my trembling fingers, I raised my glass and filled my mouth with a large gulp of wine. I wished the tart taste could wash away my past that was hell-bent on catching up with me. It didn't, but the bouquet bloomed in my mouth, and I closed my eyes, enjoying the sensation as the liquid slid down my throat.

"Mind sharing?"

I opened my eyes and looked into Asher's smiling face. Up close, he was even more striking. His long brown lashes shielded his hazel eyes, but his lips quirked in typical Asher fashion. I shouldn't know what that was—I barely knew him, really.

"My wine?" I asked, confused. "Isn't that a little forward? Even

1

for you?"

He grinned, showing straight, white teeth. "If you want to. But I meant the table. There aren't any other seats open."

"Oh. Sure. Good to see you, Asher."

"You, too, Dahlia. It's been a long time."

I waited until he sat before I asked, "You here to listen or is this a special top-secret performance?"

"Just to listen."

We shared a love of music. It had been my refuge for years. When Dad died, I played his old records, pretending they were his last hug. As Doug learned to play on that first, battered guitar, I'd sit, rapt for hours, feeling the vibration of the strings, daydreaming about our future together.

Much as I wanted to quit listening to music after Doug died, I hadn't been able to. It was too much a part of me, a reminder of better days.

"I've heard good things about this guy," Asher said.

"Simon will be thrilled you've heard of him."

A waitress walked up and looked at Asher, her expression expectant but without a flare of recognition. His shoulders relaxed as he placed his forearms on the table. The sleeves of his dark button-down were rolled up, showing off his tanned skin. Light brown hairs glinted where they caught the light.

"Pike IPA on tap, if you have it."

The girl nodded and headed back to the bar.

"You know Simon?" he asked. His gaze sharpened. "Oh. Dorsey. Related to Doug?"

I nodded.

"I should've known."

I'd raised my glass to my lips for another gulp of liquid courage, so I shrugged. He waited for a real response. My heart pounded in my chest as if I'd danced the Samba. Silly as it was, the anxiety suffocated me.

Just a conversation. I had them every day with other people. I was fine. This was fine.

No, nothing about the situation was fine. Why did I have to run into Asher tonight? I cleared my throat. "Yeah. Simon's my brother-in-law. I'm here for moral support."

The song ended, and I clapped, adding a loud "woo-woo!" Simon glanced over and raised his beer. His eyes narrowed when he saw Asher sitting with me, but I waved back, smiling.

Simon got the message. I'd known my brother-in-law since he was a gawky thirteen-year-old; he wasn't going to do something to piss me off when I had photographic proof of his late-90s hairstyles.

"You stayed involved in the music scene?" Asher asked, surprised. "I haven't seen you around." He'd leaned forward a little so I could hear him over the growing noise of the crowd.

"Not really. Doug quit playing about ten years ago."

Again his gaze sharpened. "I heard about that."

Asher sat back, letting the waitress set a napkin and his pint glass in front of him. He chewed on his lip. Would he get up and walk away?

"Where is Doug tonight?"

"Dead." At Asher's look, I continued, "It's okay." Abbi's stricken face flashed through my mind, and I struggled to maintain a reasonable tone. "He passed away almost three years ago."

I took another big sip of my wine. At least the panic had receded. I wasn't sure if it was because I was comfortable with Asher or because of the wine I'd already consumed.

"This is the problem with touring so much." Asher ran his fingers through his hair, causing it to flop against his brow. "I hadn't heard."

I turned my face toward Simon, who had just started the song he'd written with Doug for our wedding. We would have been married fifteen years in February. I tipped my glass and polished off the wine.

Asher shifted, as though he was getting ready to stand. I turned to look back at him, trying to banish the melancholy that lingered so often these days.

"Don't leave. Please. It's good to see you. Really." I smiled. "If I'd known you'd be here, I would've worn my groupie shirt. I'm proud to say mine is from the first round of shirts you ever had made. From Cactus Arrow. It's pretty tattered, but I like to wear it when I read."

"You seriously have a shirt from that band? We were together for all of two months." He shook his head. "Who came up with that name anyway?"

I laughed. "You did."

He smiled and turned his attention back to the stage, his eyes intent on Simon's fingers sliding up and down the guitar frets. He clapped when Simon finished the song.

"I can see why people are talking about him. Beautiful melody."

"Thanks," I said.

Asher's gaze slid back to mine.

"I'm taking credit for that one," I announced. "Simon wrote it for my wedding. It's the oldest in his repertoire. He doesn't play it often anymore. He asked if I'd like to hear it tonight."

"You two are close."

"Closer since Doug's death. Before that, we were all leading our own lives."

Simon slid into one of his newer, bluesier tunes. I tapped my foot and rolled my empty wineglass between my hands, shocked to realize the alcohol had bubbled into my head.

Hmm, it'd been a long time since I was buzzed. I'd missed this feeling. I'd also missed talking to an attractive man.

Asher had left Cactus Arrow within a few weeks of creating the band. Doug had never forgiven him for walking off the stage with his guitar in its case right after he sang the most beautiful song I'd ever heard. Chills rippled across my skin as I thought of how Asher had looked at me that night as he stood on the stage.

I'd willed him to look again, before he walked out of the venue. He didn't. And... that had been a long, long time ago.

———◆———

Asher clapped when Simon took his final bow nearly an hour later. I tapped the stem of my second glass of wine. The lights stayed dim, but female heads turned in our direction, the murmur of Asher's appearance making the rounds.

"You're going to be inundated now that they've figured out who you are."

Asher rolled his eyes. He slammed back the last of his beer. I clasped my hand over his where it gripped the glass, surprising us both. I'd never been pushy or forward, preferring to let the situation come to me. I dropped my hand from his warm skin.

"I'll play the knight-errant if you want me to," I said.

His mouth turned down. "It's been a shitty week. I'm done

with people."

A little grimace twisted my lips. "Okay. Well, good to see you."

His eyes widened. "You're not leaving me. You said you'd help me out."

"I thought—"

"You still like to walk on the beach?"

I turned back. "I do." I tried to keep my voice neutral, but I probably failed, because Asher smirked.

"Let's go."

"You don't want to listen to the rest of the bands?" I asked.

"Simon was the only one I came to hear."

I pulled out two twenties and laid them on the table.

"Thanks for buying my drink," Asher said.

"Thanks for sitting at my table. If you want, I'll introduce you to Simon. He'd like to meet you."

"You sure? I don't want to impose." We both knew Doug had made some terrible comments about him when Asher left the band. He glanced around, his eyes darting too fast to catch anyone's. Asher probably assumed Simon wasn't his biggest fan.

"You're not." I hefted my bag onto my shoulder, took Asher's hand, and led the way to Simon.

I wended my way through the tables, passing by a cute blonde two tables over. Had I ever been that young? My daughter Abigail was nearly the same age as the girls here tonight. I wasn't ready for her to move away to college.

I had to swallow down the panic. Abbi was smart and capable. She'd proven that by taking on a counselor role on a trip with her aunt this week.

Simon finished buckling his guitar case, concern seeping into his eyes.

"Great job tonight," I said. "Thanks for playing my song."

I embraced my brother-in-law, needing a second to compose my emotions. Simon rubbed his hand up and down my back like he'd done each time he hugged me for nearly ten years, ever since Doug started showing symptoms. I pulled back and cleared my throat.

"This is Asher Smith. He sat with me for part of your set."

Simon held out his hand, which Asher shook, but I caught the look Simon shot me from the corner of his eye. "Wow. Great to meet you. Lia gave me one of your albums when I was in high school. It's amazing." Simon always used my nickname, just like Doug had.

"Thanks. Always good to hear you appreciate the music. Makes it worth doing."

Simon still had his other arm wrapped around my waist, an annoyingly protective gesture. Because of my dad's stiff formality, I'd never been much for public affection. Except with Abbi.

I sidled away, pointing up toward the speakers. "Too loud," I yelled as the next band started tuning their guitars.

"I'm planning to catch the next act," Simon said as he moved toward the back of the club. "Sit with me."

I frowned. "I'm good. I think Asher and I are going for a walk."

The cute blonde I noticed earlier intercepted Asher as soon as Simon pulled me away. She clutched his arm. He smiled and nodded, but he shot me a look under his long bangs, his eyes begging me to save him. He took the pen from the blonde's other hand and autographed the napkin she held out.

Four more people—three men and a woman, all in their late twenties—gathered around him. The woman was gorgeous, and Asher had a reputation as a lady's man. One he'd built over the years after leaving Cactus Arrow. Much as I'd hated hearing about his exploits, I read about them all. Every single one.

Unlike Asher, Simon didn't like dealing with the fans much. He knew it was part of the performer job, but he was in love with Ella. In. Love. The kind of love I used to write about.

The kind I thought I had with Doug back when I was young and naive. I locked that door, refusing to let the melancholy overcome my burgeoning good mood. Doug and I had made our choices. I had to live with the results.

"He's married, Lia," Simon scolded me, while Asher was occupied with his fans.

I turned back to Simon. "I'm not interested in an affair. Especially a sordid one with a famous married man. Key words there are 'married' and 'sordid.' In that order."

I tossed my long auburn hair over my shoulder. The weight slid across my back, the ends nearly to my waist. Just one more piece of myself I hadn't maintained. I wasn't willing to go to the effort of being social even with my hairdresser.

Abbi was right. I'd been hiding. Not just from other people but also from my own needs.

"Doug didn't like him, Lia. He was wild, and he writes about his affairs. Each album is chockfull of them. Even after he married." Simon scowled at the growing crowd swarming around Asher, whose face was now as blank as his eyes.

"Maybe like you and me, he writes what his audience wants to hear, not necessarily what's true. And Doug was jealous."

Asher wasn't enjoying the attention lavished on him, especially by the young women. Good. That meant he'd be happy when I rescued him in a few minutes.

"I'm not looking for anything romantic." I turned back to Simon. "And I'm not into casual. You know that."

Simon settled into a chair at the table I'd recently vacated. He tugged my wrist so that I was seated next to him, our knees touching.

"He'll turn your relationship into a song when he leaves you."

"I don't plan to be anyone's muse, Simon."

"It's been almost three years. You'll want to go out again sometime."

"Not yet. I need to focus on Abbi. She's my priority."

"And Ella and I applaud you for that," Simon said, his voice careful. "But I want you to be happy. If that means finding someone…"

"What brought this on?" I asked.

"I want you to be safe. Asher Smith isn't safe. He's a time bomb waiting to explode all across your life. Don't get me wrong. Meeting him is cool. I was always so mad Doug played with him for a while, and I didn't get an intro."

I smiled at Simon. "No need to worry. We're old friends."

Simon's brown eyes were shadowed with worry. "He'll hurt you, Lia. We're just starting to see you emerge from wherever you've been hiding. Ella pointed out you've smiled on this trip. We haven't seen you smile in years."

I patted his hand. "I'm completely safe from doing anything that might come close to be called living."

"That's what worries me. What's going to happen when you pop the grief bubble?"

I'd have to finish mourning the life I'd lost. I'd known those last years together would be hard, but I'd chosen to stay. While

Huntington's was a slow and painful descent, my relationship with Doug suffered many little deaths, some more painful than others.

Simon rubbed his hand over the fashionable jet-black stubble bristling his chin. He looked good in scruff. Doug's beard had been patchy at best, making him look like a guy with a bad case of mange.

I'd always wanted to run my hand over a man's cheek, feel the short, silky hairs prickle my fingers, or better, my breasts or the sensitive skin of my stomach.

Huh. Must be the wine. Or maybe Simon's continued push to talk about Asher. He looked good in scruff. Really good.

"Just… be careful."

"I always am," I quipped. I searched his eyes. "Are you okay? Doug's death hit us all hard."

"Yeah. Ella and I, Jeremiah, we've gotten our feet under us from Doug's death. It's you we're worried about."

I pushed down the sadness. I never would've chosen to become a widow at thirty-two. Half my friends hadn't even married at that age, and I'd already lost my lover. "Thanks. You know I appreciate you looking out for me."

Simon swallowed hard, his eyes brightened by a sheen of tears. "We've been family a long time."

"We have," I said. If he cried, I wasn't sure I'd be able to keep my own emotions in check. "So give me a little space now, please. This may be stupid, but I want to talk to Asher. We used to be friends. Good friends. I'd like the chance to reconnect."

Simon tugged at his lower lip. "That's what upset Doug. Your friendship with Asher. It worries me now."

Asher glanced over, fatigue pulling at his mouth and eyes.

"I'll keep that in mind." I touched Simon's shoulder. "See you in a bit."

Making my way back to Asher's side, I grabbed his left hand, planning to pull him forward. He threaded my fingers through his, and the contact, palm to palm, stole my breath. I couldn't remember the last time I'd held Doug's hand.

The bubble of grief Simon had just mentioned cracked, and something thick and ugly seeped through my chest. I loosened my fingers. I needed to go home and go to bed.

I needed to quit feeling. This was too much, too soon. I wasn't ready.

Asher gripped my hand more firmly. My breathing turned raspy. This was bad. Really bad. He must have felt my shiver because he let go of my hand and wrapped his arm around my shoulder, supporting most of my weight when I staggered against him. Instead of relief at the fresh air, black dots formed in front of my eyes.

"This was a bad idea. I-I should go," I said. My voice was hoarse as tension crawled up my throat. I was about two seconds from a full-blown panic attack.

"We're taking that walk. You look like you need a distraction from whatever you're thinking about, and there's no way I'm going back in there with those fans. They're rabid. C'mon."

His arm still slung over my shoulder, I stumbled along next to him as he towed me down the block. I tried to force down the weight in my throat. I couldn't take a full breath, not with his arm around my shoulder. My heart battered my ribs so hard tears welled up in my eyes.

"Can't," I whispered, yanking away from him. "I'm sorry."

"Dahlia, don't you dare run from me. It's almost ten, and this is not the nicest part of town."

"Panic attack," I said, my voice hoarse. "Don't want you to see this." I turned, trying to dash toward my car.

Asher cursed, but then his long fingers wrapped around my forearm. He spun me around. He must have dipped his knees because my nose was pressed into the side of his neck, his strong arms banding around me. His touch, the caring in it, unleashed the monster I'd tried so hard to chain.

He lifted my feet from the ground and stepped backward toward what I assumed was an alley. My vision tunneled, and I really didn't care. I struggled to get air into my lungs.

I gasped, shook, and mewled as embarrassment mingled with the panic. I'd gotten better at recognizing the signs, managing to get away from others before I melted down. Not this time.

He held my head, his voice soothing. The worst of the pain passed quickly, and I trembled with relief as tears leaked from the corners of my eyes. I willed them to stop, and I tried to pull back. Asher tightened his grip just enough to keep me tucked against his large, warm body, his arm settled low on my waist. His free hand smoothed down my hair.

He spoke to me in a low voice. Soft words, like I used to say to Abbi when she had a nightmare. His fingers continued to comb through my hair. This time, I relaxed completely, basking in his warmth. This almost-stranger was more than I could handle, yet somehow exactly what I needed. The universe was so clever with its sense of humor.

He smelled good, like summer rain.

When my brain keyed in enough to hear what he was telling me, I calmed further, resting against the solid wall of his chest. My cheek was wet from tears, and sweat bloomed across our skin wherever our bodies touched.

"I remember the first time I saw you. I looked out into the crowd gathered in that garage where they held the tryouts for Cactus Arrow and saw this long, dark hair and the biggest, brightest gray eyes. I remember thinking how happy you were, how in the moment. I looked for you every day after that. I loved seeing the joy on your face. I loved talking to you."

"I'm sorry about that," I whispered.

"Panicking? Better than being puked on. That's happened a couple of times."

"You handled it well," I said.

His eyes darkened. "My mom had panic attacks. They got worse after my father left. A lot worse. She'd try to hide them." He raised his brows, a silent question.

"Some event usually triggers them," I said. "At least that's what I've read."

"Doug's death?" he asked, his voice still soft.

I hesitated, debating. "My dad's, when I was fourteen. They got better for a while. Then Doug was diagnosed." I pressed my cheek against the hardness of his shoulder. "With Huntington's disease." I stepped out of his arms.

"I don't know what that is."

"A death sentence," I whispered. Much as I didn't want to, I forced my gaze to his. "I'm sorry. For all of this."

"It's better than being covered in vomit." He smiled.

I grinned. It was wobbly, but it was real. Damn, that felt good.

I scrubbed the heels of my hands over my eyes. I was glad I hadn't bothered with mascara. At least I didn't have black dripping down my red, blotchy cheeks. "No one else knows about my, er…

episodes. Thank you for talking me through it. That helped. A lot, actually."

Asher chuckled. "Jessica would be shocked you're thanking me. More that I actually helped you out. She says I'm selfish, always focused on me. But even an egotistical ass like me understands shitty things happen to good people."

I closed my eyes and leaned my head back against the wall. I was probably getting grime in my hair, but I was too tired to care. "Seriously, I'm sorry. I don't normally freak out in public. That's more of a good-times-at-home experience."

"Something you save for Saturday night kicks?"

The smile tugged at my lips. "No. I'm not much of a crier. Maybe that's the problem."

"That was intense. Do you normally have any warning?"

"I'm fine."

"I'm not dropping this yet, Dahlia." His voice was stern but there was an undercurrent there. One I didn't quite understand. "Do you know what brought it on? You should avoid your triggers. That worked for my mom. Most of the time."

I snorted. "I avoid life." The silence built. I met his patient gaze. "I liked holding your hand." I swallowed. "A lot." I shrugged, trying to cover my embarrassment. "Feel free to go back to the next band. I can hear the music. Seems pretty good."

I closed my eyes again and waited for him to walk away from me. It was inevitable.

"If you're feeling well enough, let's walk. My mom said endorphins solve just about anything."

I opened one of my eyes. "Your mom sounds smart. But I don't want you to feel obligated. You could be having fun. I'm so not a good time. I just proved that."

"Fun gets me into trouble. And my mom was smart, I miss her."

"When did she die?" I asked, my voice soft.

"A few years ago."

"My dad died in a peace-keeping mission in Eastern Europe. It was terrible."

"You've had your share of shitty, too. The panic attack is nothing to be embarrassed about." He tucked my hair behind my ear, his hand lingering for a moment before dropping to his side. "You didn't do anything wrong, and I wouldn't be here if I didn't want to be."

"You could be inside the bar, talking licks and chords with Simon."

"Nah, I'm all about introspection these days. Walk with me, Dahlia. Please."

A thrill shot through my chest at the sound of my name, not just my nickname, coming from Tristan Asher Smith's mouth.

Maybe we shouldn't have reconnected. If he'd picked a different seat, a different bar, we wouldn't be having this conversation now.

But if I'd learned anything since Doug's death, it was to be thankful for the moments you were given. To treasure them because they were fleeting. This moment with Asher was a mere passing-in-the-night.

That made the entire situation even more intoxicating.

He'd been my favorite lyricist ever since I heard him sing in a dingy garage not far from Doug's apartment. The band was short-lived, but I was hooked. When his first Supernaturals album came out, I'd scraped together my change to buy a copy. And for the next week, I sat close to the speakers whenever Doug was out, listening over and over to Asher's rough, sexy voice sing about depression, drugs, and unsatisfying sexual encounters.

As I matured, I'd realized he was singing about universal tropes most people identified with, at least at some point in their lives. He seemed as sad as I was, but he was still willing to express compassion.

He slid his hand against mine, lacing our fingers together. "I like touching you. This okay?" he asked.

"Yes. Really good. Especially now that I've realized how much I've missed it. Thanks."

That clasp, our hands the only thing that touched, was intimate. I couldn't let go.

CHAPTER TWO
Asher

We drove in separate cars up Seaview to Golden Gardens Park. From the parking lot, we meandered down the path bordering the water, away from the marina and its dark, hulking sailboats. The air was cooler here next to the sound, and Dahlia stopped to shrug into a long cardigan. She wrapped her arms around her narrow waist. She wasn't relaxed with me now like she'd been in the bar.

I shortened my strides to match hers, occasionally grabbing her elbow to help her avoid a depression in the sidewalk or a rowdy bunch of weekend partiers carrying coolers of beer toward a bonfire. Dahlia's conversation was sporadic. She'd drawn inward, focused on something I couldn't see. Maybe it hadn't been a good idea to push her to go on a walk.

The alternative was to let her go home and mourn the life she wouldn't get back. I didn't want her to do that, much like I couldn't face being alone with my thoughts.

"Why does fun get you into trouble?" she asked.

Her voice surprised me out of my own introspection, and I stumbled. "Fun means getting piss-faced drunk, maybe using something harder," I responded. Honesty might scare her away, but she seemed to think I was a better man than I'd ever tried to be. "Altered states of mind do not make the best decisions. And the situation with Jessica… I need to do better. No more broken bones or bad media events."

She looked at the horizon, her eyes glowing with a warm, soft light. Like moonlight on the water.

"Want to walk on the beach?" I asked.

"Sure. I won't see it again for a while so might as well enjoy my last night here."

I tried to ignore the soft line of Dahlia's hip when she leaned against me to take off her brown, heeled boots and socks. I smiled at the paisley pattern.

I slid off my shoes and grabbed them both in my left hand. I didn't like sand much, but tonight I enjoyed the coolness as it caressed my feet.

"You don't live in Seattle anymore?" I asked.

"Nope, so no awkward run-ins after tonight," she said, still smiling. "We're heading back to Idaho. It's a little town out in the middle of nowhere, but I guess that's not saying much because the whole state's sparsely populated."

"Do you miss it?"

"I enjoy the city. I used to love it, but now I find I can only deal with it in small doses."

Her panic attacks must be harder to control here, probably because she was surrounded by so much movement and the smell of other people's anxiety and needs.

"You said you're visiting Simon and his family."

"I've made a point to get Abbi together with Doug's family every few months. It's just Simon, his wife and son now. Abbi doesn't have much in the way of family."

"Abbi?"

"My daughter. She's sixteen."

I had no idea Dahlia had a kid. When my eyes met hers, she looked so small and lost. I slid my palm against hers again, offering what comfort I could. She jumped at the contact, making me gently grip her fingers tighter as I led her toward the water.

"You're going to spoil me with all this hand-holding," she murmured.

"I hadn't thought about it before," I said, shooting for nonchalance. I'd noticed how much she liked the contact, how it calmed her. "What specifically do you like about it?"

"This is silly, I know, but the connection. The fact that someone else cares enough to want to touch me for so long."

I looked down at our joined hands and rubbed my thumb across her knuckles. So many words lodged in my throat. "I'm sorry."

"For what?"

"You're still heartbroken."

She smiled a little, but it didn't reach her eyes. "Not like you think. I have Abbi. She's a great kid."

"You think it would've lasted?" I asked, looking out at the water. The waves lapped in a steady rhythm. I loved the sound, the constancy of it.

"Is this about your relationship, or mine?"

Perceptive. I wondered if she was a psychologist. No. Her panic attacks would be too ironic for her to be a therapist.

"I'm not prying," Dahlia said when I turned to study her. I raised my eyebrow at her. She looked away. "Okay, I am."

"Jessica and I…" I drew in a deep, unsteady breath. "We've been rocky for a long time. Trust is hard."

My lips firmed as I began to walk again. We'd made too many mistakes, hurt each other too many times. Especially Olivia, my biggest regret. She would always be between us. If I'd tried harder, maybe… but Jessica wasn't willing to forgive me for that night. I'd never forgive myself. I looked down, thinking how easy it would be to walk out there and not come back.

But Mason deserved a father. Even if the best Mason would ever have was the fuckup I'd become.

"You've grown apart?" Dahlia asked. Her foot slid into a hole in the sand, and I was relieved when I had to focus on her body, my arm around her waist, holding her steady.

"There's so much between us," I said. "I married her because she was pregnant."

"Doug married me for the same reason."

"Ah, that explains so much," I said, brushing the lock of her hair from my cheek. "I remember. You were high school sweethearts."

"Mmm. I met him my freshman year. He was a senior. I hit the popularity jackpot." She laughed, the first true one I'd heard. The sound bubbled out of her, effervescent, drifting across the dark night. I wished I could bottle her laugh.

"If your daughter's in high school, you must have been a teenage mom."

"I was nineteen. Young, yes, but Doug and I had already been together for five years."

She had a kid two years after I'd quit Cactus Arrow. I didn't know what to do with that information. I swallowed down a bitter mouthful of regret. "I don't think I've got it in me. The staying power." She deserved to know I was an even bigger bastard than she thought.

"With Jessica or any woman?"

"Who's to say about another relationship? Jessica's been pretty clear about her unhappiness for a while now. I'm not surprised we've unraveled."

I swallowed, thinking about her angry outbursts, about her look of triumph when I'd signed the papers that destroyed what was left of my family. Had it already been nine months? "I'm surprised by how much the failure hurts."

Dahlia leaned against my shoulder, comforting me. "You're nicer than I remember. Or your lyrics led me to believe. If you're not careful, I'll develop deep feelings for you," she said with a dramatic shudder.

"My lyrics, hmm? That's my best feature?"

I walked into the shallow water, shivering at the chill temperature. Too cold, but we stayed there at the edge of the surf, laughing when the foam lapped over the edge of our jeans.

"Do you still love it? Performing?" she asked, finally moving away from the water's edge.

That was the question. One I'd been asking for a while. "I like the energy. I'd be lying if I said I didn't like the adoration. It's great for the ego."

"You're very attractive," she said, her statement so matter-of-fact I wasn't sure if *she* was attracted to me. "It's easy to see why women throw their panties at you."

She pulled her hand from mine and plopped down in some dry sand. I sat next to her, leaning back on my elbows. Her head settled on my shoulder. I was sure it must be very late, well after midnight now. I needed to get her home, but I sat still, enjoying the warmth of her body, the brush of her long hair against my arm, the clean, soft smell of her skin. Floral. I smiled, picturing dahlias. I doubted she'd wear that fragrance, but she was subversive enough to enjoy the sly humor.

"I'm going to pull out this memory often," she murmured. "The last few years haven't been good. This is tender."

"Real relationships are probably what I miss most from my life before," I said. I hadn't meant to tell her that. I hadn't meant to tell her most of what I had tonight, but after seeing her so vulnerable, I couldn't stop myself. "Jessica doesn't understand why I don't want to be out there all the time, lapping up the attention. Doling out pieces of me. A story, an old guitar. It's always something."

"That's exhausting. You have no place to just *be*. Is that what you meant about trust and staying power? That your needs are just too different?"

"If not for Mason…"

"Your son?"

"Yeah." I tilted my head down so I could see her upturned face. "You do know a lot about me."

I'd quit following up on her years ago after she married Doug. Tried to move on. I nearly snorted. Because that had worked out so well.

She shrugged, turning to look out into the dark water. The moonlight glittered across the waves. "Lots of late nights. Not much sleeping. The Internet offered an escape."

"You, like, cyber-stalked me?" I couldn't keep the shock from my voice.

She fidgeted, sitting up. "I joined your mailing list and found a few old interviews."

I gripped my hands around my knees, rocking back and forth. "And just what else did you find out about me in your stalking?" Oh, this was too good to pass up.

She looked down at her fingers, dragged them through the sand. "Mmm. This is very uncomfortable for me."

"I'm not the stalker."

"It was completely harmless. It's not like I walked up to your

22

table in a bar."

"I thought— Never mind." No way I could tell her what I'd really thought. Not even on this night of honesty.

"What?"

I kept my eyes on hers, hoping she'd understand now what I couldn't say when she was seventeen. I'd been too old for her then. "I've never forgotten you, Dahlia."

"Puh-lease," she said, rolling her eyes, unwilling to consider I was serious. But I was. I always had been about her.

"I regretted for years you were Doug's girl."

Her eyes snapped to mine. She forced a smile and looked down at the sand. I missed those bright gray eyes focused on me. I gazed out into Puget Sound.

"Favorite song?" I asked, needing to break the tension.

"'Sweet Solace.'"

"That's not what I would've guessed. That one almost didn't end up on the album because it was so different from what we were doing then."

"I'm glad it did. That song lets me know that you've experienced pain and loss. 'Sweet solace in the dreams that can never be… You left too soon and I'm struggling to see… The beauty in a life without your smile.'"

She would be drawn to those words. "Sounds prettier when you say it."

"Don't ask me to sing because I won't." She bumped me with her hip. "Not when I'm sitting next to a legend."

"Funny. But you never struck me as someone who'd want to make music. Or perform."

"I like to listen. I've never yearned for the limelight." Her brow furrowed as she weighed her words. "Those are real emotions in your lyrics, expressing that you know what it's like to lose someone you love. That song helped me get through those early days and months after Doug died."

I opened my mouth. Shut it. Cleared my throat as I decided on a partial truth. "I wrote it when my mom got sick. Breast cancer. It ate her up for years before she finally died."

She touched my cheek, her eyes softening with empathy. I didn't tell her I'd been thinking about her as much as my mom. That sounded unrequited, and I'd never liked Romeo and Juliette. He should've moved on, like I did.

I hung my head, my turn to feign interest in the sand. A long moment slid passed, the only sound the water lapping at the shore as I searched for a safer topic. "You weren't kidding about connecting with lyrics. Let me guess—you're a writer."

"Mmm. Nailed it in one."

"Anything I've heard of?"

"Doubt it."

"Color me curious."

"You ever read a romance novel?" Her muscles tensed, probably because of the usual comments about writing smut.

I sang about affairs—mine and my buddies'—I'd heard all the shaming comments. "A couple."

"Really?"

"Reading. Yes, I do it. There's not much else to do between stops. I'm shit at Xbox." I narrowed my eyes. "You don't love 'Moonshine Eyes'?" I had to know. "'Drifting deeper in my dreams,'" I sang, my voice soft and low. Dahlia shuffled closer, her eyes widening as I continued, "'I swear I never thought you'd leave.'"

24

Her lips parted, her tongue darting out to touch the center of her bottom lip just as it had that first time I sang this tune.

I dipped my voice lower. "'I've stared so long into those moonshine eyes, sliding further in the calming sea of pleasure and mystery.'"

"Oh, God," she whispered, her breath a warm puff across my lips. Yearning was etched deep in her eyes and the way her luscious mouth opened in welcome.

"I do like that song. So much. It's beautiful," she said, her voice reverential.

I wanted to pull her close, mold her soft body to mine. "What if I told you I wrote it for you?"

She leaned back enough that her lips were no longer inches from mine, her eyes darkening with pain. "I'd say you were trying to get in my pants, and we have an agreement."

I was silent for a long moment, wishing I'd reconnected with her sooner. Later. Any time but now when my life was so totally fucked. I picked up a shell and tossed it hand to hand.

"If I wanted to get in your pants, I'd sing you 'Let's do it in the Surf.' You know, to set the mood."

She laughed, grabbing her stomach, eventually collapsing back onto the sand. "That's the song that created my daughter," she gasped between giggles.

"Wait until I tell the guys we get to claim partial credit for your daughter. And critics say our music doesn't always live up to its potential."

"For what it's worth, I was eighteen, looking for adventure, and hyped from your gig. I met Doug on the beach later that night. He wouldn't come to your concert." She sobered, her eyes distant, remembering. "The water was so freaking cold. Don't do that, by the way."

"What?"

"Try to make love in Puget Sound." Dahlia shuddered. "That's hypothermia waiting to happen."

Silence enveloped us again. Like the dark, it was comforting.

"So you really read romances?" Dahlia asked. I loved how she looked at me. I had her full attention. She cared about my answer.

"Of course. Jessica reads them, goes through them like they're candy. My mom was more literary, but she had a couple favorite genre authors. One was a romance writer."

She snorted. "I bet you read a vampire or BDSM series. Something sensational."

"Neither. My mom told me about Lia Moore's books when I was going through a bit of a slump. When Mom died, I wanted to connect with her on some level. She, Lia Moore, I mean, is pretty deep."

Her shoulders tensed, and she glanced at me from the corner of her eye. I wondered… There was no way.

"So what do you write? Anything as good as Lia Moore's books? Last I heard, she was taking some time off to spend with her family."

She stood, brushing the sand from the back of her jeans.

"She is. And no, I haven't typed a word worth reading in years."

I stood, taking her hand in mine. I was going to miss touching her palm, talking to her. We walked up the beach and sat on a bench, swiping off the sand so we could put on our shoes. We didn't talk as I led her back along the dark sidewalk.

About a block from our cars, she turned toward me. "I know you didn't ask for my opinion. This is overstepping the limits of friendship." She took a deep breath and the words tumbled out. "From someone who's been on the other side of loss, talk to Jessica. You married her for a reason. Love isn't something to throw away or let slip through your fingers."

Emotion rippled through me. I stared into her beautiful, earnest eyes, and I couldn't tell her it was too late for Jessica and me. I'd signed the separation papers months ago and had the divorce proceeding date to prove it. I forced my lips into a smile as I tapped the side of her nose. "Still a romantic even if you aren't writing about it these days."

"Writing about love, for me, means believing in it. I hope you still do."

"Tell you what. I'll talk to Jessica if you promise to write another book." I was a dick for not telling Dahlia the truth, but I wanted her to find something she loved again. The way she'd talked about my lyrics showed how much writing meant to her.

"You don't even know if I've written anything worth reading." She dug around in her purse until she pulled out a set of keys.

"I know you, Dahlia Dorsey," I said. "Your words are worth reading."

She smiled, a bright, happy beacon in the dark, weed-ridden parking lot.

"I hope life leads you back to love," she said.

I rubbed her hair through my fingers. "Same goes." Dropping her hair, loss blossomed in my chest.

She opened the door to her SUV and slid inside. So she didn't have to look at me? "I've had my chance at love."

"I still say you're too young to have loved properly or to have a teenage daughter."

"Bye, Asher. I'm glad we met again."

———— ◆ ————

Dahlia drove away. Her words slithered through my mind, sincerity dripping from her soft voice: *Love isn't something to throw away or let slip through your fingers.*

She was right. Problem was, I'd never loved my wife.

I turned and walked back toward where I'd parked. Dahlia's panic attack had been horrible to watch. Her hesitancy at holding my hand depressed me. I'd always liked holding hands—for the connection, sure, but also for the imprint of the other person's emotions.

Snuggling palms with Dahlia had been more intimate than most of the sexual encounters I'd had during my twenties. Maybe because I was sober now. Maybe because I craved a partner who saw and loved me, not my stage persona.

The constant need to guard my expression, my thoughts, animate my actions, be "on"… I was tired of all that shit. More, I was tired of trying to make sense out of my personal life.

Mason had been sullen and unresponsive when I called earlier. That wasn't anything new. He was a smart kid and knew something was wrong between Jessica and me. I was lucky my wife and her lover, one of Mason's friend's dads, weren't splashed over every entertainment station, website, and magazine. I figured it was a matter of time, which was why I'd wanted to keep our separation quiet. Mason didn't deserve to deal with any more drama in his life.

When Mason had handed Jessica back her phone, she'd told me her lover made four times more a month than I did. Owning car washes.

I almost asked her how much Car Wash Dale's soon-to-be-ex

was going to keep, but I didn't want to give Jessica any more ideas. She was ambitious. I couldn't blame her, not after I discovered the extremity of the poverty she had grown up in. Like so many others who'd once not had enough to eat, Jessica was fixated on the zeroes in her bank account.

When she had first pushed me to tour more, I agreed. I wanted some of the trappings of success, too. And I liked the screaming fans, the late-night parties.

Over time, I changed my mind about what success meant. I was thankful I was able to do what I loved. That, right there, was worth a shit-ton of money. I was even more thankful I wasn't working at a car wash all day, no matter how much Dale made. A car wash might be even worse than a soulless gray cubicle.

I headed up the elevator to my place on the tenth floor. I yanked out the key to my crap apartment as I headed down the hall.

Dropping my keys onto the kitchen counter, I pulled out the papers I'd carried around with me for the past few weeks. Jessica's first salvo in the divorce war—a list of unreasonable demands designed specifically to piss me off.

Over thirty years later, and the family cycle continued. The kid in me wept bitter tears of resentment all over again. I was no better than my father.

"Moonshine Eyes" filled my head along with an image of Dahlia in the moonlight. *Love isn't something to throw away or let slip through your fingers.*

I didn't want my soon-to-be ex-wife. Hadn't for years. No, Dahlia was the only woman I'd ever yearned for.

I left Cactus Arrow because I didn't want to fuck up her life. She'd seemed happy with Doug, devoted even. What right did I

29

have to mess with that?

I breathed out. Pulled up the e-mail I'd typed to my lawyer in response to Jessica's demands.

I didn't want to fuck up Dahlia's life now either. But I still wanted her. More after spending the night with her. I pressed Send on the e-mail.

Game on.

CHAPTER THREE
Dahlia

"How'd it go last night?" Simon asked, his voice laced with sus-picion. He slammed back a huge gulp of his drink. Simon always drank his first cup of coffee fast, the way most people took a shot.

"Well, let's see… I cried all over Asher. And I mean snot and near-heaves."

Simon's eyes widened and his mouth dropped open. "You did not."

"Mmm hmm. Afterward, we went to the beach, and he said he was trying to work through his marital problems with his wife so his kid had a chance at normalcy."

Simon shook his head, his dark hair the same shade as Doug's. But Simon wore his longer, shaggier. Like Asher's. Clearly, the sexy bedhead look was a rock-star thing.

I liked it better on Asher.

"I was surprised you came home last night." Simon refilled his cup. No cream this time. He only doctored the first cup.

I'd spent my formative high school years in the Northwest, and I liked my coffee to taste, well, like coffee. I raised an eyebrow as I sipped from my own mug. "Seriously? I'm repressed. You know that."

"You'll cut loose one of these days. You don't just stop the sensual daydreams. Ella's made me read some of your books because she was sure you and Doug had a way better sex life than we do."

I laughed so hard I spilled my coffee. "I miss feeling that good."

"TMI, as Abbi would say," Simon said, but he was grinning.

"You still have each other," I said, my tone now serious. "Talk about what you want." I looked down into my mug, thinking about the last few years of Doug's life.

"You've never mentioned how bad the Huntington's got," Simon said.

I gripped my mug. He knew I hated talking about Doug's illness. Remembering was hard. Not just the disease, but Simon didn't know that. I measured his facial features as my heartbeat ratcheted. Simon's eyes were concerned, sad.

He didn't know. He couldn't. I turned away, struggling against the anger and anxiety.

"He would've died much more slowly, and it would've been painful for you and Abbi to see that decline," Simon said.

I fisted my hands so hard my short nails bit into my palms. "So it's fine that he went skydiving and didn't open his parachute?"

Simon came around the island and gripped my arm. "You remember how he acted when he couldn't play his guitar anymore?"

My cheeks burned with embarrassment. "That's not a day I'm going to forget."

"He shouldn't have taken that out on you, Lia."

"There were lots of things he shouldn't have done," I snapped. I sucked my lip in. I'd kept Doug's—my—secrets this long. I walked to the coffeepot and refilled my cup, pleased to see how steady my hands were despite my rapid heartbeat.

"I know he was upset, but the insurance company accepted it was an accident. Maybe you could, too," Simon said.

"I still haven't gotten all the money from them," I said, pressing my lips together hard to keep them from trembling. I hated feeling this raw. I hated talking about Doug with Simon, the only one who could understand his brother's needs and mine, too.

Simon turned and dumped his coffee in the sink. "Lia, you can say it: he was a coward."

I stared at Simon. We'd worked hard to hold it together, to build a relationship based on more than anger and grief.

"I don't want to be angry any more."

Simon touched my tense shoulder. "You've been angry since Doug got sick and started acting out, and you deserve to feel that way. I'm still angry, too." He glanced at the clock. "I need to go get El and the kids."

I grabbed the sponge and wiped the counters. "I'm coming. Be ready in ten," I promised.

———————

Abbi stood next to a boy about her age, twirling her hair the way she did when she was interested in pursuing whatever she'd started. I thrilled. She was so perfect. Her eyes were bright, her hair glossy.

She was healthy. According to the predictive genetic test, Abbi had been spared the indignity of Huntington's, and I should be more thankful for that. My daughter was worth all the pain of losing Doug, first to the anger of the disease and then to his "accident."

Abbi laughed. The boy leaned in and wrapped her in a hug. Seeing her smile, I sighed, knowing she was going to be quiet and withdrawn the whole trip back to Rathdrum. Unless she decided to once again lament her forced existence in middle-of-nowheresville.

Sixteen wasn't the age to explain concerns about crime statistics and traffic congestion so prevalent in big cities. I wasn't sure if Abbi was upset with living in a small town or if she was angry we hadn't moved closer to our family after her dad's death.

I never wanted Abbi to live with the anonymity of moving every year, or every two if I was really, really lucky, like I had done as a teenager until ending up in Seattle. An introvert unable to open up quickly, I'd found my family's moves hard even though it meant we'd seen parts of the world most other Americans merely dreamed of.

I hugged Ella. "Hey, how was the trip?"

Ella squeezed me tight before stepping back and sliding her hand into Simon's back pocket. A piece of her flaxen hair drifted across her pixie face. "Nineteen teenagers and a seven-year-old. Just about what you'd expect. My four parent chaperones were a godsend." She winked one of those bright green eyes at me, and I was charmed, as always, by my sister-in-law's Britishness.

"Perhaps next time you can offer your time along with your daughter," she pressed.

"I'm nowhere near as good with the kids as you are, Ella. Abbi and I get along because we've grown up together. I'm going to go say hi and meet her latest crush. That way Simon can tattle on me like he's dying to do."

As I walked over to my daughter, my phone rang. Bev's name popped up on the screen. Crap. "Hey, Bev. I don't have another book. Nothing new to report at all, actually. I'm your most pathetic client, and I don't know if I can actually bear you saying the words to me."

We'd had the same conversation a few times over the last few months. I figured the least I could do was spare her the pain of asking. I wasn't sure why she kept me around. My sales had plummeted in the last year. She and I both knew I needed to do something, like write another bestseller, if we wanted to see any real income.

"I can't call because I like talking to you?"

"Um, no. Wait, who is this? What did you do with my tough New York agent, scary-nice person?"

"You're still a pain in the ass. Good to know some things don't change. Fine, we won't chat. I've got news, Lia. Great news. HBO wants to buy the rights to your Gardiner series."

I stopped walking. "No."

"Yeah. Garcia Jones wants to produce it. Garcia Jones!" Bev screamed in my ear.

"Ouch. My ear's bleeding. Wow. You know how to surprise a girl."

"This is amazing. Why aren't you more excited? We sold your books to HB-freaking-O!"

"Yeah, I heard you. Cool. So now some young producer and a hungry director rip apart my stories and make them a better fit for the screen, meaning you make a ton of money, and I can't ever watch HBO again without feeling sick."

"You writers are all so emotional," Bev muttered. "Let's think about the nice fat check this is going to bring both of us for a moment, hmm? Garcia happens to love your books and wants you to collaborate on the project. He said, and I quote, 'you're a romance genius.' Take that, romance queen!"

"I honestly don't know what to say."

"Well, you say yes and sign the docs. Because you won't get a better deal than this one. I nearly swallowed my tongue when the offer came through."

"Good?" I asked.

Abbi walked toward me, concern filling her dark blue eyes. I smiled at her and opened my arm for a hug. She stepped in, and I was shocked, once again, to find my daughter at eye level. She'd grown so much in just a couple years, both emotionally and physically. We'd always been close, but there was a relaxation in our relationship that hadn't been there before. I was thankful for this new level of companionship.

I smoothed her hair from her face, and she pointed at the phone. Her eyes lit up when I mouthed "Bev."

Abbi turned and walked over to her aunt and uncle. She bent down to help her seven-year-old cousin, Jeremiah, with his sleeping bag.

"...thousand, plus creative input for the screenplay, and a big fat option for the conclusion of the series."

"I haven't written the series ending," I reminded her, not too worried about the cash amount she'd spouted and I'd missed. If Bev said it was good, it was.

"Well, get your ass on it because HBO wants it. In fact, the deal's contingent on you finishing it."

Anxiety crawled over my skin, tiny spiders of doubt and insecurity weaving a web I hadn't been able to break out of for years. "We'll see. E-mail me the details, and I'll look it over while Abbi and I drive home."

"No driving home. You're flying to Lala-land in the morning, and you're meeting with Garcia Jones and Paul Loomis, the director on the project."

My heart pounded, too heavy and fast. "No flying."

"Dahlia Moore Dorsey, do not make me come out there and hit you. I will. You know I will. And I'll bill you for the ticket and the time it takes me to find you and give you a bruise."

"I'm not flying. I can't, Bev." I didn't want to discuss this anymore. Flying, even the thought of flying, was a major trigger for me, reminding me of Doug's choice. I relived the look on Abbi's face when I had to tell her Doug was dead.

I took a deep breath and reminded myself I was safe. My eyes sought Abbi, ensuring she was well, too. The vise in my chest loosened by increments, and I drew a breath.

I'd focus on my choices, make the best one. I couldn't simply turn down this opportunity. That would be stupid, and I couldn't let Doug's death continue to have such a hold over me.

"I'll drive," I said, trying to sound firm. "So set the meeting up for this Monday." I bit my lip, realizing I had to get Abbi home for school. "Actually next Monday would be better."

"I'm sorry, Lia." Bev sounded contrite. "I forgot about your flying thing."

"If that's the only way, then I just can't." I hated to give up the money, but if this deal was contingent on the fourth book… well, I doubted that would ever happen. My ability to write died a long time ago. I'd barely finished the last manuscript.

Bev grumbled. "Can you stick around Seattle a couple more days? Garcia said they were planning to scout the area for places to film. I guess they plan to do this right: on location and everything."

My knees softened with relief. "Yes, okay. Sure." Maybe I could figure this out. I wanted to.

"Give me a few to set it up."

"You're amazing, Bev. I hope they go for meeting me here. That'd be perfect."

"It's not just you. They want to talk to some people in the indie music scene there, too. For the sound track, I guess. At least that's what Garcia said."

"Oh. Well. That'd be really fun. E-mail me the details. I'll let Ella and Simon know they aren't getting rid of me today after all."

"Good girl. And Lia, I hope you know this is a second chance most writers don't get. They're catering to you. Don't mess this up. And write the last damn book."

The phone screen blanked. I stared at it for another minute, bemused. Still shell-shocked, I met my daughter's worried gaze.

Simon wandered over. "Ready to go? Everything's in the car. Abbi said your agent was on the phone."

I nodded.

"Good news?"

I lifted my eyes to his. "HBO wants to buy the rights to one of my series. Mind if Abbi and I stay another night or two so I can go to a meeting? I'll cook."

Simon smiled. "Magic words. If you're cooking, you can stay another week."

"I can't. Abbi's already missed two days of school. We have to get back before Monday. And it's already Friday."

"We told you you were welcome for as long as you need, Lia. We meant it."

Though Ella was an amazing mom, calm in the face of just about every problem from a broken collarbone to Jeremiah's biting problem when he was two, neither she nor Simon could do more in the kitchen than warm up food. Their music teacher salaries didn't allow for many meals out. Whenever Abbi and I stayed at their four-bedroom bungalow near the beach, I always stacked the freezer full of meals.

I loved our arrangement. The kitchen was one of the few places I was still happy. I insisted on going to the market to ensure freshness of ingredients so that I could enjoy the process more.

As I'd told Simon, I wasn't big on hotels, not after moving

around so often during the first fourteen years of my life. The sterility reminded me of the apartments of my early childhood. I was thankful I could stay with Simon and Ella as opposed to some random, poorly cleaned room, and I was more than happy to buy groceries in exchange for the homey experience.

Not that I'd ever tell them, but I also enjoyed looking after Simon and Ella a little. To them, I was useful. Needed. Not just Abbi's mom.

Abbi's mom—that title wasn't going to work for much longer. My daughter only had one more year of high school left.

I should find a partner, someone I could cuddle next to on the couch. Laugh with. Maybe I could start living in this century and enjoy a man's company without a deep emotional attachment. I deserved… something more than my current barren love life.

I'd set up that dating profile everyone was hounding me about, go on a few dates. See what was out there.

Thirty-five was too young to be this incomplete.

CHAPTER FOUR
Asher

I pulled up in front of the clapboard farmhouse Jessica and I had bought in Mount Vernon, about an hour north of Seattle. All the lights were on, spilling warmth onto the porch. Dread stiffened my shoulders, causing my head to ache.

I toured and recorded, successive rounds, one after the other, to keep a steady flow of income for Jessica's desires and to cover Mason's needs. But I wanted more than four days with my son each month. I wanted Mason to remember me as an involved father.

Right now, I wanted to tousle Mason's hair and hold his solid body close to my own. That's why I was here, a day earlier than I'd expected. Problem was, I didn't want to see Jessica. Part of me felt like I'd cheated. I'd shared more of myself with Dahlia last night than I ever had with my wife. But Jessica was the one who'd chosen to dissolve our life. Now, after seeing Dahlia, I was glad. Relieved, even.

I climbed out of the car and walked into my house, my heart slamming a harsh beat within my chest.

Mason sat on the couch, the Wii controller in his hand. Jessica was right. I'd bought the stupid gaming system out of guilt. Gifts didn't assuage my shitty parenting abilities, but Mason liked the thing.

"Hey, buddy," I said.

He glanced up, his mouth in a sour line. "I thought you were coming back tomorrow."

"Yeah, good to see you, too." I sat next to him on the couch. He didn't lean into me like he used to.

40

"Mom was going to let me spend the night with Bryan Horn-sacker."

"Well, if those are the plans, I wouldn't want to mess that up."

Mason's faced softened. "Really?"

"Mason, I love you. I want you to be happy."

He sat the controller down and slid his arms around my neck. I hugged him hard, regret biting at my heart, burrowing deep. His legs were lanky, like a colt's. Before we started using Skype, I was shocked by his growth between my visits home. I kissed his cheek, and he let me. This, here, was the best thing I'd done with my life.

"I'm glad you're home," Mason said, his voice muffled into my neck. "Wanna play with me?"

"What are you doing?"

"Building. See?"

"An entire city," I said. "That's amazing."

"You should add something cool."

"Sure, let me just tell your mom I'm home."

Mason's eyes shifted to mine, his mouth turning back down. "She's next door."

"You're here by yourself?" I asked, keeping my voice controlled. Our next-door neighbor was a half-mile away. If a problem arose, no one would hear Mason's cries.

"Yeah."

"Does she do that often—leave you here alone?"

"Sometimes." He shrugged. "I get to play my game while she's gone."

Anger welled up, overriding the guilt and regret I'd felt moments before. "Well, let's build the heck out of this city and then we'll grab some dinner. You hungry?"

"Yeah."

"Wanna eat first?"

Mason turned those bright hazel eyes toward me. "Yeah."

I gripped him around his middle, hauling him into the kitchen like he was a football "Let's see what you got."

———————

I was able to get in a few hours of time with Mason before Jessica dropped her nuclear bomb into my skull.

I ended up driving Mason over to his friend's house for his sleepover. I gave Bryan's mom my cell, asking her to call me if she needed anything. Confusion filled her eyes, but I ignored it, bending down to hug Mason. He was too excited for more than a quick pat, running and shouting out some scene from a show he and Bryan liked.

Jessica's car was in the garage when I got back to the house. Great. Now we could talk.

"You took Mason to his sleepover?" she asked from where she stood in the kitchen.

"Wish I'd known he was going to be gone tonight. Maybe I would've stayed in Seattle. I had a meeting request I turned down so I could hang out with him."

"No one begged you to show up tonight." Her eyes were bright, really bright, like she was on something. Much as I wanted to ask, that would only make the situation worse.

"I noticed. Why was Mason here by himself, Jessica? He's just a little boy."

"I left probably two minutes before you got here. It wouldn't have been a problem if Mrs. Knowles wasn't sick. She wouldn't come stay with him."

"He's barely eight, Jessica."

"I have better things to do with my life than sit around and wait for you to drop by," she said. "Mason was fine. He was playing that stupid game you got him."

Neither of us mentioned that our neighbor, who Jessica had been "visiting" instead of watching our son, was a forty-something single man with an easy smile. He was fit, a runner.

I bit my tongue, refusing to point out that I'd cut back on my travel schedule years ago because I wanted to spend more time with them. After a year and a half of long weekends and extended weeks home between gigs, Jessica demanded I go back on tour. She wanted to put Mason in private school and she wanted a new car.

I opened the fridge and pulled out a beer. Not the kind I liked, but it'd do.

"Come with me on the next leg this summer," I said. Not because I wanted Jessica with me. I really didn't, especially since I got her list of requirements from her lawyer. I'd told Pete to hold off until Monday to forward over my counteroffer. I still had time to pull some of the demands if Jessica let Mason come with me. And I'd even put up with her to get more time with my son.

"It's easy, up and down the coast. Lots of beaches for Mason to play at and for you to relax on. What's the name of the fashion designer you like? Doesn't he have a store in LA?"

Jessica crossed her arms over her breasts. I noticed she wasn't wearing a bra under her thin, green camisole. She probably hadn't worn it to see if I'd get angry. I took a large gulp of my beer and wished I hadn't given up the harder stuff.

"I don't want to travel with you, watching women throw themselves at you. How many do you plan to screw while I'm in the hotel room with Mason, waiting for you to come in after the show?"

Jessica wouldn't give me what I wanted with Mason—tonight had proven that. I closed my eyes and fought to find some serenity. Dahlia's eye's reflected in the water slid into place behind my shut lids. "I don't screw any of the fans."

Jessica sniffed.

"Look, we've beaten this horse past death and into dust. Mason will never completely believe in stable, loving relationships again. The least we can do is ease the transition."

"You signed the separation agreement, and we have the trial date set."

"Let's give our kid a chance to get used to the idea," I said. I set the bottle down before facing her. "We haven't told him anything, Jessica. He's not going to understand. Especially with you screwing Car Wash Dale." I waved my hand. "And the neighbor." Jesus. Two different men.

She slammed her hand against the counter. "I'd rather have any life except this one. Any other life!"

"You'd go back to that trailer?"

She glared, eyes burning with anger. "You are such an asshole. I'll never be poor again. Ever."

Fear flitted through her eyes. I didn't know what it was like to be hungry and scared. Jessica had never told me much about her mother, but from the little she'd said, Jessica's childhood was filled with traumas I could barely grasp. Her fear was deep-rooted, a demon she struggled to overcome.

"If you won't provide me with the lifestyle you promised and make sure I have everything I need to be happy, then I'll find someone who can," she said. She was petulant but also combative.

"Fine," I said, relief replacing the brooding depression I'd felt since I pulled into the drive. At least I could tell Dahlia I'd tried without it being a complete lie. "I'll have my lawyers get in touch with your lawyers. Guess I'll see you around."

Sadness and fear swirled through her eyes. She looked like a lost puppy. She straightened and smirked, thrusting out her chest. "Enjoy your little apartment. I have things to do."

I turned to go. I should have just left. I knew it, but I couldn't keep my mouth shut. "What about Mason? Do you care what this does to his life?"

She picked at one of her nails. "He has a life. The one you wanted for him."

"I never said my life was glamorous, Jessica."

"I've known that for years. It's a slow grind."

"Then why shove this on him now?"

She met my gaze, her lips settling into that mischievous smile I used to find adorable. "I've talked to Dale."

"What's good ol' Dale up to these days? Besides banging my wife."

"Your wife. I haven't been your wife in years, Asher. Long before we officially separated." She laughed, but it was caustic, scraping against my skin and shredding my pride.

"He asked me to marry him. And he wants us to have custody over Mason."

CHAPTER FIVE
Dahlia

Garcia was a thin, well-dressed man who gushed with flamboyant happiness about my grasp of emotional nuances. By the time I was seated in a brown leather chair in front of the gleaming glass-and-steel conference table, he was my new best friend.

"I read the first book in the series at my son's birthday party. My partner hasn't completely forgiven me, but after reading your books, at least he understands why I was so captivated. He said to thank you for that bathroom scene. You sex kitten." Garcia winked. "I'd totally do that if I was a woman."

I wanted to. With Asher. But more, I wanted to see his smile, to hold his hand. I needed him to ease the panic winding into a tight grip in my chest.

I focused on how his hand pressed against mine, and my lungs relaxed. The clasp of our hands had been decadent, intimate. Perfect. I wanted to hold his hand again. Soon. I wanted more with him.

Reconnecting with Asher Smith had pushed me over the edge, reminding me of the small, lonely life I'd been leading. This sudden rush of need left me raw, unsure how to proceed. Hence, my increasing anxiety.

"So we see you in a producer role. I told your agent I want your input because your grasp of romantic tension is divine," Garcia said, his smile wide, his manicured fingers steepled in front of his short, neat beard. "But we'll need to see where you plan to take it—the final ending, you know, so we can set the tone. Paul suggested we might want to film the ending first."

"Of course," I said, squirming in my chair. The ending? I had no idea how the series would end. I'd made notes, sure, about the next book. But since Doug's death, nothing I wrote flowed. It felt stilted, unimaginative.

Bad.

I exhaled through my nose and turned back toward the director who was waxing poetic about another scene. We'd done many of the things I'd written about, Doug and I, before the symptoms started to manifest. He'd declined faster than his doctors predicted. Within months, Doug's coordination started to fail, and he'd been frustrated with his waning strength. Our sex life was the first casualty. Not that it had been all that spectacular for the previous couple of years.

I shoved my glasses back into place and then clasped my chin, forcing my attention to stay trained on Garcia's thin, tanned face. My eyes felt gritty, too tired after another sleepless night. I didn't have it in me to deal with my contact lenses this morning.

Paul, the director, had remained silent this whole time, twiddling a pen. I could tell he didn't want me on the project. He was sending out as much negativity as possible, trying to get me to agree to sell my rights and leave.

I had two options: I could pretend Paul wasn't bothering me or I could confront this situation. Panic fluttered up my throat, but if I wanted to be able to complete the series, I needed to take charge of my writing. That started with taking control of my life.

I faced Paul, both amused and ashamed that his heavy features reminded me of a basset hound. His balding head and long ear lobes didn't help, but it was his deep frown that sealed the connection.

"Are you sure you want my input?" I asked. I slid my hands into my lap and twisted my fingers together. My knees began to bounce, but I kept my gaze steady. I was in control of this situation. I could walk out anytime I wanted.

"We do, darling," Garcia answered, glaring at Paul, who'd yet to do more than blink at me. "This is going to be the hottest series on HBO. We're in agreement there. Right, Paul?"

"Of course, Garcia. But I'd like to get through the first round of screenplays that *our* writers are working on before we ask Ms. Moore for her input."

I waited for Garcia to quit grumbling. "Paul, I appreciate the offer to keep me in the loop. I really do, but I need to make sure you and I can work together. I haven't signed the contract yet because I wanted to see what your vision was for the project." And because I wasn't sure I could deliver the next storyline. "And call me Lia, please."

Paul glanced at Garcia from the corner of his eye. He took a deep breath before launching into his ideas.

"So I'm thinking we open with the firehouse scene. Viewers will be hooked."

I nodded, moving my clasped hands to the tabletop. That was one of the hottest scenes in any of my books, one Doug had laughed at when I read it to him. *You think dudes actually do that? Please, Lia. Maybe you need to recategorize into fantasy.*

I'd reminded myself that Doug had been sliding deeper into the Huntington's by then, and he probably had no idea how much his words had hurt. They still did.

Paul sputtered out and I blushed, trying to smooth out my frown.

"Sorry, you were talking about the sound track?"

Garcia leaned forward. "Bev told us you're a big indie rock fan."

I nodded. I listened to it all the time. It even played softly in my room as I slept. "My husband was a guitarist."

"Oh, I didn't know that."

I smiled. "His band was pretty underground."

"What was it?"

"Dynamite Fish."

Paul smiled, his red-rimmed eyes sparkling with interest. "Really? I have all their albums."

"I'm sure Doug would've been thrilled to hear that. Before that, he was in Cactus Arrow."

"I've heard about them. That was, what? Nearly twenty years ago?"

I nodded. "I can make you a copy of their only release. It was four songs, including an early version of 'Moonshine Eyes.'"

"Excellent!" Paul smiled, but he still looked tired.

Garcia tapped his pencil on his desk, shooting Paul a get-on-with-it look. Paul met my gaze as he scratched behind his ear.

"'Moonshine Eyes.' That's an Asher Smith song. Was Cactus Arrow one of his earlier bands?"

I nodded again, slower this time. Paul smiled, his brown eyes lighting up even more.

"I've been talking to Asher Smith's agent, Richard, about possible projects. Richard and I went to UCLA together, so when he approached us a couple years ago, I tossed Asher a few smaller gigs. He told me Asher wants to move into sound tracks, do more producing."

"Interesting," I said. I dropped my pen and shoved my shaking hands back into my lap. Just a coincidence. No way I'd get thrown back into Asher's life after all this time. Fate wasn't this cruel.

Garcia leaned forward, smoothing his gelled hair back into place. "When Paul mentioned Asher's interest, I was intrigued. I mean, the man writes about sexiness with a little roughness. Your heroes are willing to play it loose with the rules. Like Asher."

"I saw Asher Smith again a couple of nights ago at a singer-song-writer show. He's a great guy."

"Maybe you two could collaborate on the lyrics," Paul said, his droopy face jiggling with excitement. "For the theme song. That could be really cool! Not too much, just give him some ideas of phrases that'd work well for certain scenes. The two of you could make the music so intense! Actually, if you're good with that idea, Asher's going to meet with us today. His agent said he had a family thing to deal with last night, but Asher called a while ago, saying he was back in Seattle."

"I'd love the opportunity," I said. Sweat slicked my back and my heart rate escalated.

Garcia thought we were a perfect fit. I swallowed, breathed deep through my nose. I couldn't see Asher again. I couldn't. My bur-geoning feelings for him needed to stay out of whatever business arrangement we developed. He was married, and I wanted them to reconcile whatever their problems were. I needed to believe in Asher as much as I needed to believe that love could get people through the hard times.

Correction. I needed to believe in Asher even more, especially after the night we'd spent together.

I forced the tension down with brutal efficiency, unwilling to give in to the emotions rolling over me.

Paul's smile warmed. "Great! I want him, specifically, to do the songwriting, with some help from a few singer-songwriters and an-other couple of indie rock groups. Keep the mix eclectic but uni-fied. Maybe your brother-in-law, Simon. I heard him play a couple of months ago, and I loved his 'More Time' tune," he gushed.

Surprise sizzled through me. "I'll pass that along," I said. This entire meeting was surreal. First, my books were like Asher's songs and now Paul wanted to give Simon his big break. "I'm sure Simon would love the opportunity and airplay."

The door opened and a young brunette stuck her head through the opening. "Asher Smith's here. Should I send him in?" she asked, looking at Garcia.

"Please," Paul said.

Garcia nodded. I sucked in a deep breath, trying to school my features into some semblance of professionalism. I wasn't ready. When he entered, I stood, bumping into my notepad. It tumbled to the floor. "Asher, so good to see you again," Paul said, holding out his hand.

"Yeah, thanks." But Asher's eyes never left mine, even when he shook Garcia's hand.

"I wondered," he said, a slow smile curling his lips. "I remembered your last name used to be Moore."

I stared at him, the panic building. I couldn't sit next to him for an hour, not after the depth of our conversation the other night. Asher narrowed his eyes, no doubt seeing I was about to lose it. He moved around the table, picked up my notepad. He leaned in and brushed his lips against my cheek in a casual greeting.

His smell swirled around me, heightening the burning sensation around my heart.

"Breathe, Dahlia," he murmured, close to my ear. "You have this. I'm not going to let anything happen to you."

I looked up at him, his eyes soft and sure. I took a deep breath and nodded. He set the notebook on the table in front of me. I collapsed into the chair, and Asher sat next to me.

"I didn't realize you two were more than acquaintances," Paul said, frowning.

"Old friend," Asher said with an easy smile. Under the table, he clasped my hand. "Dahlia and I reconnected the other night at Simon's gig."

Paul eyed us. Asher squeezed my fingers, and I managed a smile.

"Thanks for having me here," Asher said. "Richard said this was for a sound track."

"Since you know Lia," Garcia said, his smile megawatt-bright, "I'm sure you know she writes these sexy-hot books. We want to produce her Gardiner series."

Asher nodded. "I'm familiar with those books."

I pulled my hand from his, and rested my damp palm on my knee. Much as I wanted his touch, I couldn't handle it, not if we were going to discuss love scenes.

"So here are some of my ideas," Paul said, snapping back to business mode.

I pulled my pen and paper closer, ready to take notes.

CHAPTER SIX
Asher

Once the shock wore off, Dahlia handled herself with the same poise and patience I'd come to expect from her years ago. She offered a few suggestions, but mainly listened, jotting down her notes.

I shook hands with the men before ushering Dahlia from the room. She fell into step beside me, surprising me with her acquiescence. Once we were in the elevator, I turned toward her. She was composed, but the pulse in her neck still beat at a frantic rate.

She hadn't told me her pseudonym. I didn't think it was because she was embarrassed by her work. Like I'd told her, as had millions of her fans, she wrote intriguing stories with deep, compelling characters. Something I strove to do with my songs.

Maybe that was the whole of our connection. We both loved words strong enough to evoke images and emotions. It didn't encompass how much I'd wanted her all those years ago before she started creating her own art. No, I was drawn to her, the woman with sad eyes that shone bright in the moonlight.

"Why didn't you tell me you were Lia Moore?"

She kept her gaze firmly on the floor. "I don't know."

"Look at me, Dahlia. Please." When her eyes hit mine, the punch of awareness was deep. I sucked in a breath. "I keep thinking about you."

Not what I meant to say, but there it was.

"Maybe this project is a bad idea," she whispered. She clenched her tote's strap so hard her knuckles were white. "I mean, I haven't even written the ending." Her breathing became more labored, nearly a wheeze. "I don't know if I can do it in one more book. And

53

getting you involved in my mess seems irresponsible."

She thought she was irresponsible? She didn't know half of the mess I'd caused in the last few days, let alone over the past two decades.

The elevator doors opened to a crowded lobby. Before Dahlia could object, I pushed the up button, followed immediately by the close doors button. A man in a suit hurried toward us, waving for me to open the doors. I ignored him.

"I didn't tell you the full truth the other night either," I said, fighting the urge to fidget. "That's not right. Everything I told you was true. I just didn't tell you the whole story."

She scooted back into the far corner, her breathing escalating again. I moved close enough to touch her shoulder. I slid my fingers up to the soft skin on her neck, my thumb against her pulse. She melted into me, her body finding its place against mine. I wrapped my other arm around her, holding her there for a minute.

"Jessica and I have been separated, officially, for nearly a year. She instigated it. Had me served." Dahlia made a noise but didn't try to pull away. I hoped that was a good sign. "We have the date for our divorce hearing."

"Asher." Her voice cracked. "I didn't know."

"We've managed to keep it fairly quiet. I'm worried about how the split will affect Mason. So far he hasn't asked any questions, probably because I'm gone so much on tour." A huge weight lifted from my shoulders, easing the constant tightness there. "See, you need to know you weren't part of that decision. It's been made. Was made long before I met you the other night."

"But you said—"

"I said we were in a bad place. We are. The divorce is going to be difficult. I want custody over Mason. Jessica knows that. She wants money, security. I'd give it to her, but she's been counseled that she'll do better financially if she keeps custody." I unclenched my fists. "I'm pretty screwed there."

Her mouth softened and her eyes finally came back up to meet mine. "I'm sorry."

"I want to work with you on this project," I said. "Not just because I'll get to see you. That's a major perk, by the way. But I've been transitioning into a more stable work situation. To show I'm capable—and willing—to take on Mason's school schedule."

She pulled back, and I let my arms fall to my sides, though I wanted her warmth against me again. Her, there, it felt right.

The door opened and two people entered, deep in discussion. Dahlia and I stood quietly at the back. We rode up another few floors before the pair stepped off, never looking back. I nearly groaned with relief. I didn't need to deal with a fan right now. I needed to talk to Dahlia without distractions.

"I told you I always thought Doug was a lucky bastard. What I didn't tell you was how much I loved and hated that you were Doug's girlfriend." I scratched the side of my head. "Loved it because you were at so many of the practices. But I wanted to talk to you. I knew I shouldn't. But I did. I always did."

The pulse in her neck sped up. She wrapped an arm around her waist. "You can't say this to me now."

"I should've said it then. I wanted you, Dahlia. I dreamed about you. Fantasized you dumped Doug and slept in my bed."

Her eyes were huge, her face so pale. I pressed my thumb to that spot at the base of her neck. She inhaled sharply.

"I had to leave," I said. "The band. I wanted you enough that I

55

was willing to fight for you. I did."

"What?"

"Doug knew how I felt about you. He taunted me about the fact you'd just moved in with him. How he was going home to you. I went after him but Bill stopped me." Bill, my best buddy even then. He'd left Cactus Arrow and helped me form the Supernaturals.

The elevator chimed. We were at the top floor. The doors opened. Neither of us moved. We started the descent back to the lobby.

"That's why I left the band. I was too old for you then. Hell, I'm probably too old for you now. But I always—*always*—wanted you."

The doors slid open. Four young women entered.

"Oh, my God! You're Asher Smith," one squealed.

Turning toward the ladies, I smiled. I managed to sign a paper for each of them, sidestepping their overt offers for a drink and easy sex.

The whole time, Dahlia stood in the corner. Her knuckles white where she gripped her bag, her eyes huge.

She deserved to know she was the one woman who'd stuck with me all these years. Seeing her again had just reinforced how much I wanted her. That desire was still there, buried under the years of poor decisions and too many memories I wished I could forget.

We collected another few people on the elevator. I moved back to stand next to Dahlia. She didn't move closer this time. She didn't look at me. I didn't try to touch her again. Much as I wanted to push for more, Dahlia needed to come to her own conclusions about us.

When we arrived at the lobby, I waited for her to exit the car and followed her to the parking garage. She pulled her keys from her purse, her mouth in a firm line that spelled trouble.

"I'd like to work with you, Asher," she said, her voice steady. "I want to help you with your son. But I can't be some ideal. I'm not the same woman I was eighteen years ago."

"I know that." But did I? I paused. She'd been my dream for so long. What if the real woman now couldn't live up to my memories of her?

"I need to go," she said, her shoulders folded in. I hated seeing her so defeated.

"I want to ask you something. Will you answer me?"

She tugged at the ends of her hair and shuffled back, giving herself the emotional space she was trying to build between us. I got that—it was smart. I was in a bad place emotionally. I shouldn't push this. I knew I shouldn't. But like so many of my decisions, I was compelled to push forward.

"Did you feel it, too? The attraction between us? Isn't that why you liked my music?"

She sucked in a breath. Then another. I stepped in, but she held up her hand. "I'm not panicking." When she lifted her eyes, they were dark with concern. "Yes. I did. I still do. But I could destroy your chance at custody of your son if I can't fulfill my contract." Her pleading eyes met mine. "Let me focus on our career goal first. Please."

She slid into her SUV and shut the door. I turned toward my car, knowing she wasn't going to give me anything further right now.

She'd already given me more than I deserved.

CHAPTER SEVEN
Dahlia

"How'd the meeting go?" Ella asked when I opened the door.

"Good. I think it's going to work out well. As long as I can figure out an ending they'll like for the series." I tried to stretch out my neck, but it was too tight to find relief. Great, I'd probably end up with a killer headache soon. "Where's Abbi?"

"She and Jeremiah walked up to the corner market for ice-cream cones. That's okay, right?" Ella asked, worry filling her eyes when she caught a glimpse of my face.

"Yeah, fine." But the familiar anxious flutter beat its way upward from my stomach at the thought of Abbi walking through the city unsupervised. I took a deep breath and remembered the feel of Asher's hands on my cheek, his long, lean body pressed to mine.

Until he'd talked me through those moments, I hadn't realized how anxious I was all the time. When I thought about him and his whiskey-roughened voice, my pulse slowed and my muscles unclenched enough for me to function.

"She's careful. More careful than any other sixteen-year-old I know," Ella said.

I closed my eyes. "That's because she knows one bad decision can cause death."

"I'm sorry, Lia. I didn't think it was a big deal. They were bored, and it's just to the corner. We walk up there with Jeremiah most weekends. And Abbi's old enough to drive."

I smiled, but it felt forced, like a fake attempt at happiness.

"It'll be fine," I said. This time I made my voice firm. "I'm glad Jeremiah wanted to hang out with his cousin another day."

"Are you kidding? He loves Abbi. He cries whenever you leave."

I needed to change the subject and distract myself. I dropped my bag in my room before heading toward the kitchen. "So Paul, the director, likes Simon's music. He asked about him specifically for the sound track."

"Really? That's bloody brilliant!" Ella hugged me before stepping back. She jumped up and down a few times, her hands clasped under her chin.

I smiled as I opened the fridge. "What did you want for dinner tonight? Anything in particular?"

"Whatever you feel like making, we'll gladly eat. You know that. Tell me more about the meeting. It went on for hours. How cool is it that you met with HBO execs?"

"They're planning to make an entire season's worth of episodes. Well, if I can give them an ending." I delved deeper into the fridge, needing a moment to settle the emotions twisting in my chest. "I guess that's abnormal to put so much money into a production at the get-go. But they're shooting it like a movie. I don't really under-stand. Paul, he's an indie rock geek, wants Asher Smith to do the sound track. Garcia said Asher's songs complement my writing."

I pulled out a bunch of packages, set them on the counter.

"Interesting," Ella said. She hopped onto the island and swung her short legs back and forth. She looked like a teenager sitting there, cheeks flushed with excitement. "You and Asher Smith com-plementing each other. Simon told me about your night out while we were gone."

"I knew he'd tattle. Nothing happened."

"That's too bad. Asher Smith is scorching."

"Ella!" I squealed.

"What? He's always been GQ cover material. I'd let him in my knickers."

"I don't know what part of that to address. Did you just say *knickers*?"

"I'm British, darling. Not even your lovely family can change that."

"I'm glad," I said, giggling.

"I'll open a bottle of that gorgeous Rioja you bought, and you can tell me all about how Asher Smith brought you back to the land of the living. I owe that man a debt of gratitude. I haven't seen you this animated in years."

"Yes to the Rioja. Paul and Garcia have some fabulous ideas for the series. I'm really excited." I bit my lip. As long as I didn't think about the writing. I shook my head. I wanted this—for my career, yes, but also to help Asher. He deserved to be happy, and I'd do what I could to ensure that.

"But?"

"There's no but."

Ella made a skeptical sound.

"Asher was at part of the meeting."

"What? And you're just getting to this *now*?"

"Look, there aren't any details to share. This is business. He wants the project so he can have stable work hours for his son."

I turned away, unable to face Ella's all-too-knowing eyes. Asher's words still swirled through my head, just as they had since he'd said them an hour ago. *I always*—always—*wanted you.*

Something more beautiful than panic fluttered through my chest. He didn't really mean them. He couldn't. Not when I wanted him to. So badly.

"What about your walk on the beach?" Ella asked.

"We talked. He's easy to talk to. I'd forgotten that." I tugged at the ends of my hair. "I told him he should work things out with his wife," I said in a rush, fighting the familiar anxiety.

Ella slammed the corkscrew down on the counter and turned back toward me, her creamy cheeks cresting with furious color. "Please tell me you're kidding."

She'd used her teacher's voice. The one that made an entire room of high schoolers sit up and listen. I was in so much trouble. "No. Why wouldn't I tell him to work things out with his wife?"

"Because you had the *perfect* opportunity to burn up the sand with him. And we both know you've been at least half in love with him for years."

I always—always—*wanted you.* I tossed my hair back, glowering. "You're insane."

"No, I'm telling you the truth." She thrust her finger at my chest. "One you don't want to hear."

"I'm *not* in love with Asher."

"Yet." Ella's smirk was triumphant.

Why did he have to tell me he'd wanted me for years? Seeing him the other night brought back all those yearnings I'd tamped down. Knowing *now* he'd felt the same... I mashed my lips together, hard, to keep from saying something stupid.

My life could've been so different.

"He's the first man since Doug died to make you realize you're missing life," Ella continued.

"That's not true." I feared, however, Ella was right.

I'd forced down my interest in Asher for years, just as I'd done again the other night. I pressed a hand to my queasy stomach.

"Bollocks. You're sex-starved. It can't be good for your brain, let alone other important body parts. At the very least, you could have reestablished a connection with the great O.

"You—I can't believe you."

"When was the last time you had sex?" Ella asked.

I pulled out pans I didn't need. "I'm not answering that."

"The last time you even mentioned sex was over six years ago, Lia."

"Doug was sick," I whispered. But there was more than that. I ran my hands up and down my chilled arms.

"You weren't, darling. That's my point."

"We had good years."

I hated that I always came back to that. Hated more that the words were a smoke screen to cover up the disaster our relationship had become.

"You loved Doug the way a man can only dream of being loved, better than most women could have. But I've seen the look on your face when you're listening to Asher sing. Why do you think Doug hated him so much?"

"That's crazy," I breathed.

But it wasn't, not after what Asher told me today. Doug had known of Asher's attraction. He'd known I'd shared it, and he'd used my guilt to keep me pinned in our relationship. If not for Abbi...

Ella narrowed her eyes. "I hear how your voice vibrates with passion when you talk about him. You had the opportunity, and you passed on it? I am so angry with you, Lia Dorsey!"

"What's going on?" Simon asked. He walked over to the wine bottle and poured himself a glass. He glanced back and forth between us, taking in his wife's ruddy cheeks and firm jaw.

"Ah. You're discussing Lia's rock-star boyfriend."

I gasped. "Simon! He's a friend. And your wife"—I pointed a

finger at her—"is upset I didn't have sex with him."

"Course she is. I was worried you would. So, naturally, she's upset you didn't."

I flapped my hand in front of my face in an ineffectual effort to cool my now-burning cheeks. "You two are getting too personal."

"By pointing out you have feelings for him? Even I have to admit, he's super cool. A lot mellower than I'd expected him to be," Simon said.

"He exudes that melancholic sex appeal you favor," Ella added.

I downed my wine, unwilling to lie. I had feelings for Asher. Strong ones that I'd been trying to hide, both from him and myself.

Now, on top of the fantasies I'd already created, Simon and Ella had stuffed more in my head. Hot flesh, soft lips, and deep release.

I picked up the pepper mill. "Sorry to disappoint you both, but Doug is still the only man I've ever slept with."

"Drink the wine, darling." Ella refilled my glass. "No need to take your frustrations out on the pepper grinder or that gorgeous steak. We'll think of something to relieve the tension," she added, her voice sly.

"Who says I'm tense?" I asked.

Simon and Ella exchanged a glance.

"Lia, even I think it's time you started dating," Simon said. He sipped his wine, his gaze steady. "You deserve more than… than… widowhood. You're beautiful, funny, smart, and successful. Men are idiots if they don't see what a catch you are."

"Date a few," Ella said. "That doesn't mean you have to fall in love again. You don't have to get married."

"Are you ganging up on me on purpose?" I grumbled.

"Yes," Ella chirped. "Because we want you to have one of those happy endings you used to write about."

"There's a reason I write, Ella. Well, used to write. It's fiction. Make-believe. In real life, there's no guarantee for anything other than an ending. I've learned they're rarely happy and most often painful."

Simon leaned back against the counter and considered me over the rim of his wineglass. "So Lia Moore's been reduced to bitterness. You know, losing Doug hurt us all."

"We didn't lose him," I interrupted, my voice low and vicious as some of that poisonous anger spilled into my chest. "He can't come back because he isn't *lost*. He died. He went skydiving and didn't open his parachute. He didn't tell me where he was going, didn't tell Abbi good-bye. He left me *alone* to raise a broken teenager."

I bit my lip before more venom spewed out. I turned away. I needed to go. Ella placed her hand on my shoulder. Grief and anger tangled with the panic pounding through my chest. I wanted Asher's arms around me, his voice whispering in my hair. I wanted what I couldn't have.

When would I learn?

"You should be angry, Lia. We've been waiting for it. Grieve what you lost. Please."

My shoulders fell inward as the fight went out of me. "Doug took the choice from me, so why should I mourn him?"

"Be angry with him," Simon said. "I am, too. For hurting you and Abbi, for not talking to any of us about how he was doing. But, totally separate from Doug's death, you deserve to find someone to share your life with."

"I don't see the point of trying again. Most loves don't last. They might not end as dramatically as mine, but they end—in divorce or a car accident or cancer or cirrhosis of the liver."

"You love because it's worth the risk," Ella said. "You know that better than anyone."

"Don't quit believing in something beautiful just because Doug fucked it up." Simon set his glass on the counter. He held my stare. "He fucked up, Lia. Bad."

He had. Worse than Simon knew.

Simon leaned over to peck Ella's cheek. "I'll walk up and see what's keeping the kids."

I stared at his back, so similar to Doug's, and the piece of me that had broken through the bubble when I took Asher's hand at the bar shattered. I leaned forward, struggling to get enough air. No good. The grief and anger weren't contained any longer. They spread through my chest, outward to my limbs, up to my brain.

And then the image I'd buried deep bubbled up: Doug looking down at baby Abbi, his smile so proud on his young face. *"I'm going to love her better than any other man ever could, so she'll keep feeling it even after I'm gone. Like I love you."*

I missed what we'd had then, during the good years before unwarranted jealousy and sickness broke us. I missed feeling wanted.

Hands pressed to my mouth, I tried to breathe myself back to safety. *I wasn't doing this.*

The Doug who'd killed himself hadn't been the Doug who'd loved Abbi and me.

"What is it?" Ella asked, gripping my hand.

I shook her off. "Just tired."

I turned on my heel and walked quickly to the bedroom. I fell onto the bed and struggled to contain my breathing. Bad idea. I needed to get up and keep going or let the anger pull me all the way under.

No way was I giving Doug the satisfaction of knowing I was still broken. Even if he was dead… No, he hadn't broken me. Not completely.

So I got up. Cooked dinner. Drank too much wine.

Later, I struggled to stop the few silent tears that slid past my tightly shut eyes when I finally went to bed. And I hated my weakness nearly as much as I hated what Doug had turned me into.

CHAPTER EIGHT
Asher

"Lift your back elbow more," I said. I lobbed another baseball toward Mason. His swing was jerky, but the crack of the ball hitting the wooden bat told me he'd finally gotten what I'd been trying to explain about using the middle lane.

Mason *whooped*, jumping up and down as he watched the ball arc over the apple trees toward the house.

"Home run!" he shouted, running in a circle like a flustered chicken.

I chuckled at his enthusiasm. He didn't know he was about to be in the middle of the next battleground between Jessica and me, the only fight I really cared about.

I took off my ball cap and slapped it against my leg while I waited for Mason to quit celebrating. I resisted the urge to check my phone again to see if my lawyers had reached a settlement with Jessica about the house, our joint retirement accounts, all those messy details detangling lives that no longer meshed.

I didn't care about the money or the house. I never had, not like Jessica did. I wanted to make music and I wanted my son. No way Jessica was letting some asshole in pleated pants gain custody. When I'd made the mistake of telling her that, she set off higher than a firework on Fourth of July.

I was still pissed she expected a percentage of future record sales. She was leaving me now, so I figured any judge had to consider what a well-regarded musician had to offer. I was more than happy to give her the paid-off house, a new car, and split time with the child we'd had the good sense to create. But Mason was my son, and he'd know I loved him.

Even if she stopped the custody nonsense, I didn't want to give Jessica sole custody of Mason because she would always have an excuse to keep me from my son. Especially if she found out I wanted to see Dahlia again. Jessica would assume I'd been having an affair, which would make these painful proceedings downright nasty.

Didn't matter that I'd worked hard not to look at other women for years because I'd determined at the age of eleven that I wasn't going to be a cheating asshole like my dad.

I'd read enough websites to realize judges liked continuity, and Jessica had been Mason's main guardian for years. I wondered, not for the first time, if she'd pushed me to go back to recording and touring for this eventuality.

I hoped like hell I was wrong because that made her even more calculating than I'd thought. And I knew she'd fucked around with the band, trying to break us apart or no longer trust each other. The guys and I, we'd worked through those issues years ago. We were in a good place now. I wanted it to stay that way.

But if the media dug into Olivia's death again… I couldn't imagine what that story would do to my son. He grinned and I counted the freckles on his nose. Damn, I loved this boy. I'd throw in the whole of my retirement account and all our cash as long as I got equal time with Mason.

"Mom's home," Mason said, looking over my shoulder.

I turned. Jessica's mouth was set in a thin line, her hands on her hips.

"She's mad," Mason said. He scooted closer to me.

"At me, I bet." I ran my hand over Mason's sweat-dampened head.

He glanced up, his brows furrowed. "Why is she so mean to you?"

Shit. Not a question I wanted to answer. "Because I'm sure I did something to make her angry."

"I don't like it," Mason muttered, sliding his small hand into mine.

I rested my other hand on his shoulder and hugged him tighter to my side. I'd missed this. I needed more time with my kid.

"Mason," I said. "Why don't you go get a drink?"

He scampered into the house without responding. I wished I could follow, but instead I braced myself.

Jessica crossed the yard in quick, jerky strides. Pissed didn't cover the look on her face. Awesome. This ought to be fun.

Jessica had a pretty smile, all dimples and straight white teeth. I'd loved to see her turn those brown eyes toward me in the beginning. I'd written songs about her and for her. I'd kissed her eyelids and rubbed her expanding belly. I'd held her as she wept.

"Were you going to tell me about your new sound track project?"

"I don't have a new project," I said. "I have an inquiry for a new project, and I really don't see how that's your business."

Jessica's eyes narrowed. "I'm your wife."

"Correction, you *were* my wife. We're legally separated, which means anything I do in the future has no bearing on you, especially now that I have the newest settlement agreement in writing as of this morning."

"All the years I spent waiting for real fame, and now that you've been asked to work with HBO—"

"Which you'd only know by checking up on me. Who'd you sweet talk? Richard?"

My agent and I would be having words. And if he didn't listen, I was firing him. No way was I giving Jessica more access to my life. What was next? Hacking my e-mail?

She tossed her short, brown waves back from her cheeks. She flicked her fingernail against my chin, scraping my stubble. "Your career was always supposed to open doors for me. I want that, Asher. It's what I've always wanted. Fame. Money. That's success, security. That's what people respond to."

Sure, I could provide those, but Jessica didn't want *me*. And that was the hell of it—I couldn't rescue a marriage that had long been dead. More, I didn't want to.

"I thought you were marrying Dale."

She glared at me. Like I had done something wrong by bringing up her new lover. "No, I said he asked me. Now that you're doing this big project I might just stick around, like you asked me to the other night."

She batted her eyelashes at me. Sickness swirled into my throat. I was such a fucking idiot. I'd made an offer I had no desire to keep.

I wanted to spend time with Dahlia, and this project offered the perfect excuse. I didn't, however, want to keep spiraling into negativity each time Jessica and I tried to have a conversation.

I wished I'd met Dahlia a few months later.

No, I didn't. The night on the beach was the most honest one I'd ever had. I wanted more of those moments. So I did the most natural thing I could do with Jessica: I lied. "I told Richard the HBO project's a no-go."

CHAPTER NINE
Dahlia

Our drive back to Rathdrum started off quiet, Abbi staring out the window. While I should have been considering methods to get beyond my writer's block, I spent too much time thinking about Asher. I couldn't wrap my head around the fact he wanted me. *Still* wanted me. The way he'd held me, the concern in his eyes—those moments were real, almost too perfect.

"Don't let this go to your head, but I've missed our place."

"Glad to hear that," I said. "How's school going?"

"Good. Kinda boring."

"Nothing interesting at all?"

"I like one of the baseball players."

"More than that boy you went on the trip with?"

Abbi wrinkled her nose. "He was cute, but he isn't the varsity's best pitcher. Plus, I actually see Luke. You know, once we're home."

"Luke who?"

"Watson. His dad owns the big spread near us."

"Jim Watson's a nice man…" I quickly glanced at Abbi, who was wearing a smug expression. "Oh, I know that look! Stop those wheels turning right now. Jim and Evelyn just split up in January. And he's not my type."

"Because he isn't Asher Smith?" Abbi giggled. "I overheard Aunt Ella talking about him. It's hilarious that you have a crush on a rock star."

"Your dad was a musician. So's your uncle."

"Different league, Mom."

True. Doug's band had been successful, but not enough to make much of a living.

"I'm setting up a dating profile when we get home," I said. "But I'm not dating Jim or Asher or probably anyone else either of us has met before."

"Why?"

Because I wanted Asher too much for us to actually work out. Because I was afraid he was projecting feelings onto me in an effort to get over his wife. "Because... ," I replied, not being able to muster a real response. "Asher lives near Seattle."

Abbi cocked her eyebrow, calling me on my pathetic reasoning.

I cleared my throat. "Back to school. The advance placement classes still aren't challenging enough?"

Abbi shrugged. Her finger followed a raindrop across the glass.

"I know that look, too. Your dad got it when he was about to say something he was pretty sure I wouldn't like."

She turned in her seat, pulling her foot under her other thigh. "I don't have many high school credits left. I could finish those in the morning either during the summer or during the first part of next year. I could start some college coursework online, too. Mr. Jameson said I could probably tutor in math and science. I could save the money."

"What about your senior year?"

"Besides Sally, most of my friends are graduating this year. I want to apply to Marin Tech, and I think this could help my chances."

I clutched my empty coffee cup, wishing there was another sip of cold coffee. I needed something to help with my dry throat.

"Say something. It's a good idea, right?"

"Unh," I managed to croak out. "Give me a bit of time to process. Marin Tech?"

This was the first I'd heard of her desire to go to California for college. California was so far away. No weekends home to do laundry and veg out in front of the TV for *Breaking Bad* marathons like I'd envisioned.

I sucked in a breath, trying to stave off a panic attack. I needed Asher's arms around me, murmuring words into my hair. How could I crave him so intensely?

I was losing everything. My daughter, my career, maybe my sanity. Abbi wanted to leave me, just like her father had. Just like my mother had all those years ago. The thought struck, hard and vicious: I wasn't lovable.

"Your face got all pale."

"You want to leave?"

"I want to go to Marin Tech. That doesn't mean I won't come back to visit, Mom."

"Of course."

Abbi huffed and shoved herself back into her seat while I struggled to breathe and drive us home.

———◆———

As soon as we cleared our bags from the car, Abbi went up to her room to call her friend Sally. They'd spend the next hour or two texting, talking, and otherwise social media-ing about Abbi's latest crush.

I spent some time lurking on Abbi's social media accounts, finally deciding this Luke was a reasonable kid.

I stared at the swirly screensaver for a few minutes before I forced myself to open the writing program I preferred. Panic bubbled up in my chest. I'd been sitting at my computer finishing the last scene of the third book in the Gardiner series when I got the call telling me Doug was en route to the ER.

I hadn't seen Doug that day because he'd left before I woke up. Just like when I lost my father and I hadn't had the chance to give him a last hug, tell him good-bye. Would I have done so with Doug? I'd like to think I would have. He'd held an important place in my life, even with all of the problems we faced later in our marriage.

I stood and walked into the kitchen. I pulled down a wineglass and opened a bottle of my favorite red. I watched the liquid spill into the glass, the bottle emptying with a gurgle of pleasure.

I set the bottle down on the counter and lifted the glass. I filled my mouth as full as possible and leaned my head back to swallow. I could do this. I was a writer, dammit. I walked back to my computer, set my hands on the keys. I pulled them off, my breath hitching. I sipped more wine. Finally, closing my eyes, I ignored my fluttery stomach and started typing.

The words were disjointed, not so much a story as feelings I'd been trying to grasp and understand. A paragraph of nothing.

I stood and walked to the window, staring out at the mountains.

Where was Doug? Could he hear me? My eyes remained dry, but my heart hitched a little. "I wanted to be perfect for you," I said to the room. "You broke my faith. My trust. Me."

The night and my house were quiet. I walked back to my desk and picked up my wine. I drained the glass before I sat back down.

I placed my hands on the keyboard once again.

Nothing.

I slammed my laptop closed and went to bed.

I couldn't sleep. Asher, the way his face looked in the moonlight, taunted me. I should have been honest. I should've told him I was scared. That of course I cared about him.

Ella said I was half in love with Asher. I bit into the pillow to keep the hysterical giggle from exploding forth. Another musician. A more successful musician. And I'd sworn off that breed years long before Doug died. I didn't want that type of relationship, always waiting for him at home.

But I did want Asher. He'd said he wanted me, too. Wanted me in his bed. The ache built in my belly, but more importantly, hope grew in my chest.

I looked up at the clock, shocked to realize I'd been lying there for more than four hours. I stood, stretched, and forced myself to get up.

I peeked in Abbi's room. She was curled up in her bed, asleep.

I wandered back into my office and stared at my laptop for a few minutes, emotions roiling through me. I snagged my notebook and trotted down the stairs. I'd watch the sunrise, use it as a writing exercise.

I was forcing myself through another line of description of the changing colors, when Abbi strolled into the living room.

"Did you go to bed last night?" Abbi yawned. She shuffled into the kitchen, and I forced my pen to continue across the page. *Fading into burnt umber.* Yeah, that was going to win awards.

I tossed down my pen and walked into the kitchen. Abbi raised her eyebrow as she bit into one of the whole grain waffles she'd toasted.

"Yeah. Just couldn't sleep." I waved the notebook in my hand. "I was trying to sort through my thoughts so I could send Bev and the HBO people a decent outline. Bad news is, it's got to be two more books. I don't know if they'll go for that."

I'd stared at the notes for at least an hour before the sunrise, willing something, anything to spark inside me. I flipped back to the scene sketches I'd written years before. They didn't feel right anymore. I wasn't sure I could write one, let alone two, more novels.

Abbi leaned over my shoulder, reading my notebook. She inhaled sharply.

"Please tell me either Dad or Asher Smith said that to you."

"It's fiction, Abs. Poetic license."

"I want a man who's that romantic."

"Romance is what you make of it. You're not old enough for a man. Stick to Luke boy-almost-guy for now."

"You're tied up in knots, Mom. I don't know if that's a good thing." She considered me as I set my notebook on the bar. "Hmm, it's almost seven. I need to hop in the shower and get my bag together."

I walked to the big windows and stared out, cup of coffee cuddled in my hands, staring out at the view without really seeing it.

"My ride's here, Mom. See you after practice."

"You don't want me to take you?" I asked, blinking. It was almost eight. Wow. I took a sip of my coffee; it'd gone cold. I headed into the kitchen to reheat my full cup.

"No. I called Luke and told him you were working on your HBO miniseries," Abbi said as she shouldered her messenger back. "Thanks for that, by the way. Now I get to show up at school with him."

She pecked my cheek. I noticed she was wearing the new ripped jeans we'd bought in Seattle. Her dark auburn hair was braided down the side of her head and hanging over her shoulder. My you-don't-need-much-make-up lecture had taken hold. Abbi had on some mascara, which highlighted her vibrant blue eyes. Lip gloss coated her smiling mouth. She looked pretty and fresh. I'd forgotten what that felt like.

"You should check your Facebook account. See ya. And wish me luck. I've wanted to kiss Luke forever. Today's the day!"

"As long as it's just kissing," I said.

Abbi laughed as she walked out the front door. "I set you up a dating profile," she called back.

I frowned, watching as Abbi greeted Luke, who was both cute and muscular. I'd told her I would start dating, but I wasn't sure I wanted to date anyone. Well, I did. But Asher was off limits.

———✦———

"You still sitting there?" Abbi said.

I yelped, falling back in my chair.

Abbi moved back away from me, laughing. "Dude, you're jumpy."

I turned to her. "School's out?"

"It's after five, Mom."

"Really?" I gasped.

Abbi laughed again. "I'll make dinner. You looked totally engrossed. Have you been sitting there all day?"

"I guess so." I was thirsty and trailed behind Abbi to the kitchen. I grabbed a glass, filled it with water, and downed it quickly. I refilled the glass and drank again.

"Slow down there, lady. No reason to get crazy. Did you check your Facebook account?"

"Was I supposed to?" I asked as I filled my glass again.

"I told you this morning." Abbi cocked her head, pointing toward my office. "Still nothing, huh?"

I shook my head, feeling even worse now that Abbi knew I'd failed to write anything new. Again.

"It'll happen. What did you tell me? Writing's about creating my own fantasies. Why don't you just start there?"

"Because I don't have any."

Abbi raised a skeptical brow, and I had to agree with her knowing look. I did have fantasies. About Asher. Which I'd locked down tight because I wasn't sure I could handle how much I'd yearn for him if I let my imagination and hope run free.

"Fine. Don't write, and lose your deal."

"I don't need more pressure, Abigail."

"Now to the good news, Luke asked me out!"

"Really? Well, that is news."

"Not as big as your new Facebook friend. Would you check it all ready? I've been dying to know your reaction all day!"

I pulled up the page, expecting it to be Garcia Jones, maybe Paul Loomis. It wasn't. My new friend was Tristan A. Smith. His private page, not his public Asher Smith page that linked back to the Supernaturals.

My stomach dipped. "Did you do this?" I asked, my voice hoarse.

"No. How could I? He must've looked you up."

He'd sent me a private message, too.

"Did you read this?" I asked Abbi.

"No!"

Relief flooded my system. My relationship with Asher—Tristan... no, he'd always be Asher to me—was confidential. I needed to keep it that way.

"What does it say?" Abbi asked.

"I'll read it later," I said, closing my laptop.

"You're so mean," Abbi moaned.

"Did I ask you about your conversation with Pitcher Luke?"

"I'd tell you if you'd share your sexting with me," Abbi said, crossing her arms.

I gaped at her. "You did not just say that!"

"Too much? 'Kay, I didn't. Am I cooking dinner or can we go out? I really want some manicotti. Practice kicked my butt."

"Out. But I need a shower."

———◆———

The private message from Asher lingered in my mind the entire time I was showering and through dinner. I enjoyed the building anticipation.

I'd missed the heady feel that came from a new relationship. Not that I was in a relationship with Asher. I had to remember he was just a friend. A friend who maybe was going to become a business associate.

I pushed my plate away, no longer hungry.

"Read the message, already," Abbi snapped. "It's not going to change what he said to you a few days ago."

I pulled out my phone but made a point of frowning at my daughter as I did so. She just grinned, all smug, and forked up another bite of her dinner.

My hands shook, and I had to set the phone on the table. I opened the app, holding my breath. I clicked on the message before I could chicken out.

I've been thinking about you though I probably shouldn't. I want to know how you're holding up. Any more panic attacks?

Much as I want to do this sound track with you, I've hit a snag. Jessica found out about it and is making noises about reconciliation. She doesn't mean it. She just wants more from me—more money, more fame.

I told you we've been legally separated for months. Our lawyers are hammering out details for our court date. It's soon. And, Dahlia, I can't wait. Because for the first time in years, I have something I'm looking forward to. I'm looking forward to spending time with you.

You better hold up your end of the bargain. Start writing.

"So?" Abbi asked.

I raised my eyebrow.

"Mom!" Abbi fell back into her chair, arms down by her side. "You're so killing my mood."

"He says he's been thinking about me, and I need to start writing." I didn't mention his divorce because I knew what she'd say, and I wasn't sure I'd know how to respond.

I pulled at my hair. He wanted to spend time with me. What kind of time?

Was it bad my mind went immediately to sex? The good, scream-his-name kind I hadn't had in years.

Abbi sat up, a large smile on her face. "Awesome! All true." She reached over and stole a bite from my plate. "Hey, this is good. I might order it next time."

"All yours."

"I told you I was hungry."

She forked up more of my linguini, slurping it a little before putting her hand in front of her mouth.

"It's messy. I'm not ordering that in front of Luke. He might get grossed out. How'd you eat it so neatly?"

"Practice. So tell me, why doesn't Varsity Pitcher Luke have a girlfriend?" I asked as I pushed my plate closer to Abbi's side of the table.

She shrugged. "He did until just before spring break."

"And?"

"He broke up with her." Abbi's cheeks turned pink, and she was very serious about twirling a bite of pasta onto her fork.

"Do not tell me you were involved in that." My voice was sharp.

Abbi's eyes flew to mine, the fork clattering to the table.

"No! She moved. To, like, New Jersey or something."

"And you decided to insert yourself into his life. *After* he and his girlfriend broke up."

Abbi picked up her fork and shoved it into her mouth. "Yeah," she said around the pasta.

I shook my head. "Just so you know, I would never have had the guts to go after a guy I liked in high school. If your dad hadn't constantly flirted with me, I would've never had the courage to go out with him. And I'm not going after anyone now either. Asher's married, anyway." Technically. But that was enough.

Abbi swallowed her bite and set down her fork. "Word in the media is that they're having problems. They've been separated for months."

"Did you look him up?"

"Of course. With Aunt Ella."

"I'm totally mortified you did that."

"You'll get over it, especially if you start a relationship with him. By the way, there've been a couple of articles that she's seeing some other guy and filed for a divorce."

"I'm not a marriage breaker-upper."

"You do realize that's not a word, right? I don't see the harm in going after what you want, Mom."

"This discussion is officially closed."

"Fine," Abbi said, flopping back in her chair. The kid was so dramatic. "But you really need to do something for yourself. You and I both know life isn't fair. Did you look at the dating profile I set up for you?"

"Not yet, but I will."

We sat in silence, mine thoughtful, Abbi's sullen, until the waiter brought a box and the bill.

"You'd want to be the reason some kid lost one of his parents?" I asked.

Abbi glared at me, her fair skin flaring tomato-red as it always did when she was embarrassed or truly angry.

"People make their own decisions about their lives. Dad chose to get on that plane. He chose to jump out of it, too. And guess what? We're the ones who pay for his actions."

"That's exactly my point," I said. But I was discombobulated, like my daughter had faked a pass right and spun around me to the left.

"Which means we're the ones who have to find our own happiness." Abbi smiled in triumph. "May I drive home?"

I handed Abbi the keys as she stood.

———◆———

I went straight back to my computer when we got home.

"Ooh, you're going to answer him!" Abbi squealed as she leaned her hip against the edge of my desk.

"No, I'd planned to work on my proposal for HBO."

She rolled her eyes because we both knew it was a lie. I blew out a breath and leaned back in my chair. I looked up into Abbi's eyes—so much like Doug's—and saw a world of excitement I hadn't felt in years.

"I want to answer him," I said. "I think he and I can be friends, Abs. We might work together for the miniseries, but that's it. I-I need to learn to take care of myself, not lean on someone else for my happiness. You're right about that."

"Like you did with Dad?"

I bit my lip and slammed my eyes closed, hoping she hadn't seen the anger in them.

"Mom?"

"Yeah, like I did with Dad. We were so young."

I'd needed Doug's confidence, his support in high school. My father was dead, and my mom didn't want my sister or me. Doug and I had grown up together, merging into one person in some ways. Doug's opinions, laughter, even his silences had shaped the woman I'd become. And there was no way to cut out half your vital organs and survive that level of trauma. Even when that other half was the cause of the emotional turmoil. I hadn't been strong enough to do it years ago, and I was still paying the price now.

I hadn't realized—because it wasn't something I'd allowed myself to consider—my feelings for Asher Smith were simmering underneath my day-to-day life with Doug. Since he'd sung "Moonshine Eyes" at that last performance, I'd gone over the edge from awareness to caring.

I'd thought those feelings were safe because they weren't returned. He'd moved on to another band, and I'd moved away.

"I'm not much younger than you were when you moved in with Dad."

I turned my head to smile at my daughter, the set of her chin just like Doug's. "I was seventeen, not sixteen, and your dad couldn't take any more community college courses. He needed to move to go to the university across town."

"So it was no biggie to leave your high school friends, your school?"

"Here's the rub. I was so wrapped up in your dad I didn't care about any of that." I didn't add *then*. Abbi didn't deserve that much honesty.

Abbi's eyes misted. "I want that for me," she said.

I didn't. I'd overlooked Doug's faults, willing to let him sustain my happiness as he had for years before we moved in together. When he blew apart what was left of our life together, I quit trying to find any kind of happiness. Worse, I quit living.

"I want more than that for you," I said instead, gripping Abbi's slender fingers. "I want you to stand up by yourself, be proud of the woman you've become. Find a partner, someone who loves you and respects who you are. You don't need to complete the other person. You need to be your own person who is loved for who you are."

Abbi's brows drew down, and I knew she didn't understand what I was saying to her. I wasn't sure I understood myself, but I needed to find out who Dahlia Dorsey was, separate from Doug, if I had any hope of being happy again.

"I really am going to work on my proposal. I have to get something to Garcia and Paul by Friday." I said.

"Do you have depression?" Abbi asked. She studied my face with narrowed eyes.

I laughed. "I have clarity. It's refreshing." I smiled at her, then dropped her hands. "Changes are a-comin'. You think you can keep up?" I teased.

"Pfft. I'm the poster child of flexibility."

I grabbed her hand and squeezed. "That you are, and I'm sorry for it, Abigail."

She pushed off the desk. "Not to worry." She yawned. "If you won't let me read your response to your boyfriend, I'm going to go obsess with Sally over what to wear to school tomorrow."

"Sounds good. Want to go into Spokane this weekend? Shopping, hair, maybe a mani-pedi?"

Abbi threw me a grin over her shoulder. "I like these changes. We're going to make you smoking, Mom."

I didn't answer Asher's message that week though I did accept his friend request. I liked pulling up my account and seeing his face there, but I obsessed over his unlisted relationship status for two days.

He probably thought I was teasing him or, worse, ignoring his overture. I told myself I was doing neither. I wasn't sure what I wanted to say, especially after how I left it in the parking garage. I'd been scared so I chose to back away. My normal MO, one Doug had taken advantage of.

Asher and I both knew the importance of words. I wanted my response to him to be clear so that he knew what I expected moving forward. Since my head wasn't capable of finding the right response yet, I procrastinated.

Unable to make any progress with the writing, I made copies of my notes and sent them to Bev. She went through and jotted down her thoughts, which I dutifully typed up into the proposal.

"It's not your best work, but it shows that you've thought about it," Bev said. "I don't love the ending."

Neither did I, but I hadn't come up with anything better. "What if we send them these synopses but say I'm open to developing the appropriate ending for the series with their help? I think Paul would like that."

"Hmm, you mean not sell these last two books you know you need to write, just the movie rights?"

That wasn't what I wanted, but I couldn't get the words onto the page. I might not have a choice.

"I'll send them this," Bev said. She seemed hesitant, and I'd never heard Bev sound tentative before.

When Paul's response of "We need something in line with the quality of the first three books" came, I collapsed into my chair, struggling to breath. When Abbi called to me from downstairs, I fled to my bathroom, turning on the shower. I had a week to come up with the quality Paul and Garcia expected.

One week to overcome years of frustration and disappointment.

CHAPTER TEN
Asher

Last night I'd considered driving to Idaho just to make sure Dahlia was okay. A stupid impulse, sure, but she hadn't posted anything online. Like, at all. She'd been a regular user of social media until she accepted my friend request. This week nothing, even though her friends posted on her wall. And I knew from one of those posts—no, I wasn't checking my account fifty times a day—that she'd set up a dating profile. Her sister, Briar Moore, had commented on it as soon as it went live.

Why the fuck had Dahlia set up a dating profile now? She'd linked it to her Facebook account, another oddity since she ignored both.

While I wanted to talk to Dahlia about what I'd said to her the last time we spoke, I needed to discuss the sound track. The HBO guys coughed up more money to sweeten the deal, but I needed time—time to get Jessica out of my life so I could accept the gig.

Especially since Jessica had rejected my last offer, further dragging out the divorce proceedings. She was now asking for full custody of Mason and alimony from any future music royalties.

"Face facts," Jessica had said. "I'm going to get a lot of this because you weren't exactly circumspect about your drug-taking for years. No judge is going to rule against the little wifey who's been raising your kid in backwoods Washington while you're touring the world in rock-star style."

I'd walked out at that point. If I'd stayed, I would've done something stupid. Like get high just so I didn't have to hear Jessica's bitching anymore.

I drove to the crap apartment I'd rented months ago for a place to store my stuff. Not that I had much. I hadn't wanted to worry Mason by clearing out more than what was necessary. One extra suitcase hadn't made much of an impression, but now my entire music library was still at the house and Jessica planned to sell it off for cash.

I had another month left on the lease but I was too dejected to renew. I had to start making some decisions about my future. I knew what I wanted: a chance to be me, hanging out with my kid, getting to know Dahlia, the woman I'd always coveted.

With each day that passed, I stretched tighter, as if I were going to snap. The last time I'd been this wound up, I'd popped enough pills to see my world in Technicolor for three days. That'd been amazing, but I'd done some stupid shit that I was still paying for in the form of bad publicity. That was one of the reasons I'd cleaned up my act. I knew, even then, I'd lose Mason if I didn't.

———◆———

Mason flopped onto the grass, his chest heaving. I headed over and sat next to him.

"I like baseball," he said.

"Home-run derbies are the best."

"Are you and Mom really getting a divorce?" he asked. His hazel eyes were serious, his mouth turned down with concern.

"Yeah." I pulled my knees up and laid my arms across them. Now that we had the final date set with the judge, I'd told Mason about our coming split.

"Because you don't love her no more?"

"Is that what she said?"

Mason nodded, and I sucked my lips into my mouth to keep from cursing. Every situation was all about Jessica. When had she started putting her feelings, her needs first? My stomach clenched.

When Olivia died.

"She said you wouldn't go touring with the band if you loved us right," he said, the words tumbling out faster and faster. "She said you don't want to stay here with us because we don't fill your ego or something."

I had to force my hands to unclench. I wrapped them around my knees. Mason looked at me, a frown forcing his brown brows into a deep V.

"Part of the reason your mom and I are divorcing is because we don't talk to each other well anymore. If that's how she felt, she should have told me."

"So you do still love her?" Mason asked, his face lighting with hope.

I rubbed my thumb against my forehead, hoping to alleviate the building ache.

"I don't want to tell you lies, Mason. I don't want to tell you you're too young to understand, because I remember how angry I was when my parents did that to me. What I can say is that it's complicated. Your mom is angry. I am, too. She's the one who asked for the divorce. She's the one who asked me to move out."

"This is because of that guy who calls her all the time, huh?"

"What guy? Dale?"

"I don't know his name, but he'll call and Mom will talk to him and then she'll make Mrs. Knowles stay with me and she'll be gone for hours, sometimes overnight. I don't like it when she leaves me with Mrs. Knowles at night. She snores, and I'm scared."

The headache exploded. I sucked in a breath and closed my eyes. I was going to have to have my kid testify against his mom. How, in good conscience, could I make Mason do that? He loved Jessica, even with her failings. Hell, I had a ton of my own, not least of all with Jessica.

I had been the product of a single-parent household from the time I was in fifth grade. I didn't want Mason to follow my pattern. I'd been—still was—fucked up because of it.

"You want me to talk to her about that?" I asked.

Mason nodded.

"All right, buddy. I will. When she gets home."

I just hoped that wasn't until after Mason went to bed for the night. I liked my time with him—reading him a book, tucking him in. I wanted to do more of that. I wanted the every-night daddying I'd dreamed of ever since Jessica had told me she was pregnant. Thankfully, I got my time with him now.

"He's afraid, Jessica. He's a little boy."

She was at the kitchen counter pouring a glass of white wine. "I'm the one here with him. Every. Day. So enjoy your thirty minutes of dad-time for the month. Then you get to leave for another tour, screw any number of girls between the stage and the bus, and eventually saunter in here, questioning my parenting."

She glared at me over the raised glass. When she set it down, half the wine was gone.

Fuck. Mason had reason to be scared. I was, too. This wasn't the woman I'd married. She'd been spiraling for years, and nothing I did had helped.

I ran my fingers through my hair. "What do you want from me?"

"I want you to be *the* famous rock star. I want you to adore me like you used to. I want exciting vacations and lunch dates with cool people. I want the life you promised me."

"I never promised you any of that."

"You did! But I'm still in Washington. Not even the good part. Not Seattle or Bainbridge Island. No, we moved here because of the schools. To make everything better for Mason. Well, I'm done waiting for you to realize my life is passing just as quickly as yours. I need more than this. You need to do your job."

"I have a job," I said through gritted teeth. That was the button she knew to press.

"You have gigs. You sing to maybe a couple thousand fans, have sex, get high, and move on. That's not enough anymore, hasn't been since your twenties. I don't want to share your attention, and I don't want to worry about bills."

"I sing. I put on a show. That crap—I haven't done that in years. I married you. I meant my vows. We have enough in all our accounts to keep you from worrying about bills for years."

Jessica scoffed. "I've watched the women plaster themselves on you, Asher."

A wave of exhaustion slammed over me. "I can't make them stop coming on to me. And they don't want me. They want the front man of the Supernaturals. You know my parents' split messed me up for years. I told you I wanted to be married forever."

"Then you should have lived up to your promises."

"You served me with papers while I was on the fucking road. I was touring to pay for whatever the hell it is you do here, and you kicked me out."

"I had plans, too, Asher. Big plans that did not include staying hidden in Nowheresville, fifty miles from the shit-hole I grew up in."

"What plans? Come on, Jessie. I want you to be happy. I'll do what I can to help you. Just don't take it out on Mason. That isn't fair to him."

"What would make me happy, *Tristan*, is for you to upgrade my situation." Her teeth pulled back in a feral grin. "And now I have insurance to make sure you cough up what I want."

My stomach pitched like it was at the top of a twenty-story roller coaster. The plummet, when it came, would be intense and horrifying.

"What do you mean by insurance?"

She blinked prettily around her wineglass. Did she get her eyelashes enhanced? Was that even possible?

"What does that mean, Jessica?"

"You'll see," she said. "I'm sure we'll both enjoy the spotlight then."

"Is this about Olivia?"

"Don't say her name," Jessica snapped.

"We never talked about her. Maybe we could have worked through our problems then."

"Shut up!" she screamed. She threw the glass, missing my head by inches. Glass and wine exploded across the counter behind me. Her eyes were wide, her face pale.

Hopefully Mason hadn't heard her screaming.

"Fine. We'll ignore the actual problem that's been there for years. What about Mason?"

Jessica shrugged, and anger burned through me, visceral and

ugly. I stepped back and shoved my fisted hands into my pockets.

"Mason's fine. Parents get divorced all the time. He'll probably be more normal now that we're splitting up. Soon as you give me what I want, I'm fine not seeing you again. You keep disappointing me. I didn't think that was possible. But you do."

"I meant about you going out and leaving him at night." I wanted to ask if she'd ever cared about us at all, or if I was just a stepping-stone to something bigger. She was more than willing to trade in everything we'd built for money. Problem was, I'd never make enough for her. Fuck of a time to realize that.

"He's always safe, always fed, and mommy usually even reads him a book at bedtime after he's had his milk and cried for his daddy. Every. Night. You're gone. You can't pin this all on me."

I ran my hands through my hair. I was tired. I'd been running on fumes since I received the separation papers. No, in truth, I'd been a mess since Olivia died. Jessica was right. This situation was my fault. I hadn't been worried about emotional depth when I met Jessica, hadn't realized how important it was because I'd wanted a bed partner, not a life partner.

"We both fucked up."

She glared at me until I couldn't stand the accusation anymore. She had every right to be pissed at me.

"I'm taking Mason to my place." I turned my back on Jessica and went up the stairs.

CHAPTER ELEVEN
Dahlia

Saturday morning, Abbi popped into my room early, as was her habit. She stopped short, surprised to see I was not only awake but also showered, dressed, and pulling my long hair into a high ponytail. I had on a pair of comfy jeans I'd stolen from her closet.

One of the side effects of Doug's death was losing my curves. For the most part, I looked like I always had, just skinnier. My eyes were still gray, my hair the same dark reddish-brown. My skin was relatively smooth.

Not too old to love again. Not yet.

After another sleepless night, I knew I'd have to face Asher and my jumbled feelings for him if I was going to work through my writer's block. Now downstairs in the kitchen, I smiled at Abbi, toasting her with my now-empty coffee cup. I didn't tell her it was my third. "You ready for a full day of mom-makeover?"

Abbi's face was serious, her hands on her hips. "I've been waiting for this for years." She snatched the mug from my hand. "I'll put this in dishwasher. Let's hit the road."

Abbi plugged in her charger to set a playlist from her phone, and we hummed along to a variety of current artists. Like most of her peers, Abbi stuck to the four-count rhythm and breezy lyrics so common in the pop genre. I tapped my finger along to the constant, easy beat, not really paying attention.

Then… the distinctive revving riff of a Supernaturals's lead guitar. I caught Abbi's smirk before she turned toward the window.

"Since when did you become a Supernaturals fan?"

Abbi shrugged. "Since my mom met this awesome guy who happens to be the lead singer of the band. He might be O-L-D, but he makes my mom's cheeks glow whenever she thinks about him. I owe him pretty big for bringing her back from the brink, so I figured I'd show my gratitude by buying the entire library."

"My credit card isn't going to be thrilled with that decision."

"Then take it out of my college account. I know it's all funded, thanks to Dad's life insurance. Are you ever going to answer Asher's message? You do realize you are starting to seem like a b— I mean witch."

I took a deep breath and tightened my grip on the steering wheel. "I don't know what to say to him," I murmured.

"Be you. He seemed to like that the last time. And before, when you knew him a lifetime ago."

"Tell you what. Let's get through the haircut and some new clothes, and then I'll send him a message."

Abbi glared at me. "You need to check your dating profile, too, but we'll do that later. Asher comes first. Lunchtime. That's your deadline. Or I'm hacking your account and telling him you're a chicken."

"Abigail, that isn't funny."

"It wasn't meant to be. It's called a threat."

It was my turn to glare at my daughter, but I could tell by the thrust of her jaw and the gleam in her eye, she'd follow through on her warning. This was the downside of having a child so young. I didn't have the same parental sway as many of my older counterparts. Abbi was so easygoing and fun, we'd spent more time as friends than in a traditional mother-daughter relationship.

"You will *not* touch my accounts. And you need to let me handle my life my way. Please."

Her eyes filled with disappointment, her irises darkening and the sparkle fading. "Not if you're going to hide for the rest of it. I need you to live again, Mom."

I swallowed and looked away. "I'm trying." We sat in silence for a moment. "So I figure cutting off all this weight has to be a good first step."

Her eyes stayed serious, but her mouth lifted. "I'm sure we can find something that shows off your big eyes and awesome cheekbones."

———◆———

I stared back at my reflection, shocked by the difference the multiple layers and a Brazilian blowout had made. Whoever said that confidence came from feeling beautiful was onto something.

Abbi and I spent way too much time and money in a massive shopping mall. By the time we walked out, bags pinching my fingers, my stomach growled, and my feet felt tight in my sensible flats.

"You holding up?" I asked.

"Totally. I love the marathon approach," Abbi said, shooting me a happy smile. "I can't believe you bought me that cashmere wrap. I may have to sleep in it for the rest of my life. It's so soft."

I'd bought one for myself, too, cringing at the price. But I had enough to cover the splurge even without the HBO project. Which wasn't signed. My stomach fluttered.

For long-term security, I needed to make that deal happen. I had six days.

I frowned. Paul hadn't mentioned whether Asher planned to put together the sound track when we'd talked earlier in the week. Asher had written that Jessica was causing problems. Was he waiting for me to respond to his message, to give him the okay to work together? If so, well, I'd procrastinated long enough.

Stowing our items in the back of my SUV, we headed toward one of the restaurants at the mall.

After being seated and served our drinks, I tapped Abbi's glass of iced tea with my own. "To beginnings."

"I'm in love with your new cut," she said. She took a sip of her tea, scrunched her nose, and reached for the sugar. "Get out your phone and answer Asher Smith. Now."

"I haven't looked at the menu yet."

Abbi finished dumping in sugar and set the dispenser on the table with a thump. "You're afraid."

The words sounded so much worse coming from my teenage daughter's mouth. I chewed my lip while I decided that Abbi was old enough to deal with some of my life.

"I am. I used to have a crush on him. If I leave it at the time we've spent together, I'll have the perfect little dream to pull back out and enjoy over the years."

Abbi gripped the top of her menu and leaned forward. "He's not Dad."

Anxiety slashed through me, dragging the air from my lungs.

"He probably won't die. Or leave." She sat back, completely unaware of how close I was to falling apart. I ducked behind the menu, relieved she hadn't found out. Some secrets were just too much to share.

"He mentioned he wants to be friends." Abbi snorted as she shook her head.

"You read my messages?"

Abbi lifted her left eyebrow. "But of course, Mrs. Dorsey," she said in a terrible British accent.

"That's an invasion of privacy." I was angry. Angry enough to burn away my burgeoning panic. I couldn't remember the last time I'd been inundated with this much emotion.

"How is it different than you reading my texts and messages?"

She had me there. "You're prone to do something dumb. It's instilled in your teenage DNA."

"I love you too much to do something that'll hurt myself, Mom. I'm not going to go to some lame high school party with hot beer just to get busted by Sheriff Lindon. I'm not going to put myself in danger to be date-raped, and I'm not going to come home pregnant. But you can keep checking up on me because I know you need to feel like you're doing everything you can for me. And you're less anxious when you feel in control."

I dropped the menu to the table, barely missing my glass. "You know about my panic attacks?"

Abbi nodded. "Yeah, and the insomnia. Both seem better." She cocked her head, her long, shiny hair spilling over her trim shoulder. "Since our trip to Seattle."

She waited, letting me digest that information. "I may be only sixteen, but I understand something about love." She raised her eyebrows as she took a sip of her drink. "Maybe because my mom writes romances. I know it's the trust part that's a leap of faith. Right now, Asher is asking for you to trust in friendship. Did it ever occur to you that maybe he needs a friend just as badly as you do?"

Abbi sat back in her chair. The waitress ambled over and Abbi ordered us salads and a double order of onion rings. I nodded my approval, my mind whirring.

"When did you get so smart?" I pulled out my phone, and Abbi fist-pumped the air.

"I've always been this awesome. Just took you a while to figure it out. Type your message. I need to pee. Be back in a jiffy."

Pulling up Asher's message caused my face to heat up, and I was shocked I still blushed. I opened the app and reread the message I knew verbatim. I started typing. This was the time for truth, not my edited thoughts.

I've read your message every day, wondering if I should respond. I worried what to say. Nothing felt right because nothing can tell you how much I needed you last week. Thank you for holding me, for listening. Thank you for caring.

I'm sorry about your marriage. This may be presumptuous, but I want to be that real friend you said you miss. I'm ready to listen any time you need me.

I can't write. I'm scared the HBO deal will fall through because I'm not strong enough to get beyond my emotional block, which means I won't get to collaborate with you on the sound track… If you've worked it out on your end.

That's part of why I haven't responded.

-D

My finger shook, and I had to press Send twice before it actually went. Abbi slid into the booth across from me, her lips pursed.

"Done." I said.

"You gonna let me read it?"

I bit my lip, considering my options. Then I slid my phone across the table. I watched her eyes slide across the screen. A little smile formed as she handed it back.

"He's calling you."

CHAPTER TWELVE
Asher

"Are you mad?" Mason asked, his voice small. We were in the field next to the small orchard that'd come with the house. My heart wasn't into playing ball. I kept replaying Jessica's comments from the other night. She wanted to nail my balls to the wall. I should've acted years ago to start this separation process, like my mom had gently suggested.

Mason climbed up in one of the apple trees. I sat beneath it, watching him. He and I had been hanging out every day for a week. This was the longest I'd been home since Olivia... I couldn't quit thinking about her.

"I'm working on the fear thing. Bryan said he still has night-mares about monsters, but I don't do that anymore," Mason said proudly from his perch in the tree.

I flopped back onto the grass. "I'm not angry that you're afraid of the dark. I was, too. I got scared again when my dad left."

My dad told my mom that leaving me with her was for the best because she was the better parent. He was right; my dad was a selfish prick. I remembered spending a weekend with him when I was maybe thirteen. He'd gotten dressed up that Saturday night. When I asked him where he was going, he'd grabbed his keys off the counter and tucked his wallet into his expensive slacks. "I'm going to pick up a woman and screw her brains out. You'll get the itch when you're a little older."

"But what about me?"

"What about you? Oh, here's some money for some pizza." He'd tossed a pile of bills on the table. "See you later. Might be tomorrow if she's any good."

My mom might've worked long hours and taken business trips she dreaded nearly as much as I did, but she made sure I had a qualified adult to watch me. She made huge piles of my favorite foods and stored them in the fridge and freezer with sticky notes on each container telling me to enjoy and how much she loved and missed me.

"Promise, Dad?" Mason's voice brought me back to the present.

I blinked at my son. He'd climbed down from the tree and was sitting next to me in the grass. I wrapped my arm around his shoulder.

"What was that, bud?"

"You promise you won't leave me alone at night?"

I swallowed hard. I couldn't fulfill his need as long as Jessica had custody.

I looked down into his little face and held out my pinky, hooking it slightly. "Pinky swear."

I poured Mason some lemonade, glad Jessica had decided to drive into Seattle for girl time with one of her giggly friends who I hated.

Mason wanted to hang here at the house. As long as Jessica was gone, I was good with that. Though, I'd learned that the guestroom mattress was lumpy and my back wasn't as forgiving as it used to be.

It was just after noon. Good. I needed a beer.

Snagging it out of the fridge, I also pulled out the sandwich fixings Mrs. Knowles brought over that morning. If I was hungry, Mason had to be, too.

"You want a sandwich?"

"I'm really hungry."

"Why didn't you say anything?"

"Mom says it's annoying to always be making another meal when I just finished the last one."

I slammed the plates onto the counter with more force than necessary, breaking them both.

"Oops," I said, hoping my voice sounded normal. "Get me the broom, will you? What about Mrs. Knowles?"

"She makes me whatever I want when she's here. I love her quesadillas."

After cleaning up the porcelain shards, I made Mason two sandwiches and loaded his plate up with apple slices and some chips. We carried our plates onto the porch and ate in companionable silence. Mason finished well before I did, my appetite ruined.

"Can I get something else?" he asked, his hazel eyes, the one feature we shared, hopeful.

"Course, buddy. After you get another snack, we'll head down to the lake."

"Awesome!" he squealed. He picked up his plate and carried it into the house. I waited until his feet pounded up the stairs before I pulled out my phone and called my lawyer, Pete Nelson. After laying out what Mason had told me earlier, I said, "Figure out how to get me custody."

"That's not going to be easy, Asher. She's already pushing hard for the money and primary custody."

"I don't give a fuck about money. I want my kid."

"Her lawyer said she'd be more amenable if she had a percentage of future earnings. She wants a full twenty percent."

"She's crazy. There are four of us in the band. That'd leave me with five percent on all the work I do after she's out of my life." A growl rose in my throat. "I'm not her indentured servant. That's after the house and all the cash we've managed to put away, right?"

"That's her current demand, but each time it's for more."

"She's said she's willing to ditch Mason for the money and future earnings. Can we use that?"

"She's his primary caregiver, always has been. You know judges like continuity. We'd have much better leverage if we could show she was an unfit mother. Something concrete, not your kid's comments, though those will help. You have a nanny. Get her to document neglect."

I closed my eyes, warring with myself. "Kinda hard if the nanny's here, taking care of him."

"Yeah, and Jessica will claim she needs the money to keep the nanny. That happens a lot. You're going to have to do more, Asher. Talk to your nanny. Leaving the kid home alone—get someone to take pictures or something. We have to build the case."

"Mason might love Jessica, but he's suffering," I said. "That has to stop. You said we had a better case because she's the one who filed, both for the separation and the divorce."

"True, but your past doesn't endear you to a judge."

"The partying? I haven't done that in years. I was never busted. I don't have a record."

"I'm talking about that huge spread with that rock magazine fifteen years ago to showcase your rowdy lifestyle, which Jessica's lawyers have already mentioned. You're smoking pot in the picture, Asher. Hell, half your songs are about pills and easy sex."

I closed my eyes, tilting my head back.

"Once again, that was before I was a parent. There isn't any recent story or magazine spread to add. I have a stage persona, one I cultivated in my early twenties. That's not *me*."

"I'm not the judge, Asher. I'm just telling you what he's going to be thinking."

"What about Jessica's affairs? Use them. I pay you a lot of money. I want my son. Figure this out."

Mason came out, carrying a bag of Oreos. Those were Jessica's favorite. I smiled at him, knowing we were both going to catch shit when she realized he'd raided her stash. I snagged two cookies. They tasted like sawdust, but I ate them anyway.

I opened the web browser on my phone, intent to do some more cyber stalking. Happiness rocked through my chest when a tiny headshot blinked up in my message app. Dahlia had answered me. I could almost imagine the hesitancy in her eyes as she wrote her reply.

"I'm gonna put on my suit!" Mason said. His mouth was coated in the chocolate powder.

"Be right in, buddy," I said, dialing the number I'd finagled out of Paul Loomis.

I headed inside, my heart lighter and a smile splitting my face.

CHAPTER THIRTEEN
Dahlia

"What?" Thank goodness I was shocked into breathlessness because otherwise I would have screamed.

The waitress brought our food. She set it on the table and glanced back and forth between my flushed, gawking face and Abbi's smug one.

"You ladies doing all right here?"

Abbi waved her away as she picked up her fork. "My mom's just surprised at how much other people like her. It'll be fine."

"Promise?" the waitress asked, twisting her fingers into the hem of her top. "We had a guy have a heart attack in here last week."

I turned to the girl. "I'm fine."

My phone started ringing again.

"Mom, you have to answer this time."

I peered at Abbi before picking up the phone with a shaky hand. "Hello?"

"Dahlia. I've been worrying about you."

"You don't have to."

"But I do. I thought either our walk meant more to me than to you, or Simon talked you out of continued contact with me. I'm glad I was wrong. I hope on both counts."

"Asher, I—"

"What I said in the elevator? I know the timing is terrible. I know you're nervous. But, dammit, Dahlia. This may be my one chance to get this right."

"This?"

"Don't give up on me. Please."

His voice, so filled with emotion, slithered through my defenses. If I was smart, I would step back, push him away. I'd been with a musician before. I looked over into Abbi's eyes, saw her hope reflecting my own. Stupid though it was.

"I'm here," I whispered. My heart pounded slow and sure in my chest.

"I want you to meet Mason. I want to meet your daughter."

"I have commitments, Asher. This project. I need it to work out. I know you want it nearly as badly as I do." The uncertainty built, pushing away the pleasure and peace I'd just derived from his words.

"Just write. It'll start out rusty and horrible, but push through. I have faith in you. Can I read it when it's done? I know it's going to be worth reading, Dahlia Moore Dorsey."

That was the problem. I no longer had faith in myself. "Thank you for saying that."

"I'll always tell you the truth. That's my promise."

"Bye, Asher."

"Think about what I said."

I chewed my lip. "I haven't stopped," I blurted out.

"Dahlia? You're not just an ideal."

I hung up and set my phone on the table. I ignored the fact that my hand was still shaking.

"I'm no longer going to feel so lame when I'm dying for Luke to call me. Not if Asher's doing it with you."

"Abbi. Stop. Please."

Abbi ate the rest of her salad and most of the onion rings while I nibbled and thought. I mourned the end of Asher's marriage, just as I had my own.

106

"I'm going out with one of the guys from the dating site." I snagged a cold onion ring and munched.

"What? Asher Smith likes you, and you think there's some other guy that's better for you?" She picked up her phone and texted someone, completely ignoring me as I ate another onion ring.

My phone rang, and I groaned when Ella's number popped up on my screen. I glared at Abbi, who glared back, her chin tilted forward just like Doug used to do.

"Don't you dare start with me, El."

"Lovely greeting, darling. I can see where your daughter gets her charming personality. I want you to post a pic of your new haircut, love. Abbi says it's gorgeous."

"Abbi already took pictures and posted them to her page."

"But I want to ooh and ah on *your* page. Do it now. We'll talk about how you're trying to sabotage your life later."

I scowled at my phone. After uploading the new picture, I pulled out my credit card and tossed it on the check tray. "We're going home. I'm so done with your shenanigans."

Abbi smirked. "That's an old lady word."

My phone chirped. I flipped it over, and there, on the screen, was a text from Asher. *You look beautiful.* I smiled, my heart warming more than my cheeks.

Abbi'd been playing with her phone, but she grabbed mine from my hand. She let out a little squeal and fanned herself. "I'm so excited he's texting you, I'm not even going to make fun of you for saying 'shenanigans.'"

My cheeks flamed again. So that was Ella's game. I was bad at this dating thing.

My experience was limited to Doug and Patrick Johnson, who'd, in the seventh grade, wanted to shove his tongue down my throat. Seriously the worst kiss ever, and he'd had the gall to tell people how hot I was for him. Ruined the rest of my junior-high experience, not that it'd been that stellar before.

But this… Ella was taking advantage of my naïveté. While her intentions were sweet, I was annoyed I'd fallen for such an obvious ploy. Why did he have to like my haircut on Facebook? I'm sure Ella thought linking our names would scare off other potential date options. For me. Not him. As many men did, he'd remained a sex symbol even after getting married eight years ago. Some women took a wedding ring as a challenge, one they'd then flaunt in the wife's face.

My phone rang, and I huffed out the breath I'd been holding. I rolled my eyes as I answered. "Hey, Briar."

"Hey yourself, sis. How come I didn't know you'd hooked up with your favorite lead singer? You know I was always jealous you hung out with him years ago."

"He told her she was beautiful," Abbi practically yelled into the phone.

I pulled back and frowned at her, but she was bouncing with excitement.

"I don't hang out or hook up with anyone. And you were in junior high last time I met Asher. He was so wild." In that sexy bad-boy way I'd written about. I frowned as I mentally flipped through the heroes in the Gardiner series. Any of them could be Asher's twin. Why hadn't I realized that before?

"He seems to have toned down the wild. More's the pity. I bet he was all kinds of fun. You were mesmerized by him then."

"Stop it. I'm already annoyed with my meddlesome daughter."

"Aw, Abbi's a cutie. She's just worried about you, like the rest of us. So what's the scoop with you and the Supernaturals lead man? He likes you under his own name. Tristan. I got a shiver saying it."

I grunted because I knew what she meant. Thinking of him as Tristan, so distinct from his stage name, was intimate.

"So he's, like, a real friend?"

I signed my name to the bill with a flourish and stood. I didn't bother to look back. I knew Abbi would follow because she wanted to hear as much of the conversation with my sister as possible.

"I saw him a couple weeks ago at Simon's show. He's taller than I remembered. Broader. His forearms are amazing, probably from the guitar playing. He wore Converse."

"Omigod. His forearms?" Briar's giggled. "That's what you want to bring up?"

"We talked. That's all."

"That's not what Ella said."

"We may work together on the sound track for the miniseries. He sent a friend request. That's about it. So I told Abbi I'm going to start dating. I have a dating profile on Ranch Singles."

"Erm…"

"Isn't that what you've all wanted me to do? Meet a nice, solid guy?"

"Yes, but Ranch Singles? What the hell is that?"

"It's the dating website for Idaho. I'm thinking about only dating guys my age or younger. You know, in case I get attached. Men die so much younger than women, on average. That's what you told me after your last symposium."

Briar was quiet for a long time. "I have no idea who you are." She hung up on a laugh.

Sad thing was I didn't know either.

———————

Abbi helped me narrow my choices to five guys from the dating site she'd chosen once she realized I was serious. It wasn't *actually* called Ranch Singles, a name I'd made up to annoy Briar. Abbi pouted the whole time, making the process even more harrowing than I'd anticipated. Like I was begging for a prom date. I could almost hear the popular cheerleader girls at every high school in the country laughing at me.

"You want me to date Asher Smith so you can go to free rock shows. It's not as glamorous as it seems."

Abbi's brow furled. "I thought he made you happy."

Shame burned up my chest, flushing my neck and cheeks. "I'm sorry, Abbi."

"Write your own date request." Abbi stormed out of the room. I sucked my lip between my teeth. She was so angry, she hadn't even stopped to collect her bags of new clothes.

I opened my e-mail, which I'd been avoiding since I posted that picture to my Facebook page earlier today. As expected, I had a flood of e-mails, nearly all of them asking how long I'd known Asher Smith and when I was going to do my supposed friends the favor of introducing them to Asher. All he'd done was like my picture; he hadn't even written anything.

I made a new file titled *Not Friends* and crammed all the e-mails into it.

A new message from Briar caught my eye. She rarely e-mailed me, preferring the faster method of text or phone calls.

Hey, sis. Since our conversation earlier, I've gotten no less than 25 e-mails asking me when you hooked up with Asher Smith. There've been rumors of trouble in his paradise for years, but I just confirmed that his wife filed for legal separation months ago—the divorce is proceeding and was in the entertainment news in the Seattle paper a few days ago. Wasn't sure if you knew.

Call me if you need to talk—completely off record. But you should already know I would never sell you out. Hugs."

I called her. "Thank you for realizing I would never get involved with another musician."

"I don't think I said that," she said, amusement lacing her voice. "Doug played guitar in a glorified garage band, but Asher Smith is a freaking rock star. Who doesn't need to live at least one lurid fantasy in her life? Especially if you write romance."

"I don't do lurid. Not in real life, anyway."

"Maybe you should."

"Not you, too, Briar. Abbi's angry with me because I don't want to pursue something with Asher."

The timing of his return to my life was so wrong. He was in the process of dissolving his marriage, and I... I tugged at the ends of my hair. He would hurt me like Doug had.

"Look, for what it's worth, Jessica Smith's up here in the San Juan Islands with another man right now. The two of them have been seen together off and on for a couple of years."

"Years?" I dropped my head into my palm. "Are you sure?"

"Yep. I could forward you the pictures one of our people took yesterday. Others are stored at the paper's servers from their previous visits, but I could pull them out, if you need them."

"Why would I need them? Why didn't you print them?"

Briar was the editor-in-chief, the youngest for the *San Juan Tribune*, and one of the younger women newspaper chiefs in the country.

"Nothing super juicy, or I'd never be able to hold them back. I don't know how to get in touch with Asher Smith directly but it seems like something he should know about."

My chest tightened, my lungs compressed. "Why?"

"She brought her son up here," Briar said. "Those pics bothered me, but I'm not running the freaking *Tattler*."

I did not want to know. "What did she do to Mason?"

"It's what she didn't do. She left him alone at a cabin while she was off with her boyfriend. Who, by the way, does not compare to Asher."

"Focus, Bri. The pictures."

"Right. The time-lapse says a couple hours."

"She left him alone?" Censure filled my voice, and the pressure in my chest increased. I rubbed, trying to ease the building pain. "I don't think Asher knows Jessica's been cheating that long."

"My guess is no if the divorce is just now coming about," Briar said. "I'll forward the pics to you if you think they'd help."

"Do. Asher wants custody of Mason."

"So you two *are* friends?"

"I don't know him that well," I said. "I should go." I held the phone away, hoping Briar couldn't hear my choppy breathing.

"Stop hedging. What's your problem? Why don't you just go for it?"

I squeezed my eyes closed. "He's a musician, Briar."

"So?"

"Like Doug," I whispered. "You said it. Asher's more famous.

More messed up. And I need to go."

"No. Tell me why you'd pass on the one man we know you want."

"I don't want to talk about Asher," I said.

"You'd rather talk about Doug?"

"He lied to me."

"Doug?" Briar asked.

Yes. My husband. That grievous place in me cracked open all the way. My breathing hitched again as I tried to force it down.

"You can't still miss him." Exasperation laced her words. She knew. She was the only one who knew how bad it had gotten.

"He promised to love me," I managed to gasp. "But he didn't. He *didn't*." Not like I needed him to.

"You're crying."

I was. They were big, ugly tears. I slid from my chair to the floor. I heard Briar call my name, but I didn't respond.

The sobs worsened, and I pulled my knees up to my chest. I didn't believe that love trumped all. Doug took that belief from me, and I was as angry and hurt about that as I was about his death. Maybe more so.

I'd held the trust we'd had in each other early in our relationship close, nourished it for years. Until he shattered my every illusion.

"Some days, I hate him," I whispered. The words fell between my tears, heavy with the truth I'd held inside for way too long.

"Ouch!" I groaned as a few eyelashes popped out of my lids. My lashes had fused together either during my hours-long cry-fest or in my sleep. I needed to get to the bathroom before I tried opening my eyes again. Problem was, I couldn't see.

I flopped over and hit something hard, maybe a knee or elbow. I squealed, dragging the covers up to my chin.

"Need a washcloth to get the gunk out?" Abbi asked.

"Thank God, it's you. Yes, please."

"Who else would it be?" She opened a door. A moment later she laid a warm, wet cloth over my eyes. The heat and moisture soothed my swollen tissue.

"Did you sleep in here?" I asked.

"Yeah. I got you into bed."

"I'm sorry."

"Why?"

"Guess I still had some sadness to get out," I mumbled, embarrassed.

"I hope so," Abbi said, her voice sharp. "I never saw you cry after Dad died. You seemed so... unaffected by everything. Aunt Ella and Aunt Briar told me it was your coping mechanism, what you did when Grandpa died."

I pulled the cloth from my eyes, thankful I could open them now. I looked at my daughter. "I loved your dad. I loved your grandfather, too."

"You kept way too much bottled up for too long. You're the one who should've gone to counseling, you know."

"I thought it would help you work through your feelings," I said. I brought the cloth back to my eyes and rubbed away the remnants of my tears.

Her eyes were too dark, her lips flattened. She tucked my hair behind my ear. "I'm worried about you, Mom."

"I'm the one who's supposed to be worrying."

"I have healthy emotional relationships. Just ask my counselor."

"Enough sarcasm, Abs. I'm dealing as best I can."

She rolled her eyes. "Are you finally going to let Dad's death go? I need to know that by the time I go to college, you'll be healthy enough for me to leave. Better yet, you need a man who spoils you rotten so you don't even miss me."

I gripped the back of Abbi's hand, desperate for the connection. "I'll miss you no matter what. Have I neglected you? Been too distant?"

Abbi shook her head. "Nah. You've been awesome, which sucks. Because now I have to live up to your strength, and that's not going to be possible."

"I'm not strong, honey. I was hiding. I knew it was going to hurt, getting it out finally. I... I was angry."

"So was I. But he was going to die anyway. With Huntington's, it's just a matter of how horrible it gets before the end. I think it would've been a relief for us. Eventually."

I hugged her. "He didn't want us to see him deteriorate." But that wasn't the only reason.

"Did you ever consider leaving once you found out Dad had it?"

"No, never." Not by then. I was pregnant. There was no way I could take Abbi from Doug.

"What if I had it? Huntington's."

"I'm thankful you don't, but if you did, I would do everything I could to make your life the best it could be."

"I'm glad you and Dad had me, in spite of what could've happened."

"Me, too, Abigail."

We lay there together. I breathed deeply, cataloguing the shards around my heart. They weren't as sharp. Maybe I'd finally let the bitterness go.

"I wish you'd hang out with Asher again. He made you happy. For moments at least, which is more than I've seen in years. And he's so cool."

"First off, he's older than your dad," I said.

"Oh, please. By like a year or something. Not a good reason," Abbi flopped back against the pillows. "Do you think Asher Smith is cute? I heard you tell Aunt Bri about his forearms. Luke has great arms, but I'm partial to his butt."

"Yes. And you're going on the pill if I hear one more word about some guy's body parts."

Abbi propped her chin on her folded palms. "Only if you go back on it, too. We can go to the doctor together. Then have lunch and giggle about our crushes."

I slid out of the bed. "I don't think I'm ready to do that with you just yet." I pulled on my robe. "Just promise me you won't treat sex as lightly as a lot of your peers do. It should mean something."

"I'd offer to wait until you were ready to date again so we could swap stories, but if I did that, I'd die a virgin."

"Abigail Rose Dorsey!"

"Puh-lease, Mom. You won't even answer my question about the hottie rock star you spent half the night with a week ago. It's called repression."

"I did answer you. I'm getting coffee, brat." I shut the door behind me and huffed.

I opened the door and stuck my head back in. Abbi was splayed across the bed. She was a beautiful young woman. Her long, sleek legs and narrow hips were encased in her sleeping pants. Her tank had ridden up, showing off the fragile, pale skin of her waist. She'd been cursed with the same narrow chest as most of the women in my family had, but she'd managed to fill out a B-cup. I bit my lip, realizing I'd been her age when I started my sexual relationship with her father.

She peeked at me from under her elbow.

"I have to be smart, Abbi. For both of us."

———◆———

Sweat pooled at my lower spine, saturating my skirt's waistband. I wanted to tug at the fabric, but that seemed fidgety. I needed to present a collected facade.

I shouldn't be here, in this coffee shop in Spokane, waiting for a man I wasn't interested in. Correction, the second man in less than four hours. I'd bought the last guy's lunch just to get out of the restaurant quicker.

That's exactly why I'd chosen this man, Dale, and the one before, too. None of these men were Asher Smith. None had Asher's chiseled jaw, straight, thin nose, and broody hazel eyes.

I'd always loved Asher's eyes.

Dale looked just like his picture—middle-age-softened stomach, long, slightly bulbous nose, and florid cheeks. He was about four inches shorter than Asher's six-two. Brent, my lunch date, was taller than Asher, but he'd been scary-muscular and talked during the entire meal about how I needed to get into Cross Fit. When Brent handed me his card, I'd nodded, not surprised to find he owned a chain of gyms in the area.

This is what happened when Abbi refused to help me. I ended

117

up on speed dates with men I didn't find attractive or interesting.

I needed to apologize to her again. I hadn't just hurt her; I'd been immature, lashing out at her instead of dealing with my insecurities.

"Dahlia? Lia Dorsey?"

I shivered when he said my name, wishing he sounded more like Asher. Correction. I wished he *was* Asher. But I'd made this date, and I'd stick to it. Swallowing, I met Dale's pale blue eyes.

"Yes. Dale?" I shook the hand he offered. I'd pegged him as a middle manager, an accountant or another unimaginative type who liked to work with numbers. His clothes were high quality. Upper management then, if I'd judged his clothes and expensive haircut correctly.

I released his soft hand as he tried not to react to the slight dampness of mine. Good. He didn't feel any chemistry either. This should be short.

"Want a coffee?" he asked. His voice was a deep tenor, not the rich bass of Asher's. He made me think of pleated pants and loafers without socks. I cried internal tears as my libido curled back into a ball and slid into hibernation.

"Have one," I said, motioning to the to-go cup in front of me. At his raised brow, I cleared my throat. "I hate cold coffee. I always get mine in a to-go cup."

"Liar," Abbi's voice screamed in my head. I'd hedged my bets, paying for my own drink on the off chance Dale wasn't worth the time it'd taken me to drive out here, even if I did get to go to the fancy organic grocery store on my way home.

I yanked at the dampening waistband of my skirt, swallowing down the anxiety building in my chest.

"Well, I guess I'll just grab a drink then."

Dale trotted to the short line, his gaze diffident. My cheeks flushed. Score one for Ella, Abbi, and Briar. While I was finally willing to jump back into the dating pool, I only wanted to swim with Asher. Just like they'd said.

I was so not built for this process. Hell, I'd narrowed my focus and love to the first man who'd shown me enough interest and attention when I was fourteen.

I exhaled slowly, hoping to ease the ache behind my breastbone. Just an hour of my time. If nothing else, this was good research for some future novel. If I could ever write anything. Five days until my deadline. The panic fluttered back to life, beating against my ribs.

"You're Lia Moore." I turned toward the voice, smiling at the woman standing in front of me. She was about my age and held a toddler on her hip. Her hair was in a haphazard ponytail, wayward strands of muddy-brown hair escaped the tie and fluttered around a thin, tired face.

"Yes. Nice to meet you," I said.

"I love your books," the woman gushed. Her voice had risen to be heard over her noisy toddler. He smacked his mom's cheeks and kicked his feet, making airplane noises. While I remembered Abbi at this age, it seemed like a lifetime ago.

"Thanks. That's the best compliment."

"When's the next one coming out?"

"I'm outlining another book."

The woman's eyes clouded, and her lip thrust forward so she looked more petulant than her son. "I hoped for a release this year. Especially since there wasn't one last year."

Disappointing fans ratcheted up my anxiety. I sucked on my lip, trying to find some kind of balance. My cheeks heated.

I pulled up the memory of Asher stroking my hair and tried to breathe through my rising panic. "Sorry about that. I had to take a break. Personal reasons." I cleared my tightening throat. "I'm working on a TV miniseries based on the books. We start filming in a few of months."

Dale walked toward us, irritation clouding his ruddy features.

"Oh, well. That's great then. I'll look forward to seeing it. After this guy goes to sleep."

I wiggled the boy's foot, eliciting a giggle. "Probably best. If you're on my mailing list, I'll send out the details so you can be sure to catch it."

"Great!" she beamed. "I'll let you get back to your date." The woman trotted out the door, hugging her son close.

"You know her?"

My stomach slid down into my foot somewhere. "No. She's a fan."

"Fan? Are you some type of athlete?" Dale's eyes slid over my spare frame, and I'm sure I came out just as poorly in his athletic perusal as he had in boyfriend material for me. I spun my cup around.

"I'm a writer. A romance writer."

As I expected, Dale shifted back in his seat, trying to escape the leprosy of my profession.

"You write about sex and stuff?"

"Only if a story calls for it."

I didn't add that pretty much every story did, so my books were filled with steamy sex scenes.

"I see," he said in a voice that stated he was no longer interested. Asher had been interested in my career, his genuine focus alleviating the tension I normally felt when I discussed my profession.

"And what is it you do, Dale?"

He fiddled with his pocket, pulled out his phone, and set it on the table. I would've frowned but didn't want to come off as any ruder than necessary.

"I run some car washes in the western part of the state."

"Congratulations. I'm sure that keeps you busy. "

"Too busy. My ex-wife didn't like my hours. I was constantly at the office."

I took a sip of my coffee so I didn't ask him if sitting in a car wash was the most productive use of his time.

Dale glanced around, eyes furtive. "Want to get out of here? I can get your car washed so clean you'll be able to eat off the seats."

Did he expect me to screw him in a small back office at a car wash while his workers scrubbed dirt from the underside of my SUV?

"Thanks for the offer. Another time, perhaps."

"I planned to spend the afternoon with you."

Oh. Gag. He was worse than Brent, the overzealous gym owner. I wasn't going to make it another ten minutes with this guy.

"Sweet, but no. I'm sorry." I tried to lessen the blow by shifting my features into contrition. "I'll need to head out soon."

"Not yet. I'm still getting to know you."

I knew all I needed to about Dale, owner of multiple car washes. I forced a smile and repeated, "Maybe another time."

I stood, grabbed my purse as I swallowed the panic eating its way into my throat. There was something about this guy... I had to leave. Now.

I stuck out my palm, wishing I could avoid the expectation of another handshake. "Pleasure to meet you, Dale."

—————◆—————

Checking my e-mail the next morning, I had seventeen messages from Dale. The first few mentioned how beautiful I was. He said he'd enjoyed talking to me. I couldn't understand why.

He wrote my name Leah even though I'd signed my name Lia on the one—and only—e-mail I'd sent him to set up our coffee date. Little details like *my name* mattered.

His next four messages suggested dinner. The last few suggested what he'd like to do with me at the local motel. I rolled my eyes and dumped his e-mails into the *Not Friends* file. Then I blocked him from my e-mail and all social media.

Instead of dwelling on the gross messages, I fantasized about coffee with Asher. It would've been so much better than my short date with Dale.

Write my fantasies. Just write.

I closed my eyes and let my fingers tap out the memory of our outing on the beach.

I opened my eyes and read what I'd written.

Ten lines. Almost a poem.

I propped my chin on my hand. Wow. I liked these lines. A lot.

With a small smile and renewed purpose, I opened a new document and fleshed out the scene that was building in my head.

I ended up writing through both breakfast and lunch, managing to take bites of the sandwich Abbi brought to me while I was still typing.

I did a double take. "Don't you have school?"

"Teacher in-service. You're in the zone. I'll talk to you later."

I hadn't been this productive, well, ever. My fingers were one with my mind, the words filling pages, the story pouring out of me. I let myself enjoy the act of creating something I wanted to read.

"I may go out later," Abbi said from the doorway. I sat back and blinked. Late afternoon sunshine pooled across her face, accentuating her petulant expression.

I downed a glass of iced tea. "Okay. Thanks for the lunch. Just let me know where, when, and with whom."

"Not like you'll notice if I go anywhere," Abbi muttered, stomping down the hall.

Abbi's attitude bothered me, breaking my momentum. I stared out the window. I should apologize to her again. I'd lashed out at her because I didn't know how to deal with my fears. Maybe if I explained that part, she'd be more willing to let her frustrations go.

I stopped off at the bathroom, then collected my plate and put it in the dishwasher. Abbi wasn't in her room or sprawled on the couch.

The note on the kitchen counter said she was out with Luke. She hadn't asked; she'd just gone. I pulled up my phone, noting the text from her twenty minutes ago: *I'm going out. See you l8r.*

I punched Abbi's number. Straight to voice mail. She always had her phone on. It was part of our deal.

I tried Sally because I didn't have Luke's number, but same scenario. Panic clogged my throat. I left Abbi's friend a message, asking her or Abbi to call me back sooner than soon. Ending that call, I dialed Sally's parents.

"Hi, Rhonda. This is Lia. Have you seen the girls?"

"Sally's sitting right here, watching that Wolverine movie with me. Girl time." Rhonda giggled self-consciously. "I'm not sure where Abbi is." The phone moved away, and Rhonda asked Sally about Abbi. "Sal says she hasn't talked to Abbi today."

"Would you have Sally try Abbi on her cell and let her know I'm really worried about her? She left with Luke a while ago, and I can't reach her."

I wasn't going to panic. I wasn't. Abbi would be smart. She was fine. I was fine. Except for the cold sweat blooming all over my body.

"Course. Sally doesn't have Luke's number, but we could get it."

"Please. If you get in touch with Abbi, have her call me. On my phone."

"You okay, Lia?" Rhonda asked.

I mumbled an "I'm fine" as I opened the door to my garage. I'd drive into town first, look in the diner. If she wasn't there, I'd go to that secluded spot down by the creek that none of the kids thought the parents knew about. As if I hadn't spent time down by the creek with Doug. Different creek, same use. My smile turned to a shriek when something hissed at me.

A raccoon ran toward me. With its teeth bared and its fur puffed up, the rodent looked as big as a dog. Its little black eyes gleamed from the dark fur around them as its toenails scraped on the garage floor.

Without thought, I threw my phone, Rhonda's concerned, muffled voice still on the other line. The phone clipped the beast in its side, stopping its momentum. My phone bounced off, skittering under the car. I backed into the house, slammed the door shut, and leaned against it, breathing hard.

These were the moments I missed having a man in my life. I was going to have to brave the hissing monster if I wanted to get in my car.

I dropped my purse onto the kitchen counter and pulled the broom from the narrow closet in the adjoining laundry room. I took a calming breath, then another. And another. I went to get a glass of water. I wasn't ready for round two with the beast from hell yet.

Sirens wailed down the road. Red lights threw weird shadows across the room as I sprinted toward the front door.

Abbi. Please, God, let her be safe.

A fist pummeled against the thick wood. "Sheriff! Open up!"

I reached for the handle just as the door flew open, the edge catching my cheek and forehead. I flailed backward, shocked by the pain. Someone caught me before I hit the ground.

"Ow!"

"Where'd it hit you, Lia? You're bleeding everywhere."

"I figured that out already, Ralph. Why'd you hit me with my door? I was coming to open it." I hissed when I touched the spot where he'd walloped me.

"You have a cut over your eye. I'll call for an ambulance. They can be here in just a minute."

"You're the sheriff. You should be able to handle a little bit of blood."

"It's not a little bit."

Nausea rolled through my stomach. "You shouldn't have said that."

Ralph helped me toward the living room. I sagged against him, trying to keep the blood from running into my eye. I settled on the sofa with a groan.

"Rhonda called me, said you were screaming. Asked me to come out. We thought it might be an intruder. You know, some crazy coming after you because of your books."

I used my sleeve to dab at the blood. My face hurt, and I had a terrible headache building behind my eyes.

"Ice, please."

"Sure thing. I'm so sorry, Lia. I don't think it's that deep, but Charlie'll look at it when he gets here. You know how head wounds bleed."

"I don't know where Abbi is," I said, the panic clawing its way through the haze of pain. "She said she was going out with Luke, but I can't get her on her phone. She promised me she'd always answer it."

Luke wouldn't hurt Abbi. He was a nice kid. At least I thought he was. Ralph hadn't heard about another accident or anything bad. He would've told me right away. He came back with the ice, talking to someone on his walkie-talkie contraption.

"Come on in and get her, Charlie. She's got a cut on her forehead. Bleeding like a stuck pig."

"Stop fussing," I grumbled. "I need to go look for Abbi."

I stood and winced, gripping the edge of my couch for balance. Charlie cupped my elbow.

"She'll be here in a tick," Ralph said. "Jimmy saw her at the coffee shop on Main. Sitting at a table by the window, pretty as you please."

Charlie tugged me to the back of his ambulance. He shoved me onto the gurney and poked at my cut. "Thank— Ouch!" I snapped, dropping the ice into my lap. I yelped at the splash of cold as the bag spilt open.

126

"You don't want a scar on that pretty forehead, Lia. Stay still so I can finish."

I huffed but remained still. Tires rolled over gravel. A car door slammed, feet pounded up the drive.

"What happened? Where's my mom? Why's she in the ambulance? Is she dead?"

The fear in Abbi's voice was a salve to my heart. Good. She needed to answer her damn phone.

"Omigod! You're covered in blood!"

"Head wounds bleed a lot."

Abbi climbed in and snatched up the dripping ice pack and slammed it against my cheek hard enough to make me cringe. Charlie cursed and glared.

"Keep still," he snapped.

When Charlie dabbed some iodine on the area, I hissed through the sting. He finished bandaging my face.

"Done. Help your mom inside, Abbi. She needs to rest. Watch her for a concussion."

"How do I do that? Who hit you? What happened? Is the house safe?" Abbi's eyes roved our dark house with trepidation as her hands shook.

"Ralph hit me with the door. There's a raccoon in the garage," I said.

Charlie clambered down and turned to help me. "I'll call animal patrol about the raccoon. Stay out of the garage until they pick it up."

"Not to worry. I have no desire to see that thing again. It tried to bite me."

Abbi shook her head, brows knit in a tight frown. "You look like someone beat you up."

Her lip trembled. I slid off the cot and down to the driveway with Charlie's help, unsteady from the throbbing in my head. Abbi jumped out after me, steadying me as I teetered out from Charlie's arms.

"I screamed when I saw the raccoon. I was on the phone with Rhonda, hoping she knew more about where you were. She called in the cavalry. No one's in the house." Except that furry avatar of Satan.

"Okay," Abbi said. "Okay. Good." She helped me to the couch. I settled back against the cushions. She brought a blanket and tucked it around me. I didn't have the heart to tell her the ministrations made my head pound worse.

"How about a painkiller?" I asked.

Tears filled her eyes. She looked at my swollen, bloodied face. "I'm sorry."

She ran to the kitchen and brought back a couple pills and a glass of water.

Opening my mouth made my bruised cheek hurt more. I wasn't looking forward to looking in the mirror. It wouldn't be pretty.

"Raccoon's gone. Lit out soon as I opened the garage. I found this under your car," Ralph said, handing me my shattered phone. "It was making a god-awful racket."

"Thanks, Ralph."

"We'll check in with you tomorrow. I'm real sorry, Lia." He shook his head and left, shutting the door with quiet precision.

I pressed the button and waited for the screen to come to life. Squinting, I was able to make out that I'd missed three calls from Ella.

"Call your aunt Ella for me, Abbi. She must need something,

and my head hurts too much to call myself."

Abbi turned her phone on and dialed the number. Ella's excited voice blared through the phone.

"Your mother is a doll, Abbi. I need to come out there and thank her in person."

"What's going on?" Abbi asked. She sniffled, tears still clinging to her lashes.

"The Supernaturals want to record one of Simon's songs, that's what's going on! Asher invited Simon to the studio in Seattle next month. I guess the Supernaturals are recording another album then."

I tried to smile at Asher's thoughtfulness. My cheek didn't appreciate the movement, and I groaned.

"Just a minute, Aunt Ella." Abbi turned to face me. "You need something?"

"More ice," I sighed.

Abbi took her phone with her while she dug through a kitchen drawer. "Mom got beat up by the sheriff tonight," she said.

I lifted my hand, trying to tell her to stop, but it was too late. I couldn't hear Ella's response, but Abbi said, "No, it wasn't like that. C'mon, this is Mom you're asking about. Sheriff Lindon came to save her from a raccoon and slammed her face with the front door. I thought she'd broken her cheek, but Charlie—he's the EMT—said it's just a bad bruise. She has a cut over her eye. It's all nasty and she's covered in blood."

Abbi brought the ice back and offered it to me. I pressed it to my cheek, wincing a little at the pressure.

"Need anything else?" Abbi asked.

"I'm good."

"Yeah, right." Abbi held out her phone. "She wants to talk to you."

I stared at the phone like it would zap me to oblivion. "Can't hold it to my face."

Maybe my family would leave me alone if I was pitiful enough. Abbi must have put it in on speaker because Ella's voice, a little tinny, shouted out, "You're talking to me, love. Don't try to weasel out of it. What the hell did you do to yourself? Abbi said you got in a fight with the sheriff."

"She did not. She told you the sheriff hit me with my own front door."

"Somehow that means you now look like a domestic abuse victim?"

"Just about. It hurts to talk. Can I call you when the swelling goes down? Oh, and my phone is busted. I threw it at the raccoon. Those suckers are fast and huge. I had no idea. I have to get a new phone. Don't call me on mine until I call you."

"Dahlia, I'm worried about you." Ella's voice grew quieter. "Are you sure you're all right, darling? Did the nasty thing bite you? Go to the hospital to make sure you don't have rabies."

"I'm fine."

"Quit pretending. Was it a panic attack? I've read you can pass out from them."

I groaned. So much for having privacy. "Never passed out before, and this wasn't a panic attack. They've been better since Asher talked me through one after Simon's concert, but—"

"Oh, no, you don't! Asher Smith talked you through a panic attack? That man is the most delectable creature," Ella moaned.

"He is. You love Simon."

"That I do. I meant Asher was delectable for you, love. I told Abbi to send me a picture of your face. I want to see how bad the damage is. Have you called Briar? Have Abbi send it to her, too. She'll want to know."

No point in arguing. Ella and Abbi had already teamed up against me. "Fine. I'm so happy about Simon's break. I'll thank Asher."

"Do that, darling. He's a right lovely bloke. Simon's having a beer with him right now. They're talking about your sound track. I guess the Supernaturals are recording that and their new album at the same time. Don't really understand it all."

"Maybe you'll get to thank Asher yourself."

"I'd prefer you do it. Many times," she said with a snicker. "Get some rest. Call me tomorrow. I'll worry."

"Yes, ma'am," I said.

I pressed the End button and leaned my head back against the couch, which caused me to squeak in pain, the ice pack falling into my lap.

Something clicked. It sounded like a camera shutter. "Did you take a picture of me?"

"Yep."

"What if I didn't want you to do that?"

"I'm worried about your cheek. It might be fractured. And the cut's oozing, even with the Band-Aid. Charlie's just an EMT. You should probably go to the doctor. Aunt Briar's boyfriend will know if you need more care."

"Ken's an oncologist, not an ER doctor. I don't want to owe him anything." I would've scowled but my face hurt too much.

My phone made a sound. Not its normal text chirp, this sounded more like a dying sparrow. I couldn't make out the words through the busted screen.

Abbi's phone rang again. "Hi, Aunt Briar. No, Mom's okay. At

131

least she says she is. She got hit with a door. I think she needs to go to the ER and get stitches. Hmm, maybe. You think? That'd be great! She's sitting right here. You want to tell her? Fine. No. Text me. Mom's phone broke. Long story. She'll tell you tomorrow. Love you, too."

Abbi settled next to me on the couch. "Aunt Briar said she's flying out in the morning and will get you into one of the plastic surgeons in Spokane or maybe even Coeur d'Alene. Ken's working on it right now."

"This is the problem with a tight-knit family. I can't get slammed in the face without everyone freaking out about it."

"It's bad, Mom. I'm really sorry you were worried about me."

"Guilty enough to never, ever, shut your phone off again?"

"Yeah."

"We can discuss whether you deserve to be grounded tomorrow. When do I have to pick up Briar?"

"She's going to text me."

Abbi's phone rang again. "Hello?"

Her mouth formed an *O* as her eyes lit up. "She's right here." Abbi thrust the phone at me.

"I'll call whoever it is back tomorrow."

"It's Asher Smith."

CHAPTER FOURTEEN
Asher

My lawyer's office was downtown near Pike Market. I hated being in this part of town with all its bustle, but I needed to go over my options. Pete told me what I already knew: to get what I wanted, my fastest option was to roll over and give in to Jessica's demands for huge alimony checks. Full custody of Mason was worth it.

Since the meeting that morning, I'd almost called Pete four different times to give him the green light, but I'd decided to run the idea by Bill. He was my closest friend. He'd learned lead guitar so we could start the Supernaturals after our short stint in Cactus Arrow. Bill and I found the other band members together.

He picked up on the second ring. "'Lo."

"Here's the deal. You know Jessica and I split."

"'Bout time."

"Don't start. I can't do the sound track outright. I already told her I'd nixed the deal."

"I don't understand. Sounds like a great gig. Both for you and for us as a band. Three songs, right? That'd be nice bank."

"It would be. I really want to do it."

"What's the problem?"

"Jessica's pushing for a cut of the royalties on all my future work. She says that's the only way she'll give me custody of Mason."

"You can't let her have anything to do with the band, Asher." Bill's voice was serious. "She's tried to break us up for years."

Dread filled my stomach, but I managed to ask, "More than what you told me?"

"I'll be there in a week for our rehearsal. The new stuff you sent is excellent. Looking forward to getting into the studio. Should we run our next album next to this sound track? Make better use of studio time."

"More, Bill?"

"Dammit. This is hard." Bill paused, his breathing harsh. "She came to my room late one night after a show. She was really high. She cried and cried, man. Kept talking about if things were different. If Olivia lived, you'd want her again. Then, when I comforted her, she…"

I leaned my head against the bedroom wall. "What?"

"Kept trying to get me to… well, to fuck her. I ended up sleeping in Carl's room. I knew you were still working through shit from that night. You know, when Olivia died. I didn't want to tell you. But it was bad. She was a mess."

I moaned a curse. "I don't want to drag you into this, but I may need you to tell my lawyers, sign something."

"Asher," Bill said. "I got my shit together just like you did. If it comes out Jessica tried to bang me… Cammie and I are in a good place. She's happy. That shit—it's ancient history. I don't want to drag Cammie through that."

"If I can't get something to stick on her, I don't get custody of Mason," I said. "She's out of control. Apparently as far back as you're talking about. Mason's getting hurt in all this. Hell, she left him alone the night I got home."

"He's a good kid, Asher. He wouldn't do anything stupid."

"He doesn't deserve to be hurt in this, Bill."

"But what about my marriage?"

I pressed my thumb to the spot between my brows. "Jessica doesn't just want Mason. She wants to punish me for Olivia's death. I get that. It was my fault. I doubt a judge would give her all these ridiculous demands, but she's hanging Mason over my head because she knows how much I love him."

"That's not something I can help you with. I mean, she's always been crazy. Controlling. She's not gonna let this go. Not if she can gain from it."

Bill was right. I'd married her, brought her into my life. But Jessica hadn't healed from Olivia's death. She wanted to hurt me. Over and over. And that was hurting Mason.

"I know you're pissed," Bill continued. "Hell, I would be if the situation was reversed, but I swear, Asher, I swear to God, I didn't do anything with her. I mean, besides some kissing…"

"I may need you to testify," I muttered. I ended the call and sat on the edge of my bed. I tried taking deep breaths.

I'd worked so hard to keep the details of Olivia's death out of the media, and so had my record label. We hadn't really succeeded, but we got Jessica through the worst of the fallout before I had to leave again. I'd been happier out of the house, away from my own wife.

Maybe if I'd listened to my mother then… but I hadn't been willing to divorce my wife when she was suffering. I hadn't wanted to turn any further into my father. And leaving a woman who was suffering from depression was a dick move for any guy to make.

I had two choices right now. I could destroy my apartment to try to work off the rage, or I could call Simon back and talk to him more about the project I'd mentioned to him earlier.

I needed to try to find a way to move on. To keep the sound track inching forward even though I couldn't sign on. Yet. Paul said the deal wasn't complete until Dahlia sent another round of outlines and more story samples. Those were due Friday. I had a few days. Time, hopefully, to sort some of this mess out.

———

Simon met me at a little place near The Showbox, my favorite live music venue in town. His smile was uneasy, but he seemed cool with hanging out for a while.

"I didn't expect to hear from you," Simon admitted. He chewed on a handful of bar nuts, his gaze never leaving my face.

"Thanks for meeting me. Like I said, I wanted to talk to you about recording your song, 'Hiding in the Night.' I like the licks, and I think Bill can do something amazing with the bridge. We start rehearsals next week. Plan to lay down tracks in two, maybe three weeks. I want to do your tune toward the beginning."

I was moving forward, building something I could be proud of. It was Jessica I was divorcing, not the rest of my friends or my career. Bill and I would work through this. I rolled my head, stretching my neck, but tension still locked down my shoulders.

"I'd love that, man."

Simon texted his wife the news while I ordered us a couple beers.

"So this isn't for the HBO sound track? Lia told me about your offer."

"Maybe, we'll see if I can make it work. The sound track, I mean." I swallowed my grimace. Not Simon's problem. "I'm not sure I can swing it. Life's complicated."

"I heard about your divorce. That's tough."

"You have no idea." I cleared my throat. "Like I told you, Paul Loomis asked for a song. But it's not signed and sealed yet. So we're moving forward with a new Supernaturals album while we wait."

I slammed back my drink, waving my hand for another. The rage was still there, burning in my gut.

Simon nodded. "You okay?" he asked, his voice hesitant.

"Not really, but I want to talk music, not about my personal life."

Simon's phone rang, and he tossed an apologetic look while he pulled it out. "That's Ella's ring. My wife. She wouldn't call unless it was important."

I dropped my gaze to my empty pint glass. Foam slid down the side, fingers spreading through the brown dregs. I wanted to pick up the glass and hurl it across the room.

If I couldn't find a way to remove Jessica from my life, I'd continue to go through these cycles each time she wanted more money, more fame. Wreak more havoc. With Jessica, there was never a topout. She was so angry with me about Olivia, she'd make sure of it.

I liked Simon, but I shouldn't have come here, brought him into my mess. I needed to hit someone or take enough downers to pass out. Neither was a healthy option. Much as I knew it, I didn't care. That scared me.

"Hey, El. Hell. But she's okay? Did she go to the hospital? No, that doesn't surprise me either. They found Abbi?"

Dahlia's daughter was Abbi. I looked up. Simon's brows were pulled down in a deep frown, his eyes cloudy with concern. Fear overrode my anger, condensing in a cold, nasty knot deep in my gut.

"That doesn't sound like Abbi. No wonder Lia freaked out. Lia didn't get stitches? Okay, I'll look in a sec. Want me to call her? Abbi's phone. Got it."

Simon disconnected, his thoughtful expression sliding into grimness.

"Dahlia's hurt?" I asked.

"She got banged up." His eyes widened as he looked at something on his phone. His breath hissed through his teeth. He turned the screen toward me so I could see.

I yelped a curse and snatched the phone from his hand. Dahlia's eyes were dilated and her mouth pulled down in annoyance or pain. Dried blood caked her from temple to neck. A big bruise marred her cheek, and a bandage covered a cut above her eyebrow.

I handed back his phone and pulled out mine.

"What are you doing?" Simon asked.

"I'm calling her to make sure she's gotten proper care." I put the phone to my ear. It rang and rang. "Her daughter's fine?"

"Abbi's home, safe."

"Why isn't Dahlia answering her phone?" I demanded.

"It broke during a scuffle with a raccoon. Want to try Abbi's?"

"Fuck, yes."

CHAPTER FIFTEEN
Dahlia

I snatched the phone from Abbi's hand.

"Hi," I said, shifting the phone, trying to find a comfortable position. There wasn't one. "To what do I owe the pleasure of this call?"

"I wanted to hear you say you're fine. Shit, Dahlia. Your face."

"Simon showed you the picture? He's in so much trouble."

"I'll tell him," he said, the laughter building in his voice. Abbi was sitting at the end of the couch, staring at me like I was a seven-headed hydra. I kicked her with my foot, jarring my face. I wasn't doing that again.

"I'm supposed to make sure you don't have a concussion," she said.

"Part of your punishment means you need to leave now," I said to Abbi, trying to cover the mouthpiece of her phone with my free hand.

She scowled at me. "Fine. I'll go research concussions on my computer, but don't go to sleep without telling me."

"Why's your daughter in trouble?" Asher asked.

"Because it's her fault I'm busted up."

"She hit you?" Asher asked, his voice filled with confusion.

"No, her phone was off while she was on a date. I called her friend's mom who's married to the county sheriff. A raccoon was in my garage and tried to eat me. Rhonda called her husband to check on me, and he clobbered me with my front door."

"The sheriff assaulted you?"

"I live in a bad reality TV show, what can I say?"

Asher laughed, and I wanted to smile until I remembered how much it hurt to move my face.

"Seems like. Simon said you have a concussion."

"I *might* have a concussion. I declined a ride to the ER to find out."

He blew out a breath straight into the phone so it sounded like a mini tornado. "Dahlia, that's not a good idea."

"It's my decision to make."

"Are you always this stubborn?"

"Yep. I'm quietly independent and opinionated."

"Don't put words in my mouth."

I wondered if he was running his hand across the back of his neck. I'd bet money he was. And his hazel eyes would be browner at the moment, his thick brows pulled low over his straight nose. I loved that grumbly look. He used to get it all the time when the guys argued about melody and rhythm.

"Look, I'm worried about you. Simon said your place is pretty remote."

"I appreciate the concern, really I do, but..." He was silent for a long moment, probably waiting for me to finish my statement. I couldn't.

"Before you tell me it's none of my business, I'm making it my business. I care about you, Dahlia."

Warmth bubbled in my stomach. He'd said he wanted me before, but caring was significant.

"Yes, by the way," I said.

"What? I'm not following you... It's probably the concussion." His voice roughened with concern. "Have Abbi drive you to the hospital. Right now."

"You can read my new manuscript. When it's finished."

"You started?" His voice seemed to smile, causing the warmth to spread through my chest. "Put in some hot sex scenes."

"You did not just say that."

"Hey, it's the only sex I'm going to be seeing or having. Make it hot."

"I'm going to hang up now."

"One more thing."

"What?" I said, biting my lip to keep from smiling.

"I want to come out and see you."

The bubbles of happiness multiplied exponentially, spreading through my whole body, making me lightheaded.

"We'll collaborate on the sound track," he said.

The bubbles all popped. "It may fall through. I have a few days to get my ending in."

"You'll get it done."

"I'm not sure I deserve that kind of faith. I don't want to make your life harder, Asher."

"I really want to do this sound track if I can get Jessica off my back. I talked to Bill earlier, and he's on board. The other guys will love it. Look, I want to see you. I'll bring Mason. He's on his Easter break."

"What are you going to tell Jessica?"

"The truth. We'll get some work done on our project while I'm there, but I mostly need to make sure you're okay. I'm coming no matter what. I just hoped you'd want me there."

"Do you think that's a good idea?"

He was quiet for a long minute. Noise from the bar, mainly laughter, sifted through his phone. "Know how we talked about friends? You offered, and I really need one now."

I gripped the phone, feeling some of his pain through the thin piece of plastic. "Then you're invited," I whispered.

"Good. Take down your dating profile."

"How did you know about that?" I gasped.

"You linked it to your Facebook account. All those guys are ass-holes. You can do a lot better."

"Who says I'm looking for anything more than a satisfying screw?" I demanded.

"You're better than that, Dahlia Moore Dorsey. Take it down. Please. I'll send you flight details."

"You're pushy."

"And you're stubborn," he said. I could tell he was smiling. "I can't wait to see what color your face is when I get there."

I gasped once more. "I revoke your invitation."

"Too late. I accepted. See you in a few days. And call someone if the pain gets worse or you see double."

"You know a lot about concussion symptoms," I fussed.

"Too much. Night, Dahlia."

"Night, Tristan Asher Smith."

"You have no idea how much I like hearing my name from your mouth." He hung up the phone.

When I struggled to get up, Abbi was by my side, helping me.

"Did you listen to my conversation?" I asked, exasperated.

"No. Swear on Dad's grave. But I now have Asher Smith's cell number in my phone." She grinned at the device.

"Don't you dare hand out his number."

"Totally get that, Mom." Her face fell, her eyes filling with tears when she touched my cheek. "I'm really sorry about tonight."

"My head hurts," I mumbled, my eyes sagging.

"Let's get you to bed."

CHAPTER SIXTEEN
Asher

As I ended the call, Simon folded his hands on the table and met my challenging gaze. "I like you, Asher. I respect you as a musician."

"But?" I settled back in my chair, sipping my new beer.

"Actually no 'but.' I think you'll be good for Lia. She'd be pissed I said that. But you need to know that Lia's changed a lot since you knew her. Mostly because of Doug."

"Got that. She deserves to be happy."

Simon met my eyes, his holding a type of misery I knew mine reflected. We had different reasons for hurting over situations we couldn't change, but I appreciated his willingness to share.

"She does. She and Doug, they met when she transferred into high school partway through her freshman year. Her dad was killed on some military mission."

"She told me that."

Simon's eyebrow rose to his hairline. "She doesn't like to talk about her parents." Simon stared down into his beer, lost in some memory. "I've never seen two people so involved in each other. The rest of us always felt like we were intruding." He smiled. "I tried to find something like that until I realized it was unhealthy."

"If you're trying to make me jealous, it's working." I took a sip of my drink, enjoying the thick slide of hops across my tongue. At his look, I shook my head. "I left Cactus Arrow because I wanted Dahlia myself."

Simon nodded. "I wondered. 'Moonshine Eyes,' that's Dahlia?"

I nodded. Simon blew out a breath.

"When Doug found out he was sick, he became obsessive,

hurtful."

There was an underlying story there. I could hear it in Simon's slight hesitation.

"Huntington's screws with your brain. I needed to believe it was the disease and not my brother doing those things. But…" Simon's lips folded inward, and he dropped his gaze from mine.

I turned to stare out the window at the hazy Seattle night. Lights winked in all directions. A huge sprawl that balanced at the edge of Puget Sound. Sadness had filled Lia's eyes when she said she didn't believe in love anymore. Death wouldn't have stripped her of that core belief.

But betrayal would have.

Simon swallowed hard. "I'm not sure what you've got going on in your life, but Lia hasn't dealt with all the baggage Doug dumped on her. She'll tell you she doesn't want another rocker, that the lifestyle sucks."

"Noted," I grunted. I scrubbed my hands over my face. "You don't think I'm good enough for her."

Simon considered that. "No, that's not it. I want her to be happy."

"Doug screwed around, didn't he?"

"We know how easy sex can be when you're an entertainer." Simon swallowed the last of his beer, his thumb moving up to circle the rim of his glass.

"Yeah, I do." I pushed back from the table. "I think I'm going to head back to my place."

I followed Simon out the door. Stopping, I looked up at the cloudy sky. The raging burn I'd felt when I walked into the bar had been replaced by anticipation.

I'd inserted myself into Dahlia's life, which was more complicated than I'd anticipated. I was smart enough to know she was hesitant about what my visit meant. If I were honest with myself, I wasn't sure what it meant either.

All I knew was that I needed to see her, and more, I liked how much calmer and focused I was when I was near her.

CHAPTER SEVENTEEN
Dahlia

I woke up with a face inches from mine. I couldn't make out any features, but I knew it wasn't Abbi. The eyes were lighter, not the violet-blue I knew best. I screamed and flailed, managing to knock my sister in the mouth. My battered face throbbed in response, and I groaned.

"Dammit, Lia, that hurt." Briar dabbed at her lip, her brow scrunched.

"My face isn't real happy about this wake-up either. What were you doing?"

"I was looking at the cut on your forehead. You know, the reason I came to visit."

She sat on the edge of the bed and took my chin in her hand, turning my face enough to see the bruise on my left cheekbone.

"That hurts. You weren't supposed to come until morning."

"It's almost afternoon."

"Really?"

Briar nodded.

"I woke up at two in the morning and couldn't go back to sleep for a while so I worked on my material for HBO."

"How'd that go?"

"I'm not sure."

Briar hugged me, her long arms winding around me like Dad's used to. I hugged her back just as hard.

"I'm so proud of you for taking back your life," Briar said. She sat back and tipped my chin again. "That bruise is a doozy. The cut, thankfully, didn't go down to the next level of tissue. But you

146

do need to keep it clean and the scab moist to avoid scarring."

"Thank you, Dr. Moore."

The skin around her eyes tightened. "I'm dating a doctor."

"Sorry, Bri. That was insensitive."

"Premed classes were a long time ago, but I do remember quite a bit."

Doug's illness had affected my sister, too. She'd been so set to be a doctor until we found out Doug's timeline had shrunk. Briar switched her major to journalism a week later, unable to handle the idea of losing people she cared about. We'd both had plenty of grief in our lives, and seeking out more was self-flagellation. At least that's what Briar had told me then.

"So… tell me about Asher. Abbi said he called you last night."

"He's my *friend*."

"You lack some important gene. I'd say its romance, but I've read your books. It's not imagination either because some of those positions you wrote about took a lot of creative thinking."

"I like him. A lot. But he's even more entrenched in the rocker lifestyle than Doug ever was. So liking him is a huge mistake that'll end up breaking my heart. Again."

Briar pursed her lips. Instead of arguing like I expected her to, she dropped her head. "I don't want to fight with you, Lia. I came to help my big sister. This is a first for me, and I'd really like to have a better experience than pretty much any other time in our relationship."

I ran my hand over her hair, like I used to. I could tell my injury wasn't the only reason Briar was here. "Be straight with me, then. You came out here because you're running from something."

She looked up, and I wasn't surprised to see the tears in her eyes.

"You always know." She sighed, fighting her tears. "Ken wants me to get pregnant. He says I'm too focused on my work."

"You're thirty years old, Sweet Briar," I said, falling back on our Dad's nickname for her. "If you aren't ready for babies, he needs to respect how you feel."

"Why can't he see that I like my job and I'm good at it?"

"The real reason?" I asked.

"Of course."

"Because he's a selfish asshole."

Briar slid across the bottom of my bed. "He's a rich asshole."

"You aren't going to be hungry again, Briar. You're the editor-in-chief for a well-respected newspaper. You've been offered a book deal, and you can probably go to any paper in any city in the country. Plus, I won't let you starve. Once was enough."

I gripped my stomach, remembering those weeks before our mom came to get us. They'd shaped Briar and me so differently. I'd launched myself at the first person to show me affection, never wavering in my loyalty to Doug. Briar became introspective, standoffish, not the gregarious little girl I remembered.

"I needed to hear that," Briar sighed. "It's one of the reasons I came out here. Don't be mad, but it's also a business trip. I'm going to meet with the head of papers in Spokane and maybe Boise."

"Good. Build the life that makes you happy, Briar."

She gave a weak smile and said, "Back to Asher Smith."

"He's nice," I sighed. "Nicer than I expected."

"Mmm. Not the adjective I would have chosen, but go on."

"He's coming to see me. He's bringing his son out for Easter."

Briar scrambled up to her knees, her eyes huge. "Holy shit-cakes! We have so much to do."

"Why? He's just coming to hang out. We're collaborating on a sound track. Well, maybe. If I can write something Garcia and Paul like."

"Yeah, yeah. We both use language in our jobs. Think what collaborate means, Lia."

Briar ran to my closet. Clothes flew out, a huge pile forming. "You went shopping. Thank God. Abbi can spend the night with her friend Sally. You're coming to Spokane with me, and I'm getting you all sex-kittened up."

I would have gaped at her, but my face hurt too much. "You are not sex-kittening me."

"Full leg wax. Maybe a Brazilian. It's all the rage these days."

"Stop. I'm not having sex with Asher. Despite the fact I realized I miss it," I muttered, flopping back against the pillow, which made my face throb. "Speaking of, Asher made me promise to take down my dating profile. Not hard to promise when my two dates were such disasters."

Briar stared at me, looking like a fish too long out of water.

"Waxing appointment. Then new underwear. Get in the shower. I'm calling Rhonda right now. She'll understand."

I crossed my arms over my chest. "Don't boss me around, Briar."

"Then stop being an idiot. You'd really ruin a chance with the man you've pined for since you were a teenager? This is a second chance at something amazing." Briar pointed her finger at me, her voice going low and serious. "I refuse to let you screw this up. I understand why you wouldn't trust him, but he's not Doug."

My chest tightened with the old, familiar pain. "I shouldn't have told you anything."

"I was here. I saw your face when you found out the truth about

149

Doug." Briar sat on the edge of the bed and gripped my hand. "Doug hurt you, Lia. I'd be gun-shy a second time, too. But Asher is older, more established, and I bet he's looking for something that'll last."

"You can't know that." I tamped down the burgeoning hope. "He's getting a divorce."

"From a woman who treats him like Doug treated you. Marriage vows mean something. Faithfulness means something." Her eyes were earnest, her voice firm. "Get up. You're getting your head looked at by a plastic surgeon in a couple hours. Ken set it up. It's his way to try to get me pregnant."

"How is a plastic surgery appointment for me going to make you pregnant?"

"He thinks he'll weasel me off the pill if he's nice to you. He knows you don't like him, so he's sucking up."

"I still don't like him."

"He got you an appointment with the best plastic surgeon in the area so you have to say thank you. You don't want to look any uglier than you have to when Asher's kissing you senseless."

"If we get involved now, I'd just be his rebound relationship." I nibbled the corner of my lip, considering. Then I shrugged. "Mine, too, I guess."

"He'd be a gorgeous mistake."

No. Asher wouldn't be a mistake. But he could very easily break my heart. "I have to make sure whatever we have is worth the hurt when it ends."

Briar stood, arms crossed, toe tapping. "Oh, it will be. We're buying some good beer. I read he likes microbrews. The least you can do is show some hospitality."

"Sure." I stood, stretched, winced, and headed to the bathroom. "Thanks for coming, Briar. I'm glad to see you."

———◆———

The water felt wonderful, easing the tightness and removing the bloody crust from my skin. I washed my hair and even used my leave-in conditioner, enjoying the few minutes of pampering.

I put on a button-down top and a pair of my new jeans, glad to be out of my blood-caked clothes.

"Thanks for putting the sheets in the wash," I said as I walked into the kitchen. Even though it was nearly one, Briar handed me a cup of coffee, doctored with a half-teaspoon of sugar and two painkillers. I sipped and said, "Smells good. Need any help?"

"No, even I can manage toasted cheese and soup. I'm not sure your cheek'll be able to handle the sandwich, but I love them with tomato soup."

"Yeah, I remember Mom making those for us when we were little."

Briar's hand stilled. "You got the good memories. The only ones I have of her are when we moved up to Seattle, and it was obvious she didn't want her old life mixing with her new one. She was so much happier back in the Northwest. She was never meant to be an army captain's wife."

I walked around the counter and put my arm around my sister, who was nearly four inches taller than me. "Moving back to Seattle after she left Dad made *her* happy. But I'm sorry she's the way she is."

"I can't believe she let you move out at seventeen."

Mom helped me pack, relieved to get me, the rebellious, angry daughter, out of the house. If I'd left a few weeks earlier, my life may have been very different. I'd met Asher then, during the time Mom tried to shorten my leash. That just made our fights even more intense and was part of the reason Doug asked me to move in with him. I'd been more than happy to leave my mom's house and our angry altercations. By the time I was settled in Doug's apartment, Asher was leaving the band.

Briar shook her head, her lips twisting with disgust and anger. I understood those feelings. With Mom, they went together.

"I mean, who just leaves their kids to start a whole new family? That's so…"

"Mom," I said. "We can't change her or our past. Or the fact she named us after flowers while her new kids got real names."

"Preslee's not that normal a name."

I tipped my head, acknowledging her point. "She doesn't know how to connect with us anymore than we know how to talk to her," I said. "I mean, Mom and Preslee get along well." My eyes wandered to the stove. "Stir the pot before the soup burns."

I tucked away my what-ifs. Those were fantasies I'd never experience. I couldn't experience those unfulfilled wishes in real life, but Lia Moore could write an alternate life, the one I could've had with Asher all those years ago. Those fantasies were what I'd written last night.

After they were on paper, I went back to bed and slept for nearly six more hours. Even now, I felt freer, like I wasn't fighting my head for space.

We ate our lunch in silence, Briar dunking her toasted cheese sandwich into the chunky red soup. She was right about not being able to handle the sandwich. The bruise on my cheek made eating anything more than soup impossible. My face was a profusion of blue, black, purple, and even a little sickly yellow. I had a large egg-shaped bump over my eyebrow that was just as tender as my bruised cheek. Briar changed the bandage, making sure to check the edges and rub some antibiotic cream into the wound.

"C'mon. Let's go see the doctor."

"What about Abbi?" I asked.

"She's going to her friend Sally's after practice. I talked to Rhonda while you were in the shower." Briar grabbed her purse from the counter. "Can we drive your car? The rental doesn't have any shocks, and I think it'll make your face hurt more."

I tossed her my keys. "Thanks for coming, Bri. For setting this up."

"I told you, I'm using my time here as an excuse to check out other opportunities. So it's a win-win."

———◆———

We didn't get home until late, but I checked in on Abbi using Briar's phone while she was in the mall.

"What did the doctor say?" Abbi asked when she answered the phone.

"That I was lucky the cut isn't deeper. He gave me some cream that's supposed to reduce scarring. He did a couple of internal stitches, but only because Briar made him. They pinch."

"Will you have a scar?" Abbi asked.

"It's possible."

Abbi sighed. "I'll meet you at home. Rhonda's going to bring me after dinner."

Abbi hadn't asked for her own car yet, and while I was happy not to pay for another vehicle, I didn't like her being an imposition on our friends. "You're sure?"

"She said it's not a problem. Stop stressing."

"Good. Be safe. Love you."

"Love you, too, Mom."

Ending the call, I handed Briar her phone, thrilling at the words. Briar opened the trunk and stuffed it full of bags.

"What's that?" I asked.

"Every pair of sexy underwear in the mall," she responded.

"Briar! I told you. Friends."

"Well, even if it doesn't work out with Asher, you still needed sexy underwear. Your drought's gotta end some time. Consider it an early birthday present."

"My birthday's in November."

Briar slammed the trunk. I waited for her to open the driver's door. "So it's a present for selling your series to HBO. Whatever."

I pleated the bottom of my shirt between my fingers, refusing to look at her. "The HBO deal's contingent on me finishing the series."

Briar patted my arm. "I know Doug's cheating hurt you, but you managed to write through some of that. So you can do it now. You're not so... distant, I guess. That's what happened after you found out he was sick."

"No, after he slept with any willing vagina."

"I'm really, really sorry he did that to you, big sis. You said you wrote last night?"

"Just set-up and a few scenes for how I'd like to end the series. Asher told me to let the words come. I sent it to Bev, but I'm expecting her to rip it to shreds."

Briar let out a little squeal. "Asher's done more for you in a few weeks than we've been able to do in years."

"I don't want to talk about him right now, Bri. It's— I don't know what I feel. I need to focus on closing this deal. I need to write again. I miss it."

Briar picked up my hand, squeezed my fingers. "And Doug? He doesn't deserve a hold over you anymore, Lia."

"You're right. I— It's better."

I looked at my sister's fingers and wished it was Asher's hand wrapped around mine. I looked out the window and swallowed down my need. Wanting, wishing wouldn't change that Asher's life was an even bigger mess than mine. Nor would it make him stop touring and focus on me the way I craved a man to do.

"Let's get that beer and pick up some pizza. Dad always said pizza and beer was the perfect meal. Each time I drink a beer, I think about him."

I wasn't sure I could manage either the pizza or the beer, but I liked the idea of being close to my dad and my sister.

———————

We'd just finished cleaning the kitchen when Abbi walked in. She kissed my non-bruised cheek and gave her aunt a hug. "I'm glad you came. I've been worried about Mom. You know how she tries to be tough. I didn't know how hard to push her about going to the hospital."

"You did just right, Abs," Briar said, returning the embrace.

"But we're still talking about you not having your phone on," I said, my voice stern because I couldn't transform my face into its mom look.

"I feel really bad. I already put my laptop in your office. I told Sally and Luke I couldn't hang out after school this week, and I was probably going to be stuck in with you this weekend, which totally sucks because Luke's going to Coeur d'Alene to catch some outdoor concert Saturday."

"You're going to be stuck with me. We're having house guests."

Abbi's eyes flitted to Briar.

"Don't look at me like that." Briar laughed. She'd finished loading the dishwasher and was now in the process of spreading her paperwork across my kitchen table. I rolled my eyes when she smeared a drop of tomato sauce across a printout. She'd never learned to wipe up all the way.

"Who's coming? Aunt El and Uncle Simon?"

"Can I tell her?" Briar asked, her grin widening. "Nah, you tell her."

"Asher wanted to come out and make sure I'm not broken. He's bringing his son with him."

"Mom!" Abbi shrieked. One of those nuclear siren sounds that made my teeth ache. "This is a monumental. He asked to come see you?"

"He asked her to take down her dating profile," Briar said. I glared while Briar smirked.

"Abigail, I expect you to not make a bigger deal out of this than it is."

She snorted. "Whatever. Can I go take the profile down? You have like four hundred e-mails."

"Seriously? That's insane," I said.

"You're beautiful, Mom. Even the guys at my school think so."

"That's disturbing. I don't want high school boys to look at me at all. I'll deal with the profile."

"Does this mean Asher is your boyfriend?" Abbi asked, bouncing on her heels.

"No, Abigail. It means you need to calm down. He's a friend. And I think he needs to talk about his divorce. Please be cool about this. Please."

I was pathetic, begging my daughter, but I'd heard the hurt in Asher's voice.

"Fine," Abbi muttered. "I'm going to my room."

"You don't want to hang out with us?" Briar asked.

Abbi narrowed her eyes and puckered her lips. "No. I'm going to go listen to Supernaturals. Brush up on the lyrics."

"So tell me why you're looking for work at other papers," I said once Briar and I were settled on the couch.

Briar hesitated, her forehead puckering. "You really think Ken is an asshole?"

Ah. Her relationship with the doctor had been a surprise. He'd pursued her with a zeal that would flatter any woman.

"Do you love him?" I asked.

Briar's eyes clouded. Slowly, she shook her head.

"They why do you stay?" I kept my voice gentle.

Her mouth was a taut line. "I don't know. Rosie would be sad."

I squeezed her fingers. "Rosie loves you. If you stopped dating her nephew, she'd still love you."

Briar dipped her head, a small concession to my words. "He's gotten worse. More controlling."

"Oh, Briar. Don't let him take your independence or your happiness. Look, you told me to dive into a relationship with Asher. What about you? Why don't you dive into a relationship with someone you love?"

She was silent.

"You need to find someone who cares about you for the amazing person you are," I said.

"I'm thinking of leaving him."

I rested my good cheek against hers. "I'll be here if you do. Anything for you, Sweet Briar."

Eventually, she scooted back. "I need to look at that paperwork."

"Okay. I should check in with Bev." My stomach ached, but I stood. While Briar headed to the kitchen, I went to my office and checked my e-mail.

Bev had left me a half-crazed message: "You should call me when you nearly die! I need to know these things. Call me. As soon as you get this. I don't care what time it is."

Bev never told me to call her, so I fought down fear as I dialed her number. She answered on the second ring. "I'm at the trendiest restaurant in the city, eating God-knows-what with my new boy toy. I'm only answering this call to let you know I want to kill you myself."

"I'm sorry, Bev. I'll try not to scare you again."

"You're not allowed to concuss that brain of yours. Now, these chapter notes," Bev said, "they're awesome."

"Really? I mean, they're just some ideas."

"How could you send me just those? I'm dying for more," Bev cried. "Where's the rest of the book?"

"I haven't written it."

"Quit falling on your goddam face and write it then. Jesus, Lia. Priorities. Get yours right. I want the first hundred on my desk by Friday."

"That good?"

"I do *not* bullshit. I have an addiction. You have to feed it. Otherwise I get bitchalicious."

"That's your normal state, Bev. I'll do my best. Enjoy the rest of your dinner and your boy toy."

"Wait a minute. What's this about you and Asher Smith?"

I moaned. "Is there no privacy in this world?"

There was a long pause. "I was wondering about the sound track."

"Oh."

"But there's more going on... ," Bev said, inquisitively.

"He's my friend," I said.

"Does he know you set up an online dating profile?"

I growled as I switched the phone to speaker. Setting it on my desk, I opened a new browser window on my laptop. "I took it down."

"The dating profile? Because you're bonking Asher Smith?"

"Keep your voice down," I hissed at her. "You're in a restaurant, and people can hear you."

"Is that where all this creativity is coming from? If so, chain him to your bed."

"No. Will you stop it? We're friends."

"Whatever you say, Lia. Just be sure to stay friends long enough to finish *both* books. If you crap out on me after those pages, I can't be held accountable for my actions."

"Bye, Bev." I hung up the phone and stared at my computer screen. Abbi hadn't been kidding. I had hundreds of e-mails asking me for everything from coffee to lap dances to—oh, that was just nasty.

I clicked through until I was sure the profile was down, then I opened up my document and began to type.

———◆———

I sent my sister off the next morning, already missing her. We hadn't been as close as I'd like to have been for years, in part because I'd moved out so young. I'd asked her to come stay with Doug and me, but she'd refused, probably out of pride and hurt.

Just weeks after my nineteenth birthday, I was married. A few months later, I had an infant to care for. Between Abbi's needs, and later, Doug's, I didn't have anything left in me, especially once my writing took off. I hadn't been there to help Briar make her decisions. Now all I could do was support her choices.

With Abbi at school, I made the trip into town and picked up a newer version of my phone. It did things I didn't understand, but the nice pierced-and-tatted young woman transferred all my data over from my shattered one and deactivated my music and book accounts on my old phone.

"You have no idea how many people don't do that. Man, do they pay later when they can no longer access their media."

I thanked her and stepped outside. My face still hurt, and now it was an even nastier mass of colors. I wanted to go home and console myself with a milkshake and more writing, but first I texted my family to let them know I had a new phone. I sent Asher a message, too.

I wasn't sure what to think about his visit. I was drawn to him, more than any other man, ever. The fact that he cared about me, wanted me... I shivered as I considered how his voice dropped when he'd told me. How his eyes had looked when he held me in the elevator.

I loved his sensitive side that was buried under years of cynicism, stardom, and even loss. From our walk, I knew he mourned his mother as I still did my father.

But I wasn't someone who sought out attention from others. I was a writer, by my very nature, a recluse. The antithesis of his rocker persona.

Getting more involved with Asher meant stepping out of the tiny life I'd made for myself. I knew I'd be happier with the wide range of people and experiences such a life would bring, but I was also terrified of leaving my cocooned comfort zone. No one in my tiny circle would hurt me. Not intentionally, anyway. I'd made sure of it.

My lips curved up just a little when my phone chimed with an incoming text.

Got the all clear so we'll leave Friday. Be later in the day because I have another meeting with Paul to officially sign on for the sound track. He just talked my ear off about your chapter notes your agent sent.

Flight deets to follow. Mason's looking forward to meeting your daughter almost as much as I'm looking forward to making sure you're still in one beautiful piece.

I pressed the back of my hand to my flushed cheek. This was a bad idea. But I couldn't bring myself to cancel.

I drove home and walked straight into my office. I opened my writing program and hit the keys before my butt settled into the chair. I let the fantasy flow.

Four hours later, I shut down the computer, feeling a sense of accomplishment. Maybe the scenes were good, maybe they weren't. But I had twenty-five pages to show for my day. Added to last night's, I had the first four chapters written. Talk about productivity.

I went to the kitchen and looked up my favorite recipes. As part of Abbi's punishment, she was going grocery shopping with me. She hated the way I tested all the produce before picking the best ones.

Unfortunately, my punishment plan didn't work out the way I expected. She was so excited about meeting Asher, she was willing to do anything to help, a theory I tested when I made her wash all the sheets and towels in the guest rooms and bathroom.

She hummed while she folded the warm, fluffed towels. Hummed.

"So school went well today?"

"Mmm hmm. Luke feels bad he got me in trouble, so he's being extra nice."

"What does that entail?"

Abbi chuckled. "It means he walked me to my classes and held my hand at lunch."

"And the kissing?"

"Only between periods. And after school. And when he brought me home."

"Is it good?"

"Puh-lease. Like I'd be with him if it was bad."

"Take it slow. Please. I am not changing diapers for at least another decade."

"There's a long way between kissing and baby-making, Mom."

"You know what I mean. I was sixteen…"

"Once, like, a million years ago."

"And I remember how hormones rage. Your dad was a great kisser."

Abbi made a face. "That is so gross."

"I thought you wanted to trade stories."

At her horrified look, I couldn't help the laugh that bubbled out. "Ouch, that made my face hurt. Just remember sex means more than a quick release. At least I need it to mean more."

She set the towel in the basket and pulled a small piece of fluff off the edge. Finally, she nodded. "I get it. But are you telling me that or reminding yourself?"

CHAPTER EIGHTEEN
Asher

Jessica agreed to let me take Mason for the weekend. I was suspicious, but I wasn't going to push my luck and ask her why she was caving on this when she was so primed to fight about everything else. I made her sign a paper, as per my lawyer's advice, stating I had the right to take Mason on the trip, and then I hustled my son out of the house.

Nearly four hours later, I fidgeted in my seat while I waited for the captain to turn off the seatbelt sign. I hefted Mason's red backpack and pulled my carry-on from the overhead bin. Last thing I grabbed was my Taylor guitar. It was an older model and the wood had long since lost its sheen. I'd had it for nearly thirty years, and I took it with me everywhere. Kind of like Mason used to do with his blanket.

"You ready to meet my friends?" I sounded almost normal. Good.

"Her daughter's nice?" Mason asked. He was picking at the skin on his thumb.

"Yeah, very. So's Dahlia. You'll like her."

I hoped he would. Mason had a great bullshit meter. Way better than mine. He wouldn't lie to me about his reaction to Dahlia, and I wouldn't stick around if he didn't like her.

My kid and my sanity meant more than my pride. With my emotions going all intense, I needed someone with better perspective to let me know if I was caught up in lust, and the best I could come up with was my eight-year-old son. I was enough of a bastard to use my kid's talent to help me out.

I took a deep breath and motioned Mason to go into the aisle in front of me.

"You seem worried," he said.

"Me. Nah. I'm just thinking about the fact our plane landed late."

"Flying's a bitch."

"What did you say?" I asked. The flight attendant and pilot standing at the exit had heard him, too. Their friendly expressions twisted into looks of shocked disapproval.

"Mom says flying's a bitch. She told me that's why she doesn't like to tour with you."

I nodded to the flight staff and hustled Mason up the air bridge.

"Probably not the best time to mention that," I said. "And what's up with the language?"

"You use bad words."

"Yeah, well, I'm an adult."

"So that makes it okay?"

———⋆———

My first reaction to seeing Dahlia was relief. I hadn't realized how much I missed her until that moment. I hated the fact that she'd hurt herself, but I was thankful she seemed lighter and happier than when we'd walked on the beach. Maybe she'd gotten as much out of reconnecting as I had.

Dahlia felt something for me. Probably undeserved. But I was going to grab it with both my dirty hands. As long as my kid was on board.

I tugged Mason over to Dahlia and a teenager with reddish-brown hair and a pair of big, dark blue eyes. I assumed the girl was Dahlia's daughter because they had the same posture, the same expressive mouth. They even tilted their chins the same way. But where Dahlia's smile was guarded, her daughter's was open. I liked the kid, and I got the impression she felt the same way about me.

"Hi," I said, stopping in front of them.

I put my finger under Dahlia's chin and tilted her face up to catch the light better. She hadn't tried to cover the bruises with that concealer stuff most women used. That shit never really worked, just made a woman's face look funny.

"Quite the knocks to the face. You feeling all right? No headaches or blackouts?"

Unable to resist the temptation, I bent and brushed my lips across her bruised cheek. Her breath hitched, and when she pulled back, her eyes were a brighter, deeper gray. Good to know I affected her as much as she affected me.

"Hi back at you," she murmured. More like purred. Damn, that was sexy. "I feel fine." She dropped her gaze to my son. "You must be Mason. Nice to meet you."

Dahlia stuck out her hand. Mason looked at her face, then put his hand out with cautious politeness. My heart thumped hard as I tried not to be too hopeful for the meeting.

"Dad said a policeman hit you with a door."

Dahlia inhaled through her nose and exhaled through her pursed lips. "That's true. The cut bled a lot. You ever had one?" she asked Mason.

She was used to talking to kids and seemed interested in Mason's answer. But then, there wasn't much Dahlia wouldn't be comfortable doing. I frowned. Except being happy. She really sucked at that.

"Yeah, I busted my chin a couple years ago. Had to get, like, a million stitches."

Dahlia opened her eyes wide. "A million! That must have hurt. I got two stitches because the doctor didn't want me to have a scar. My cut's kind of crusty and gross. Was yours?"

Mason nodded with more enthusiasm. "Real crusty. I liked to pick at it, but my mom made me stop."

Dahlia shrugged. "Might've made a cooler scar, though." She turned to her daughter who was watching the interaction with interest.

"This is Abigail. Abbi, meet Asher and Mason."

"Hey," she said. She shoved her hands into the pockets of her denim skirt. "So what do you like to do for fun besides bust your chin open, Mason?" Abbi asked.

Mason sidled closer to me. I placed my hand on his shoulder, letting him know I was there if he needed me.

"Um, I don't like to bust my face open," he said.

Abbi smiled. "Didn't really think you did. Pain sucks. I broke my foot skiing last year. That hurt."

"Did you get a cast?" Mason asked, his cheeks reddening with excitement.

"Sure did."

"Did people get to sign it?"

"Sure did," Abbi said with a smile. She had a pretty one with lots of straight white teeth and a small dimple in her right cheek. If she wasn't a cheerleader, she ran with the popular crowd.

"Aww. I wanna cast," Mason said, looking at Abbi's sandaled foot with longing.

"Signing a T-shirt is pretty cool, too," Dahlia said. "With less pain and blood."

Mason pursed his lips. "I don't like blood." He looked up at me and said, "I'm hungry."

"All right, champ," I said, shouldering our bags. "I'm sure we can find something to tide you over. What would you ladies like?"

Abbi and Dahlia exchanged looks and started laughing.

I frowned, wondering what I'd said was so funny.

"I'm sorry, Asher," Dahlia said, still giggling quietly to herself. "We're not laughing at you, just the circumstances. There are exactly three places to eat in Rathdrum, and you'll be recognized wherever we go. So will I," Dahlia said with a shrug as she tugged at her hair. I was learning that was a self-conscious gesture she used to try to control her anxiety.

"Still not seeing what was funny," I said. I tried not to sound defensive, but I must have failed because Mason stepped on my foot.

"Be nice," he whispered. "They're pretty."

"Thanks, Mason," Abbi said, slinging her arm around his shoulder. "I love hearing compliments. Be sure to compliment your girlfriend when you get one."

"You could be my girlfriend," Mason said.

I blinked, shocked at how quickly my son was making the moves. I didn't hear Abbi's response because they'd moved off toward the double doors and out into the cool night air.

Dahlia looked up at me, her large gray eyes waiting with patient promise. For what, I didn't know. Nor did I care. I was just thankful to be here, with her, in this moment.

"I'm buying you dinner. As a thank-you for having us out here. And because I want to. So where are we going?"

Dahlia bit her lip, her eyes searching my face. "I live in a small town," she murmured. "If we drive there to eat... well, locals consider it their right to ask questions, make sure you have honorable intentions toward me." She wrinkled her nose at the last words. "We were laughing because Abbi was sure you'd want to go out to eat, and I was sure you'd want to take a break from your fame. I find the little bit I have—and I'm not recognized anywhere near as much as you—exhausting. Abbi wins our bet. We could eat here in Spokane, but then the interruptions will be worse. I think."

She tipped her head toward a small group of people nearby, taking my picture on their phone.

"Will it be bad? The interrogation, I mean." For some reason, I wanted to please Dahlia's friends, wanted them to want me around.

Mason could sit still through a whole meal without doing something insane. Usually. He had way too much energy, even compared to other boys his age. Jessica said he had hyperactivity disorder or some other shit. I considered him more like an eager puppy. He needed to be run hard, then he slept even harder. Perfectly normal kid behavior. Sure, it was exhausting, but that's what parenting, in general, was.

"I don't think it'll be as bad as trying to eat in Spokane. But it's a forty-minute drive. That okay for Mason?"

"Should be. He ate a sandwich on the plane."

Dahlia smiled, and before I realized what I was doing, I'd slipped my hand against hers. I calmed at the touch, but she inhaled sharply, her eyes snapping up to mine. I dropped her hand, immediately missing the warmth of her palm even as hers slid from mine. As my hand hit my side, my mind bursting into action at her rejection, Dahlia slid her fingers back through mine, our skin recalibrating.

I loved touching this woman. I didn't want to consider why. I just wanted to accept that it was so.

"You wanting to touch me shocks me," she said, her voice

pitched low.

"I'm good for a few shocks."

Her lips flipped up. "I bet you are."

I tugged her toward the double doors.

CHAPTER NINETEEN
Dahlia

Panic flared in Asher's eyes as we stepped outside.

"Abbi took Mason to the car."

I waited for his brief nod, watched the tension drain from his face. I didn't like how my heart warmed at his concern. There was too much I already liked about Tristan Asher Smith.

I scooted closer, loving the way my skin shivered and zinged.

Abbi and Mason stood on the sidewalk nearby. The little boy, whose brown hair and hazel eyes reminded me so much of his father, was practically dancing around Abbi, love shining in his eyes. Abbi'd clearly made quite the impression. My daughter was a beautiful, funny young woman. She tended to collect trophies without realizing it. Mason was her newest in what I assumed would be a much longer line of admirers.

Abbi's eyes zeroed in on our clasped hands, but she didn't do anything, and Asher's skin felt too good against mine to let go. He squeezed my fingers just a little, a tiny curve to his lips. I felt mine lift in response.

"Mason wants to hit the diner back in Rathdrum. I told him they serve buffalo burgers. He claims never to have tried one."

"The diner it is," Asher said, but his voice had lost a bit of confidence, and he was sucking on his lower lip. This show of vulnerability did something to me, creating a warm, gooey slide in my chest.

"The car's over here."

Asher stowed their bags while the rest of us buckled into the seats. I'd borrowed a booster from Rhonda—that woman never got rid of anything. Mason sat next to Abbi in the back, asking her about the diner, the town, what she did for fun. I smiled at their easy banter.

Asher slid into the passenger's seat, stretching out his long legs, crossing his sexy motorcycle boots at the ankle. He was so at ease sitting there. Doug always drove us around, whether he knew where he was going or not. I appreciated the small nod to my autonomy Asher provided.

We drove to town and pulled up in front of the diner, which was busy even though it was still early. I felt the stirrings of nerves but shoved them down. I wasn't doing anything more than having dinner with a friend and his child.

That would be fine if my friend wasn't a rock star and didn't look like he could, and had, graced the covers of many magazines for nearly twenty years.

I pulled into a spot, and I caught Abbi's eye. She shrugged a little and opened her door. This was new territory for both of us. I wouldn't have told Asher, but I was glad we were being seen together here in my town. This, these people, I could handle. I hoped. I straightened my spine and stepped out.

Mason and Asher did the same. Mason darted forward, slamming himself into his father's jeans-clad legs. My heart tripped. If what Briar had said about him was true, this little boy had it rougher than he deserved.

I was still waiting for Briar to send the pictures she'd promised. She'd said it would take some time to retrieve them from the server. While I hated prying further into Asher's life, I'd do what I could to help him.

The sun was low, banking against the horizon, and the temperature had dropped.

"Cold?" I asked Mason.

"Nah. I don't get cold. My mom says that's because I won't keep my butt in its place."

I kept my eyes on Mason's face, willing him to look at me because I wasn't sure I could handle Asher's expression at hearing Mason's words. From what little he'd said, Asher was just learning about some of Jessica's neglect and thoughtless comments. Those bright hazel eyes, his dad's eyes, tripped up to my face. I smiled, and Mason grinned back.

"Abbi was the same way. Now she runs track, dances, and is a cheerleader."

Mason grabbed his dad's large hand. Even from here, I could see the calluses on Asher's fingers. His hand was devoid of any rings, just like mine.

"Wears me out enough to fall asleep pretty quick," Abbi chimed in.

"I couldn't be prouder of Abbi. Do you like sports?" I asked Mason.

"Sure do. Baseball's my favorite, and I play on a team. I'm gonna learn to pitch maybe next year. But I really wanna learn how to ride horses. Dad says he's gonna be around more and get me lessons."

I tucked that little nugget away as we entered the diner. Abbi beelined over to some of her friends. I was thankful Luke wasn't there and Abbi'd kept her promise not to tell him about our company this weekend. She waved Mason over. He trotted up to her, the lovesick puppy expression back on his face.

I gestured to a booth and waited for Asher's nod. He placed his hand on my back as we wove through the tables. I loved that little gesture, the warmth it evoked. He smelled good, like I remembered.

"Hey there, Lia. Watching doors?"

I nodded to Mike, who guffawed at his joke. "I shouldn't have to watch them in my own house. Ralph needs to be less quick with those hands."

"I'm sure Rhonda wouldn't agree with that." Mike laughed again.

I resisted the urge to roll my eyes. Instead of introducing Asher, I walked forward to the booth and slid in. He sat opposite me, his brows drawn down just a little. His lips, slightly chapped, were pulled into a tight line.

"You don't want to introduce me to your friends?" His voice was low, filled with hurt.

I leaned forward. "Mike isn't a friend. He's been trying to get into my pants since Doug's funeral." I turned when Wendy, the waitress and co-owner of the diner, popped over. "Hi. This is my friend Asher. He and Mason, his son, are visiting for the weekend."

Asher smiled, showing off the dent in his chin, and Wendy rocked back on her heels, her mouth falling open to show off her cracked front tooth. Yeah, I felt the same way.

"Y'all want something to drink?" she managed to ask.

"Four waters to start," I said, gesturing to Abbi and Mason who were still with Abbi's friends a couple tables over.

"Got it. And glad you have a man-friend, Lia."

I turned back to Asher, the humor still tugging at my lips. "I am, too."

"That makes three of us," Asher said.

I felt warmth spread to my face, so I picked up the menu to cover my flushed cheeks.

"So Abbi's making Mason feel included. Thanks for talking to her about that."

"I didn't. She's used to hanging out with Jeremiah, Simon's son. He's almost the same age as Mason."

"Good job with the whole sensitivity thing, then," Asher said, that little furl pulling at his brow. He moved the menus so Wendy could place the water in front of us. "I hear the buffalo burgers are good."

"They're pretty good when Frank doesn't cook the hell outta 'em. I keep telling him we're a ranching community and most of us like our meat just after the moo-stage."

Abbi was chatting, her eyes bright. Mason still looked comfortable. She caught my eye, and I tilted my head to toward the menu. She leaned down to Mason and asked a question. His head bobbed in quick succession. Abbi held up two fingers, then tilted her head toward her group of friends to let me know she wasn't finished socializing yet.

"If you're ready, Asher, I think the rest of us are going to order the burgers. How does Mason like his?"

"Loaded. Medium well. Same goes for me," Asher said, tucking his menu behind the napkin dispenser.

"Aw-righty, then. Four specials. Be back in a tick."

"Specials?" Asher asked.

"The buffalo burger is the daily special. Always. They have other items on the menu," I said, "but I've never seen a local order anything but the burger. I shudder to think how long the chicken soup's been in that freezer."

Asher looked over at Abbi and Mason, who were laughing at something one of the boys was saying. Some of the tension around his eyes lessened. His profile was strong, his clean-shaven cheeks beginning to bristle with tiny sand-colored hairs. His long, brown lashes lowered, concealing his eyes. "I'm going to fight Jessica for custody."

My heart tripped. Briar'd been right. I was going to have to tell him about the pictures her paper had taken.

"I told my lawyer I don't care about the house or the bank accounts, but Jessica can't touch Mason or the band."

"How did that go over?" I asked.

"Worse than you'd imagine. She's still so angry with me." He swallowed hard. "And I get it. I fucked up bad back then, but I can't let her take it out on Mason."

I nodded. I couldn't resist laying my hand over his fisted one.

The spell broke when Mason leapt into the booth next to Asher. "One of the boys over there—he lives on a ranch—he said he'd teach me to ride his old pony tomorrow. Can we go? Please?"

I laughed. Abbi slid in next to me, making sure to bump me with her hip. I ignored her.

"Cameron's going to talk to his dad when he gets home, but I don't think it'll be a problem," Abbi said.

Mason stared at me with big, pleading eyes. I held up my hands and glanced at Asher, who was looking a little uncomfortable.

"There're lots of horses in the area," I said to Asher. "If that's something he wants to do, I'm sure we can find one."

"Yes!" Mason shrieked, fists flailing in happiness.

"Watch those hands," Wendy said as she came up to the table. "Only one of us getting bruised up 'round here is Lia, and that's 'cause the sheriff's so desperate to rescue her."

I noticed Abbi's friends lingering in the corner, darting glances in our direction.

"Are they waiting to talk to you?" I asked.

"They want to get Asher's autograph and a picture," she said, her face apologetic. She munched a fry.

"After we finish eating," I said.

"That's what I told them."

Conversation was light while we ate. I still had to be careful not to open my mouth too wide, which meant I took forever to eat. Halfway through, I tossed my burger back onto the plate, annoyed. I wasn't that hungry, but I wished I didn't hurt. More, I wished Asher was seeing me at my best, not all battered and the brunt of the town's jokes.

He signaled to Wendy, who was chatting with a tourist couple. "Would you mind bringing me the check? Dahlia's tired."

I thanked him with a glance, glad he understood. I was tired, but more than that, I wanted another dose of painkillers and a glass of something to smooth out my nerves and the jitters gathering low in my belly.

As Wendy walked up with the check, Abbi's friends also appeared, a passel of eager puppies fighting over a chew toy. Ian Johnson led the way, probably because he played tackle for the high school football team while Cameron Ames, the boy behind, headed up the 4-H club. The pecking order was ridiculous, but these kids took it seriously. Their girlfriends, Heather and Jen, pressed close, excitement shining through their big smiles.

Asher handed Wendy his card without even looking at the bill. I frowned. I hoped Wendy hadn't miscalculated the total again. She was terrible with math.

"Hi, Mr.... er... Smith. Would you mind signing some stuff for us?"

"You famous, then?" Wendy asked. She beamed. "Figured with those looks you must be one of those movie people Lia's going to start working with. Burgers were good?"

"The best!" Mason said.

Abbi sighed, loud and long, which she did when she loved being cooler than the rest of the kids. "This is Asher. He's a musician and a singer. He and Mom are working together on a sound track for Mom's miniseries. The one they both signed on to today." Abbi smiled at me, her eyes sparkling with pride. "He's a totally cool rock star. I already introduced you to Mason, the awesome guy here on the end."

"Yeah, hey, Mason. I'll text Abbi tomorrow about the pony ride. You'll love Darlin'. She's a sweetheart," Cameron said. He smiled, and some of the tension drained from my shoulders. These kids could be kind when they remembered to be.

"So, um, Mr. Smith, we were wondering if you could, like, take a picture with us?" Heather said. Everything she said turned into a question. I wanted to tell her to be confident in herself, but that would backfire, making her even more tentative. I slid farther into the booth as I sipped my water.

"Call me Asher." He said it with an easy smile, but tension pulled at the skin near his eyes.

CHAPTER TWENTY
Asher

I couldn't escape my fame long enough to get Dahlia back to her place, especially now that I knew she was tired. I shouldn't have suggested eating out, not with her bruised cheek. In my defense, I'd wanted to keep things simple for her, but I'd managed to fuck that up—first with the meal she could barely eat and then with the fawning kids who wouldn't let us leave.

I signed a few napkins and even one piece of waxed paper—hard to do—for Wendy. Posed for a few people. Other people came over once they realized the crowd was gathering for a reason.

I nodded to Mason, who jumped up. Abbi followed his lead so Dahlia was able to escape the booth.

"Thanks, but we gotta go." I put my hands on Mason's shoulders, hoping the group would think I meant Mason needed to get away from the crowd or something.

I slid one hand behind Dahlia's back and ushered the four of us toward the exit. I could feel the curious eyes following us, but I'd learned years ago not to look back. If I did, people took it as an invitation to invade my space. I didn't want to subject the kids or Dahlia to that.

I was surprised at how protective I already was toward Abbi and Dahlia, how right it felt being here together as a unit.

I'd come here as her friend, to make sure she was healthy. But I'd lied to myself. I wanted her. Not just sexually, though I'd have to be blind to miss her beauty.

Dahlia wrote books, beautiful ones brimming with emotion and depth, like the songs I strove to write and perform. She had fans, and I'm sure she had detractors. But what mattered was the art and the emotions we evoked in ourselves.

I wanted to sit with her and talk about how to push those emotions. How to transcend the bullshit in life. Each minute in her company—each look, each touch, each shared breath—my need grew. I was stewing in it, and it felt fucking amazing.

———◆———

The ride to Dahlia's house was quiet. Mason was drooping now that the excitement wore thin. He did best when he was in bed by nine o'clock. We'd hit that tonight, which meant he'd be up before eight. After a bowl of cereal, most mornings he'd play with his Legos for a while so I could sketch out a new tune or catch up on my work messages. He was an easy-going kid as long as he slept well, something I understood completely.

Abbi stared out the window, also quiet. I hoped she felt like I'd done her friends right. I'd tried to be jovial and happy. I'd put some effort into trying, at least.

Dahlia drove the SUV with ease, her hand gripping the bottom part of the steering wheel, her far hand in her lap. I liked how relaxed she was right now. Her serenity filled me up, expanded in my chest, let me breathe.

I exhaled in a slow, soft hiss, trying to keep the rising tension to myself. I was back to how much I wanted her. But I didn't want to push into a physical relationship here, in her house, where she'd lived with her husband.

Years ago, I'd left without telling Dahlia how I felt in some misguided effort to be noble. The chemistry between us was still there, explosive, rare, and beautiful. I'd waited so long for this chance, and I wasn't willing to fuck it up. And I wasn't leaving until I knew what we could have.

We turned into a drive. Dahlia's house was fantastic. Cedar siding and lots of windows glowing with a soft yellow light. Thick river stone was stacked along the bottom story. The front door was black with a silver handle and knocker.

Classy. Understated. So Dahlia. I hadn't gone inside yet, and I was already half in love with the place.

She pulled the SUV into the garage. I opened the car door and stepped out. When I opened Mason's door, he blinked at me with blurry eyes. Unbuckling his seatbelt, I pulled him into my arms. He nestled his head into the curve of my neck, his breath puffing against my throat.

Man, I loved this kid. I hated how much of his day-to-day I missed out on while I was touring. Not wanting to dwell on the old, irritating argument, I glanced around.

Tools hung above a custom cedar workbench. Fancy German ones, covered in a layer of grayish dust. The two bays to the left were empty. An older refrigerator hummed on the end. Three fishing poles leaned against the dented almond-painted walls. A couple of mountain bikes hung from S-hooks, their tires still coated in a dried layer of mud. Equally abused pink helmets hung from the handlebars.

Abbi flounced in front of us, opening the door to the house. She had her phone whipped out of her tiny purse and was hunched over, her thumbs flying across the screen.

"Gotta go answer these texts. Luke is so mad I didn't tell him to stay in town." She giggled. "See ya in the morning."

"You've further elevated her social standing among the kids out here. She may very well be unbearable to live with." Dahlia wrinkled her nose then cringed. She tossed her keys onto the granite-topped bar and shoved her purse onto one of the stools.

The kitchen, like the garage, was uncluttered. This space was well used; the dishwasher blinked its finished load. There were two large ceramic pots with a fancy French name scrawled across the bottom in the drain tray. The appliances were all high-end, but in a glossy white. The cabinets were a smooth honey maple in a simple design, the silver pulls functional.

"Face hurt?" I asked, turning my attention back to her.

"Yeah, the bruise is deeper than the cut," she said. "I'll show you where Mason's sleeping."

She led me through a living room, an open great-room concept with a large wood stove tucked in a corner so that the wall of windows gave an uninterrupted view of the mountains. The stairs were tucked in another corner. No great, sweeping statement for Dahlia. The wood-and-wrought-iron balustrade was simple, free of curlicues and fussiness as was the wool rug lying over the wide-planked hardwoods. I didn't know what type of wood. Something expensive and sustainable, I'd bet. I was getting a better sense of the woman walking up the stairs.

I grinned as I noticed her ass was right at eye level. It was a mighty fine specimen in those jeans. The pockets were stitched in simple yellow thread, but the design shouted "Look at me!" I was happy to oblige.

Mason snuggled in closer, his breathing a light snore that told me he was down for the count. Nothing, not even taking off his shoes, would wake him up now. I wished I had that level of innocence.

182

Or maybe I didn't. I followed Dahlia into the spare bedroom. As she turned on the light, her shirt pulled tight across her back, accentuating the curve of her waist. She glanced back, noticed Mason's closed eyes, and her face softened. She went to the adjoining bathroom, flicked on that light, and closed the door two-thirds of the way. She came back, turned off the overhead light, and then went to the bed to pull down the thick blue comforter.

I settled Mason in the bed, taking in his sprawled limbs and slightly-parted lips. His brown lashes, so similar to mine, made a thick wedge of shadow on his freckled cheeks.

Dahlia unlaced his sneaker and slipped it off with quick efficiency. She'd gotten the second one off while I was struggling with Mason's jeans snap. I slid his pants down his spindly, pale legs. Dahlia pulled the sheet up to his neck, the comforter to his shoulder.

I watched her as she brushed his hair off his forehead. Her eyes were still soft when they met mine.

CHAPTER TWENTY-ONE
Dahlia

Asher's gaze was filled with yearning. His face was shadowed, his breath warm as it hit my cheek. I shivered and eased around him, heading toward the door.

I heard his cursed exhalation, but it was more of a prayer. My heart sped up. I quickened my pace, needing to get out of the room.

He followed, catching my hand before I managed to escape down the stairs. As always, his touch was soothing, and some of the rising anxiety slid away.

"You're sleeping in the other spare bedroom that connects to Mason's through the bathroom. I'll help you bring up your bags."

I extricated my hand and headed down the stairs. I made it to the small laundry room between the kitchen and garage.

"Dahlia, I didn't come here to seduce you."

I turned to face him. "I'm not ready to be seduced."

"I want us to be more than mutual pleasure." His voice was low, the words careful. His eyes were darker, more brown than hazel. The cleft in his chin was so close, and my gaze went back to it again. I'd always liked that spot. My resolve unraveled. It—*he* was right there.

"I like pleasure," I whispered.

He backed me against the door. I could feel the heat from his thighs against mine. "If you say that again, I'm going to kiss you, and screw the consequences."

He touched his forehead to mine. Need unfurled, fast and painful. My neck arched as I searched for his lips. My hips angled closer, but he kept his body from mine.

184

"I've waited for this chance for years, Dahlia. I'm not going to fuck it up."

I gripped his forearms and leaned in. My lips brushed his once in a light welcome. He slid his hand over my waist, bringing my chest flush against his. He braced his legs on either side of my thighs as he opened his mouth, the tip of his tongue sliding out to touch mine.

I moaned, the sound as primal as the need spiraling from my core, heating my skin. He slid his other hand up into my hair, his palm warm against my scalp. He tilted my head with gentle pressure to plunder my mouth.

I pressed into him harder, fingers flexing into his arms as I opened my mouth wider. More. I needed more of Asher's taste, his warm mouth. The sweet, drugging desire of a long, slow kiss.

His thumb rubbed the bottom of my ribs, and my nipples hardened. I slid my tongue over his and lifted my right leg, snagging my knee on his hip and finally feeling his hardness pressed there, where I needed him. His tongue slicked over my teeth, the inside of my cheek, before coming back to tangle with mine.

When he tried to open my mouth farther, my cheek burned. I flinched, the pain ripping through the haze of passion. I eased back and dropped my leg. I pressed my fingers to my lips, trying to capture the intensity of our kiss for another moment.

My body was primed. I couldn't remember wanting to be touched more. My nipples begged for Asher's long, callused fingers to pluck them. My thighs quivered with unfulfilled need. I was so close... so damn close to release. From a kiss.

"That was amazing," I said, trying to find my equilibrium.

His hand slid from the back of my neck to my jaw, his thumb

moving up to sweep my fingers from my lips.

"This need I have for you, Dahlia. It's intense."

I let my lips drift up in the little smile I could manage. I pressed a kiss to his thumb. I stepped back but let my tongue drift over the sensitive skin before breaking contact. He closed his eyes, nostrils flaring.

"Not yet," he said.

He was right. Much as I wanted him, he'd already told me that night at the beach that he didn't know if he could do forever. I wasn't willing to settle for less, not with him. I dipped my head in acquiescence, unsure of my voice.

"I'll get our bags," he said.

"Want a beer?" I stepped away from the door, rubbing my clammy palms on my thighs. Asher's gaze followed my hands. I stilled. He raised his gaze to mine, his eyes dark, his features sharp with lust.

"Love one." He opened the door and walked into the garage.

I pulled out the local brew Briar'd found at the store and poured myself a glass of wine. I popped the lid off his beer and brought it, a pint glass, and my Syrah to the living room. I curled up in the corner of the couch as Asher came down the stairs two at a time.

"That was too fast. I'm sorry," he said.

"The kiss?"

He glanced at the couch with me tucked as far from him as possible. I picked up the glass and took a sip of the wine, enjoying the feel of the dark liquid rolling across my palate. The taste of ripe cherries bloomed across my tongue.

"Dahlia, I'm not looking for a quick, easy lay."

I set my glass down, my lips twitching upward. "I wouldn't have agreed to you visiting if that's what I thought you expected. That kiss was really hot, and I enjoyed it." I blew out a breath. "Too much, maybe."

"Is that possible?"

My lips still tingled, searching for another round of tasting, testing. I shook my head. "Sit. Enjoy your beer. Tell me the rest of what's bothering you."

I patted the spot next to me. He eased down, careful not to jar my cheek, and grabbed the bottle. Tilting it, he took a long pull. He leaned back and shut his eyes so that those long, brown lashes hugged his high cheekbones.

I leaned my head against his shoulder, and he moved a little so that I was snuggled into his side. He pressed a kiss to my temple near my healing cut as his free arm snaked around my waist.

"Thank you," he said.

"For?"

"Being you. Being here."

"No worries. I'm good at being me." I paused, then added. "Most of the time."

"I think Mason's going to pay for my past. I can't leave him with Jessica. The things he's told me… She's neglectful."

I bit the tip of my tongue. I couldn't add to his pain by telling him what Briar had confided in me. Not yet.

"Why do you think you've made mistakes?"

"I've been touring for years. Home in spurts. Gone for maybe eight, ten weeks at a time. That's hard on a marriage. It's getting harder on me, too. I love what I do. Fucking love it. But that doesn't mean I don't want to be home on Christmas and see my kid open the presents I bought him. Coach his baseball team, be the one to go to the parent-teacher conferences, and buy his back-to-school crap."

"You only mention Jessica in conjunction to Mason." I lifted my head, my heart slamming faster. "What about your relationship with her?"

"What about it?"

"Was there intimacy?"

He sipped the beer and leaned forward to set it on the coffee table. I noted how careful he was to get it on a coaster. Little, thoughtful gestures that meant so much to me.

"The sex was good. In the beginning."

I swallowed with difficulty. So not what I wanted to hear after he'd just kissed me like that.

He tipped my chin up, waiting until my eyes met his. "It's different with you. Everything is just… better."

His thumb brushed across my lip, and my breath caught. Oh, I wanted this man.

Bad idea. He led a life I didn't want. I eased out of his hold, missing his touch even before the warmth faded from my skin.

"I meant your ability to share. Not just your body. Your thoughts, concerns," I said.

"Jessica likes flashy," he said. "She thought I was going to be *the* rock star, not *a* rock star. Hell, we were poised to make it huge. But we haven't climbed that last piece. Maybe we weren't supposed to." He shrugged, and I was pleased to see he wasn't bitter about the shifting surge of fame and influence. "I'm doing pretty damn well in my profession. Have the loyal fans and healthy bank accounts to show for it. I know tons of guys who'd love to be where I am now."

I sipped my wine. He ran his hands through his hair.

"I don't want to try to be something I'm not. I want to write songs I like to sing and play. I want to perform because it's fun and interesting, not because it's for some paycheck or to make some rich record exec richer." He turned to look at me, his eyes earnest. "I want to be Tristan Asher Smith. Not Asher Smith, the Supernaturals's front man. You know?"

"I think I do."

"I wasn't looking for anything when I walked into that bar. Well, except some good tunes and a cold beer." His lips kicked up a bit, not a full smile but with a hint of humor. "I found you again. It's been the best. Dahlia, I mean that. The best. That night with you was perfection."

I sipped again and considered him over the rim. "I'm not perfect," I murmured.

"I know. That's what's so great. You have your own issues. They're completely different from mine. I want to see where we can go. From here. Would you do that? Just see what we can make of us? Slowly. Because that's what I need and you deserve."

His face filled with trepidation, and I thrilled to see this sexy, self-assured man flustered.

"I don't want to be your bounce-back girl, Asher. That would hurt me. Deeply."

"You couldn't be. You... this... I told you. I haven't felt this way about anyone but you. Desire's always been there between us, and I can't let you go this time."

I smiled at him and set my empty glass on the table next to his. I pressed my lips into his neck and breathed him in. We sat quiet, connected. I rolled his words around, feeling them out. "I need you to understand I don't care for or about your fame. Not for its sake. On some level, I feel like I've known you forever."

"Dahlia," he groaned, "you have. I've thought about you, even when I knew I shouldn't. But if we'd had then, we might not be here now. I was selfish and definitely way too fucked up for a nice girl like you."

"You may be right. I wasn't me then either. I loved my husband, Asher." I didn't add that had been early in our relationship. "He hurt me, but he also helped me when I needed him."

"I know. That's why I left Cactus Arrow."

"Please tell me you're kidding." He'd said almost the same thing before but I hadn't believed him. Not really.

The silence thickened. I didn't want to leave the comfort of his arms. Didn't want to see what the truth did to us.

"I wanted you then," he said. "Leaving was the best way I could handle it."

I, at least, had been too young, too wrapped up in breaking free from my mom, getting past my father's death. My hand lay on Asher's chest, my fingers ringless and pale against his shirt. I'd taken off my wedding ring right after Doug's death, unable to stand the sight of the lie I'd perpetuated for Abbi.

"You have to understand," I said, my voice soft. Hesitant. But he'd shared with me, so it was my turn to be honest. "I hadn't been on tour with Doug since before Abbi was born. A baby didn't keep with the whole indie rock vibe."

"Hard to take kids on the road."

"Right. So I was excited when Briar offered to stay with Abbi. She was five, nearly six. I planned to surprise Doug, hadn't told him I was coming. I showed up to find some girl in Doug's hotel room. She was young... younger than me. She wanted to know why I was so angry. Said that Doug always brought her back to his room after a show in Portland."

190

Asher rubbed his thumb across the back of my neck. He waited, letting me tell the story in my time.

"Doug admitted she wasn't the only one. And he wasn't going to stop having sex with them. I had to make a choice. I chose my marriage, but he destroyed something vital in me. I'd already been writing, but it became my escape. I needed to believe in love for someone, even if the people were make-believe."

"He was a selfish bastard."

"Sometimes. Especially after the diagnosis. But he also saved my life."

"How?"

I drew in a shaky breath. Those days weren't easy for me to talk about. "I was suicidal when I was fourteen. My dad, my rock, had just died. My mom took weeks to come pick me and my sister up. If not for some of the other wives on the military base, we would've starved. We almost did anyway, because I didn't want to tell them I couldn't access any money." I twisted my fingers, hating remembering that time, Briar's cries of hunger and her anger when I told her Dad wasn't coming back.

"Helping you work through a hard patch didn't mean you owed him your future happiness. Didn't mean you owed him anything you didn't want to give." Asher sounded angry. I sat forward and met his eyes, the hazel darkened with frustration. For me.

"I looked you up. On my way home from Portland. You were in New York. I'm glad you weren't nearby because I don't know what I would've done if you'd told me you were interested in me, too."

Saying the words, admitting I'd been unhappy for all those years, felt good. The pain was muted, almost gone. I breathed deep. "That scares me. I'm questioning those choices I made then. Which

191

means I need to question my feelings for Doug and for you, too."

He tightened his arm around my waist and pressed a kiss into my hair. He breathed out a "thank you." The steady thrum of his heart lulled me to sleep.

———————

I woke to the sound of a camera clicking over and over. I blinked, my bleary eyes focusing on my daughter's shiny and gleeful face.

"What are you doing?" I murmured.

"I'm photo documenting the first night you slept with Asher," Abbi said in a near-whisper.

I turned, beyond thankful to see Asher still asleep. I couldn't help but smile at how carefree he looked. And hot.

I eased off his side with painful regret. He turned into the cushions. I stood, surprised by how well I'd slept. Doug had fought his demons in his dreams. There wasn't one night of our marriage when he'd slept as still as Asher had.

I beckoned Abbi to follow me, glad to see she did. I walked to the coffeepot and flipped the switch. One of my rituals was to immediately refill the machine for the next pot. It wasn't so much for the drink itself—yeah, I needed a shot or two of caffeine most mornings—but I'd always loved the smell, which reminded me of Doug's parents' home, one of the few places I'd ever felt safe and accepted. Sadness weighed on me. John had died years ago, before Abbi's birth, Margaret a few years later.

"You will *not* show those to anyone," I grumbled.

Abbi smirked, holding her phone tight to her chest.

"Abigail," I sighed. "I don't know what's going on between Asher and me, but you have to understand that the media is interested in what he does. They'll find any picture you post online. That could mean Asher doesn't get custody of Mason or that Jessica can screw him over further in the divorce settlement. Don't be the reason for that. I won't be able to punish you enough."

Something I needed to remember myself. He'd just told me he was fighting for Mason. I couldn't mess that up for him. If that meant denying my growing attraction, then I'd deny. After all these years, I was good at it.

Abbi frowned. "I hadn't thought about how you two together could hurt his chances to get Mason. Is that what he wants?"

I was glad Abbi was keeping her voice low. I didn't want Asher to walk in and hear us discussing this. I kept my gaze level as I nodded. "There are extenuating circumstances I'm not sharing with you, so don't ask. Be smart about any photo of the two of us. Any comment or note even. For now, the only thing you can tell people about us is that Asher is a friend. That's the truth."

I poured a cup of coffee and added the dash of cinnamon I'd come to enjoy. My stomach gurgled in appreciation.

Abbi nodded, her mouth turning down. She fiddled with her phone. "I'll delete them."

"I'd really appreciate it. But send me one before you do that."

She bit her lip, eyes shining, and I smiled at her. She grinned back.

"I like that you're more open. Aunt Briar said the same thing when she was leaving."

"Thanks. I think."

A surge of energy zinged across my skin. My body warmed, my skin flushed and tightened. Asher was close by. Abbi glanced up at him.

"I checked on Mason," Abbi said. She was unaware of my reaction to Asher's presence. Thank goodness. "He's still asleep. I thought I'd go for a run."

"Thanks, Abbi," Asher said.

"See you in a bit."

Asher waited until she closed the back door before stepping up to me, not touching, but his body curving into mine like a magnet closing in on its mate.

"Smells good. Where are your mugs?"

"I'll get you one," I said, using the excuse to step away.

God, I was mortified Abbi could have seen my reaction. It was primal, instinctive. I poured him a cup that he accepted, making sure our fingers brushed. He raised it to his lips, his hazel eyes darkening as he brushed the hair from my temple.

"I like seeing you in the morning."

Asher sipped his coffee, and I watched the long line of his throat swallow.

"I'm going to run to the bathroom and wash my face. I'll meet you on the porch," I said, tipping my head toward the deep cedar-framed porch I'd had built a couple of years ago. I loved sitting out there with my notebook, jotting down ideas as they flitted across my mind.

"Good place to work," Asher murmured.

I smiled. "I'll grab a couple pens."

<hr />

We sat next to each other, not touching but hyper aware. His hair was tousled, his lashes damp from washing his face. He'd taken off his button-down and untucked his gray T-shirt. His jeans were worn, soft, and faded on the thighs, right where I wanted my hands. When Asher picked up his mug, I thought about what his hands would feel like running down my throat, unbuttoning the top two buttons of my blouse so he could run his fingers over the swells of my breasts.

I started writing out the next scene for my book. I bit my lip, scribbling fast. I needed to fan my face. I peeked up at Asher from under my lashes and realized he was looking at me with as much hunger as I'd just saturated into the last few pages.

He set down his pen and smirked. "Writing something good? Want to share?"

"Um, no. More coffee." I scampered into the kitchen, needing a minute to regroup. I came back out a few minutes later after giving myself yet another lecture on why pushing our connection now would be a bad idea. Mason, my heart—there were so many reasons.

"What are you working on?" I asked.

"Sound track. You?"

I pursed my lips. "Whatever you want. Paul suggested we talk about the feelings we want to evoke. Any ideas?"

He looked at me through those lashes. "Lots of passion. And kissing."

My heart rate kicked up. "Asher. Please."

"I'm thinking about running my fingers over that throbbing pulse. Have been ever since your cheeks went so red. Give me something back. You want to. I need you to."

I scooted closer, tongue bathing my lower lip. His eyes darkened as he brought his coffee cup to his lips.

"Fingers touch, learn. Take my hunger, crumble walls." The words poured out of my mouth.

He wrote as I watched his quick, efficient strokes. The long tapered fingers, callused tips. They were warm and rough and felt amazing on my skin.

"Good. Anything else?"

I blinked, wishing I could be as collected as he appeared to be.

"How many songs are you writing?" I asked.

"Three. I have a few indie groups you'll like. I'll play them for you later."

"What else do you have in there?"

He passed over his battered spiral notebook. My heart slammed hard into my chest as my eyes darted over the page.

"You read the script," I whispered.

Asher shook his head. "I read the real deal. Your books, Dahlia. Remember? I told you my mom was a huge fan. I pulled out all her old copies once I realized you were Lia Moore."

I froze. He knew just what to say to me. Every time.

He picked up my hand, smoothing his fingers over mine. "I need to tell you something. It's why Jessica's so angry."

The rain took us by surprise. Quick drops sizzled on my skin before leaving me feeling icy and dazed.

"Inside," Asher said. He gripped his notebook and mine in one hand as he pulled me to my feet. "Move."

The rain shifted, driving into my face. I squeaked and whirled into motion. We tumbled through the screen door.

"That's cold," Asher muttered, his teeth chattering.

"Take your shirt off. I'll get towels," I said.

"You didn't have to freeze me to get me naked."

I laughed. "Not naked, but shirt off, you're dripping on my floor."

Pulling his soaked tee over his head, he shook the rain from the dripping strands. The damp cotton dangled from his fingers. Droplets clung to the hairs on his strong arms and chest. He seemed even broader without clothes covering him, and his toned chest intrigued me. Better than his forearms.

"Enjoying the view?" he asked, amusement lacing his voice. He laid the notebooks on the bar, spreading out the pages to help them dry more quickly.

I wanted to push him onto the floor and press my cool skin to his, warming us both. I nearly whimpered at my building frustration. Even the weather was conspiring against me.

"Yes."

My eyes darted upward. Seeing the need gleaming from his eyes, I forced my feet backward, finally breaking eye contact as I darted into the laundry room. I yanked my top over my head before wrapping a thick towel around my shoulders. I walked out and offered Asher another one.

"Your free time on tour—you spend it in the gym?" That couldn't be my voice. It was so breathy.

"Some," he said, rubbing the towel over his hair. He dropped the towel around his shoulders and met my eyes. "Good to know I'm making the right impression. I like to walk, run, hike, and cycle. I try to spend a couple hours a day outside. Helps me get my head on straight for a performance, but it's best when I want to write a song."

"Does it work?" I asked. I'd inched closer, drawn to his exposed skin. His heat leached onto me, and I breathed in Asher and rain. My new favorite scent.

A droplet slid down his temple and cheek. I reached up with the edge of my towel and wiped it away. Asher stood still, his gaze focused on the gap in my towel.

"You have lickable skin, Dahlia. Like cream."

My breasts were visible, and from the position I was in, they were straining out the top of my bra.

Asher moved forward, until our bodies touched, his warmth a counterpoint to the lingering chill. I moaned at the contact.

"Where are you, Dad?" Mason called from upstairs.

"It's pouring out there," Abbi said. I jumped back as the back door slammed shut. "I'm freezing!"

"You too?" He pulled my towel tight across my shoulders. "We got caught on the porch." He raised his voice, "Down here, Mason."

Asher stepped in front of me before I scurried away. He waited until I tipped my head back and met his eyes.

"Good thing the kids are here to run interference," he said.

I flashed him a smile as I pulled the towel tighter around me. Abbi raced by us, shivering.

"I need to warm up. Be down in a bit."

"Don't leave your clothes on the bathroom floor again," I called.

"Got it. Hey, Mason."

"Hi." Mason trundled down the stairs, and I ran back into the laundry room. I didn't want Asher's son to see me topless. That was just too awkward to contemplate. Exactly why I needed to get my libido back under control.

One of Abbi's camisoles with a built-in bra was still in the hamper. Score. It was tight, but it was better than the wet bra and towel. I yanked it over my head and stepped back into the kitchen to see Mason in the doorway. He glanced up at me, a lock of hair falling onto his brow and into his eyes, tangling in his lashes. Just like his father. I wanted to brush it back but wasn't sure how he'd react. Just like his father.

"Morning, Dahlia," he said.

"You should call me Lia. Everyone else does," I said. "And good morning. What do you like for breakfast?"

"My dad calls you Dahlia. He said it's a pretty flower. One of his favorites. He said you're prettier than any flower."

Asher was watching me with an intensity that completely disarmed me. Being attracted to a troubadour was one thing, being attracted to a sensitive man was more dangerous. The towel slipped, showing off more of his tanned chest.

"How about waffles?" I asked, using the bright happy voice of Abbi's childhood. "I made a bunch yesterday. I'll change while they warm up."

After the rain ended, we drove Mason over to try out Cameron's pony. Mason's grin as he stroked the horse was brighter than the warm spring sun. Cameron was conscientious, making sure Mason's helmet fit and the saddle was cinched tight to the stocky pony's belly.

Asher watched from the edge of the corral, his long body settled into a relaxed stance, but tension gathered around his eyes. Abbi was on the porch, chatting with Cameron's mom and sister, so I moved closer to Asher. His fingers were white where they gripped the slatted wood.

I dipped my head to his death grip. "He doesn't have to ride if you're concerned about it."

Asher grimaced, relaxing his fingers. I slid my hand against his, this time offering Asher the comfort of my presence. His breath stuttered out.

"No. He wants to do this. It'll be fine."

Asher's eyes never left Mason's small form. Cameron helped Mason onto the pony's back and Mason laughed, arms flying upward as he tipped his head back. Cameron stood next to the little boy, a grin spreading over his face, too. Asher's grip on my hand tightened to the point of pain, and I leaned into him.

"Hey," I said, keeping my voice soft. "Cameron's got him. Darlin's not going to buck him off."

Asher turned his head, and I was shocked to see the brown bleeding out from the green, pupils too dilated for the bright day.

"You're right."

"But if you want Mason off the pony, we'll get him off."

"Dad! Look at me. I'm riding a horse," Mason yelled. Darlin' took advantage of Mason's excitement and leaned down to munch a clump of tender grass at the edge of the pen.

"Good job, buddy. How about you hold the reins?"

Mason bounced in the saddle and Darlin' huffed, still munching. Cameron stepped in and showed Mason how to hold the reins. Asher's body uncoiled with slow, painful shudders.

"He's all I have. Watching him do these things… Sometimes it really freaks me out."

I pressed my cheek into his chest, listening to the steady thud of Asher's heart. "I understand."

"I know you do," Asher whispered, sweeping the hair off my forehead. "You make carrying the burden easier. I couldn't handle it if something happened to him."

I wrapped my arm around his waist, uncaring what the people around us thought. "You'll do everything you can to make sure he's safe. That's all any of us can do."

"Sometimes it isn't enough."

I blinked up at him. "You're right about that, too. But you've taught me to not let fear control how I live life."

"Have I?" His eyes brightened as the corner of his lips curled up. "That's good."

"It is. Thank you for that."

Asher pulled me closer. "Back at you, Dahlia." His gaze drifted toward Mason who was walking in a slow circle around the large corral, Cameron holding the lead rope.

When Luke and his dad showed up in the early afternoon, along with Sally, her younger brother, and parents, Cameron's mom suggested a barbecue.

"I don't have anything with me," I said, flustered.

"Abbi told me you cooked up a storm," Rhonda said. "So we swung by your place and picked up some of the food in the fridge. You made more than enough for all of us."

I leaned over to Abbi. "You planned this, didn't you?"

Her eyes were wide and innocent. I narrowed mine in response.

"Leave that girl alone." Rhonda swatted at my arm. "Lydia and I came up with the plan this morning when you called to see about Mason riding Darlin'. Abbi said you ate a late breakfast so you have to be hungry. This'll be a fun way to spend the afternoon and evening. Plus, we wanted to meet your new men." She poked Mason in the stomach, and he giggled.

"Can I have a s'more?" he asked.

Rhonda stood, hands on her generous hips. "You sure can. More than one if you stick by me."

"Okay!"

We all laughed as Mason danced around the yard, hyper enough to make Asher comment that he didn't need sugar.

"He's fine," I murmured. "Just excited."

"Yeah, he's wheels-off when he gets excited."

"This is the perfect place to live it out loud."

"You make it so easy, Dahlia. Thanks for today."

I smiled, memorizing the planes of Asher's face and the sparkle in his eyes.

Replete with food and laughter, Asher picked up Cameron's shiny, new guitar. The boy had brought it outside with the last load of food but hadn't actually asked Asher to play. Everyone leaned in, focused, when Asher tuned the instrument.

"What do you want to hear?" he asked.

"What's your favorite song?" Rhonda asked.

"Well, for the longest time, it was 'Moonshine Eyes'," he said, strumming a soft, light melody. I shivered as his eyes met mine, heat simmering in his gaze. "But I've become rather partial to 'Sweet Solace' once again. Tell you what, I'll play both, and you tell me which one you prefer."

Firelight drifted over Asher's skin, bathing him in its golden hues. His whiskey-soaked voice drifted over my skin, sliding deep inside me, just as it always did. My favorites, besides his own, were the old Bob Dylan songs. His voice was clear and pitch-perfect, melting into Dylan's lyricism.

Each minute, each interaction with Asher, built upon itself, reverberating through me.

Sure, the timing was terrible, but I wanted him. I wanted this easy space we fell into. I blew out a breath, looking out into the star-filled night, wishing I'd been smarter with my choices.

I don't think I've got it in me. The staying power.

Whether he had it in him or not, I wanted more of this. If I wasn't careful, I was going to want a life with Asher.

CHAPTER TWENTY-TWO
Asher

"You're quiet. Everything okay?" I asked as I stepped into the kitchen. I'd read Mason a book from Dahlia's impressive library while she puttered downstairs with Abbi.

"That's my cue. I'm outta here."

"I didn't mean to cut your conversation short with your mom, Abbi."

"Oh, believe me, you weren't interrupting a thing. Mom's being stubborn. It's the unattractive side of her personality. Plus, I have to answer all my social media messages that I couldn't check for the last few days, thanks to Mom grounding me. Popularity is a real time suck." She kissed my cheek on her way out. "Thanks for a fun day. I loved hearing you sing."

She took the stairs two at a time before I could even raise my hand to the place her lips had touched. Dahlia's elbows were on the bar, her face smug.

"Another admirer," she said. Her voice was warm. Good.

"She's great, and I'm glad we get along. But I only really care about one woman's admiration."

"Oh?" She pulled back and turned to the fridge. I followed, a magnet to the loadstone. "Want a beer?" she asked, her back to me.

I placed my hands on her hips and pressed my nose into her hair. "I meant you, Dahlia."

She turned slowly, her hand coming up to rest on my chest. "Asher…"

"Do you have any idea how much I like my name coming from your mouth? The way your lips form the syllables. I've wanted to kiss

204

your lips since I first saw you. And when I did, it was magic." I took a deep breath. "I'm not going to push you. But you have to know I've thought about you. Fantasized about you. I told you that. In the elevator. Now, being here with you, my dreams are richer."

I picked up her hand that held the beer. I took the bottle, set it on the counter, and shut the fridge behind her, leaving my arm next to her head. "I've thought about the smell of your hair. Your eyes get that faraway look when you're thinking. How they sparkle before you smile. I've thought about the little dimple in your cheek. The way your hips sway in heels."

"This isn't slow," she murmured. She sounded tortured.

I stepped back, giving her the space she needed. "I've thought about you being alone, and how scared you are even though you're capable of taking care of yourself and your daughter. I've thought about your injury," I said. I ran my fingertips across the healing cut over her eyebrow before cupping her other cheek. "I've worried about you, Dahlia. Especially your panic attacks."

Her gray eyes were wide, filled with longing.

"You have enough to worry about right now without adding me to the list."

"I know what I need to worry about."

Her lips parted. I could take her now, if I asked. I knew I could just as I knew it was too soon for her, for us. So even though I wanted to bury my fingers in her silk hair and plunder her mouth, I grabbed the beer from the counter instead.

"Are you still in love with Doug?" I asked.

She blinked. I could tell she was trying to bring her head out of the sensuality caused by my earlier words. I bit back a smile.

She opened a drawer and handed me the bottle opener.

"I—no," she said. Her eyes never left mine. "I haven't been in love with him for a long time."

My throat was dry, my skin itchy. "Because he cheated?"

"Yes." She blew out a breath. She met my eyes, and I wanted to fall into all that luscious silver. "By the time Abbi was in school, we were struggling. Not just because of Huntington's, I don't think. Not that it helped."

I rubbed my thumb across her petal-soft lips. She wore some kind of sheer gloss I liked. A lot. Dahlia wasn't superficial. She was herself, and I respected her for being strong enough not to hide behind lipstick or fake tits. "I'm glad I don't have to compete with the perfect image." I smirked. "We both know I'm not perfect."

She wanted to raise her eyebrows, but she managed to stay the motion with a slight grimace. "Compete?"

"Yeah."

I took a long swig of my beer, trying to look like I didn't have a care in the world even though my heart was in my throat and my hands were all clammy.

"You're nervous," she whispered.

"Well, this is more important than asking Carey Newman to be my girlfriend in high school."

"Because?"

"I care a fucking lot more about your answer."

"You cuss when you're upset."

"Maybe. Are you going to ignore the fact that I want this to go somewhere?"

"This?"

"Our relationship," I said.

Setting down the bottle, I put my hands on her upper arms.

I pulled her toward me. Her lips parted and her eyes dilated. I smiled, letting my lip curl up the way she seemed to like. Her breath hitched and her chest expanded so that her breasts brushed my chest. Best feeling in the world.

"You just got out of a relationship. Or are working on finishing it. Why would you want to jump right into another one?"

That was the big question, one I was trying to work out in my mind. I was pretty sure of the answer, but I was scared shitless to go there. Still, Dahlia deserved to know the truth. "You think I'd be here if I didn't care about you? This is more than attraction, Dahlia. Always has been."

She kept her eyes on mine as she nodded. "It is. For me. I-I wanted you then. But I was with Doug."

"Last night you said you were scared. I am, too." I blew out a breath.

She smiled, her eyes warming, but she hesitated. "You might hurt me," she said, voice low.

"Are you going to fight this chemistry because you're afraid?"

I ran my thumb along her soft jaw down to the leaping pulse in her neck. Her lips parted and a breath puffed out.

"I need to see you," I said. "Often. Every day."

Her pulse jumped as the panic attack tried to wrestle away her control. I waited, knowing she'd want to handle this her way. She closed her eyes while her breath fluttered across my hand in sporadic bursts.

"You'll leave. Once you're stable. If nothing else, you'll tour." She ducked her head. "You'd break me if you cheated. I can't do that again, Asher."

"I don't want anyone else. You can come with me on tour. So can the kids. We run a big enough operation it won't be an issue. Bill brings his kids sometimes. Mason came as an infant. We make it work. It changes the rhythm, sure, but it's good."

I wanted to show her how much I wanted her. But more, I wanted to soothe her fear. I slid my thumb up her smooth cheek. Her eyes were full of sadness and longing, the color of the thunderheads that had burst upon us this morning.

"Doug collected women after he'd promised to love only me forever. How do you know what you feel for me could last?"

"How do you *not* know that?"

"Don't do that," she said. "I'm serious. I've had one relationship in my life."

"You're comparing what you feel for me to him. I don't like that."

She shook her head. "Doug cheated me out of a lot. If I loved a selfish man once, I'm afraid..." She looked away, tilting her head away from my grasp.

"You'll do it again." I stepped back and snagged my beer. "Fuck, Dahlia. I am selfish." I stepped back further to ensure there was lots of space between us. I met her steady, gray gaze with my own.

"Pour yourself a glass of wine. We'll sit on the couch, and I'll tell you a story."

CHAPTER TWENTY-THREE
Dahlia

"I was going to tell you this morning, but the rain sidetracked me," Asher said. He waited until we were settled on the couch. Much as I tried to stay away, my head found its way to his shoulder, and his fingers combed my hair with an absentminded gentleness that made my heart stutter.

"Mason had a twin sister. Olivia."

I reached out, gripping the hand clenched on his thigh. He accepted the comfort, turning so we were palm to palm.

"She died of SIDS, right?"

"Accidental suffocation." His voice was raw. "In our bed. Jessica said I slept through it while she was dealing with Mason. I…" He swallowed hard. "I don't remember much about that night."

"Oh, Asher," I whispered.

"I wasn't on anything. Just tired. The babies took turns waking up, and I dealt with a lot of it because Jessica had postpartum. Her doctor said she needed help. So I helped. But that night I fell asleep."

"How old was she?" I asked.

"Five months." His Adam's apple bobbed. "When Olivia died… Jessica didn't ever recover from it. She's become hell-bent on hurting me."

I nodded, waiting. There was more to the story. Much as it hurt to hear it, he needed to tell me.

"I hired Mrs. Knowles to help out, but we were scheduled to tour about a month after Olivia's funeral. I couldn't wait to leave that house. Jessica wasn't talking to me. First night out, I hit the pills hard. Shit I'd never done before. I spent months drunk and high, just to make the pain go away."

I wanted to pull him out of the place he'd gone, but instead I waited, my heart aching.

"My mom got pissed and flew out with Jessica and Mason. I hadn't seen him in months. He was crawling, babbling. So cute I could barely stand it. I didn't want to hold him at first. Mom said I needed something to focus on, something other than the hole from losing Olivia. Jessica wasn't making any sense. Talking about how she could still hear Olivia crying."

He paused again, gathering himself for whatever he needed to say next.

"That's why you stayed with her," I said. "Because of the guilt."

He gripped my hand, his anchor in a sea of grief and loss. "I wouldn't have made it through that time without Mason and my mom. I rocked him every night. For hours. He'd sleep in my arms. But I couldn't sleep. I was too scared I'd hurt him. Like I did his sister."

I gripped his hand, tears pressing against the back of my eyes. This was painful to hear, so much worse than my spiral with Doug. Asher's demons, and Jessica's too, were buried with a tiny body in a cemetery in Seattle.

"The guys and I were fighting about whether to extend the tour. It was going well, really well, but Bill's wife was unhappy and Carl hadn't seen his son, Seth, in months. We extended. Ran another four months. As our music hit bigger, our private lives tanked. Jessica flew back out for a few weeks. She brought Mason again. She was on so many meds, she couldn't keep them straight. I had to hide the bottles and dole them out each morning. Mason didn't sleep through the nights."

"And you performed?"

"Most nights, yeah. But the worst part was that Jessica wouldn't touch Mason, wouldn't look at him. It was like she'd built a wall, unable to connect with her own kid."

I waited, my palm pressed tight to his.

"We finished our last month and came home. The guys wanted a break, needed to focus on something other than the music churn. Cammie, Bill's wife, wanted out."

He finished his beer and set it on the table. "I wouldn't have made it through those years without my mom. Then she was diagnosed with breast cancer. I'd pulled my shit together so I could hang out with Mason, be a parent. Made a point of being home for my mom as she got sicker."

He rested his face in the side of my neck and shuddered. "We've always made decisions as a band. We needed a break to put our lives back on track. Our next album didn't get the same traction."

"And she blamed you."

"Jessica always blames me. I didn't follow through on the promises I made her. I didn't make enough money. The one thing we never, ever did was discuss Olivia."

They needed to. If for no other reason than to gain closure and accept her death. Hopefully, they could find some happy memories to share, too. My heart ached for Asher but, for the first time, sympathy welled for Jessica. I knew all too well what it was like to build walls you didn't know how to push through.

"I'm so, so sorry. For all of you."

"And I'm telling you as bad as it got, I never fucking cheated on my wife or went against my vows. I'd seen what that did to my mom, and I wasn't going to be like my dad." He leaned his head back against the sofa's rounded top. "Jessica didn't believe me. Bill told me she visited him in a hotel room one night toward the end of that big run."

"Sounds like she was trying to get your attention," I murmured.

"I think it was more to get back at me. She wanted to hurt me— like she was hurting—by gaining control over me, my band. Something she's never been able to do. Problem was, we were all too stretched to keep reaching. The next album was two years later."

I held his hand, my heart aching for him. What he'd been through... He still held so much guilt.

"I've never asked Mason about Olivia. I'm scared of his answer."

"Tell me," I said. My hands were in his hair, stroking gently. "Something else is bothering you."

"I think Jessica's started using again. Probably meth or something like that. I checked her arms and there aren't any tracks, thank God." He paused. "If I put that out there," his voice was quiet, "it's going to get sordid real fast. We met at a party. It was so wild, the press talked about it for weeks afterward. All that shit's going to be out there for Mason to see. I can't do that to him. What if the judge decides neither of us is capable of raising a kid?"

His fear was rooted deep and was painful to witness. I wouldn't offer a platitude, not to Asher. He deserved better than that. "Then why don't you give her whatever she wants and cut your losses?"

"Because she wants more than money. She wants attention." He dropped his head back against my neck. "She said the only way she'd walk away, not cause a fuss, is if I give her all my future royalties for the band. But it's a lie. She said that to drag the divorce proceedings out further, keep us in the media churn. The one thing

Jessica thrives on is attention. Fame."

I tried not to stiffen in anger. I didn't manage it, and Asher clutched me tighter. His words from the night we met at the bar came back to me. *Shitty things happen to good people.* I'd thought he was talking about me, and maybe he was, but he was also talking about his son. Asher didn't seem to consider himself one of the good guys.

Maybe he hadn't been. But that hadn't stopped my interest then, and it didn't scare me as much as it should now.

He rolled his head toward me, and I looked into his beautiful hazel eyes.

"My parents' divorce fucked me up. I stayed in a really bad relationship because of it. Out of guilt."

"You can't blame yourself."

"If I'd woken up in time, maybe Olivia would still be here. Maybe Jessica would be healthy and sober."

I took his face between my palms and pressed a soft kiss to his mouth. "You aren't anything like your dad, Asher. You didn't destroy your relationship or hurt your child. At least not intentionally. Were you the one who brought Olivia into your bed?" I asked.

He shook his head. "No. They had cribs. Upstairs. Jessica didn't want the babies sleeping with her."

"Then how did Olivia get there?"

He scratched his head. "I don't know. I didn't bring her down. At least I don't remember doing that." He blew out a harsh breath. "I just want to be done. I tried really fucking hard to make it work, but she wants to drag me down into that user hell with her, and I don't want to go there again. I don't think I'll crawl back out."

I rested my head against his chest, listening to the steady rhythm of his heart.

"Briar has pictures of Jessica with her lover."

"Who's Briar?"

"My sister. She's the editor-in-chief of the San Juan paper."

"I'm not surprised," Asher said. "Think I could get the photos?"

"Yes. She already offered. Will they help?"

"I need enough leverage to get Jessica to back off. And to keep her mouth shut so our pasts don't hurt Mason later," Asher said, exhaustion clear in his voice.

"You shouldn't have to pay her with your future."

"If she'd leave quietly, it'd be worth it. But the guys said no. They're worried she'll have a voting share, and they won't work with her. The band'll fold. And I love those guys. After all we've been through, they deserve better than that. So I have to come up with another option."

I shouldn't ask, but I had to know the answer. "You haven't been intimate with her in years?"

Asher sat up and looked at me like I was insane. Though my chest ached, I couldn't help but giggle at his expression. "Yeah, it's been a long time for me, too. There are days I feel like I'm going to explode."

"I could help with that."

"I'm sure you could." I narrowed my eyes. "So the whole bad-boy image is just that? I have to admit I'm a little disappointed. I always wanted you to pull me over to the wild side."

The mood now lighter, he threw his head back and laughed so hard he clutched his stomach. "Oh, that hurts. You surprise me, Dahlia. I love that about you."

I stilled, staring at him. He didn't seem aware of what he'd said.

So I smiled, but it was shaky.

"My image was very well deserved for a while." His voice was dry.

"The image is what the fans expect, though. A portion of the truth."

"Pretty much." He wrapped his hand around my waist and pulled me onto his chest. "We keep this up, and I'll never find out if your guest bed is comfortable."

"It is," I assured him.

We didn't get up. I traced small circles on his chest. "Do you know what you're going to do?"

He shook his head. "Not yet," he said. He tightened his arms around me. "I wish I'd ended my marriage then. After Olivia died. I wanted to. Hell, I never should've married her in the first place. But I have to think about what Mason needs. And now I have you and Abbi."

I built up my courage and met his eyes. Sincerity shone from them, easing the panic that had been building in my chest. "Is that what you want?"

"Yes."

CHAPTER TWENTY-FOUR
Asher

We made it to our respective beds that night. A smart move, but I missed Dahlia. I woke up clutching a pillow, which I shoved back against the headboard in disgust.

I rose, stretched, and headed to the bathroom to take a quick shower. I couldn't remember the last time I'd enjoyed the luxury of hot water and a good night's sleep. After I dressed, I checked in on Mason. He was laid out on the bed, spread-eagle, feet dangling off the side. Tire him out with horses and a sing-along, and the kid slept forever.

Abbi's excited voice floated up the stairs. "They're doing a show next month in Seattle."

I raised my eyebrow. I wondered if she was talking about my band.

"That's great. Coffee, you need to get in my cup. Right now," Dahlia practically growled. I stopped at the bottom of the stairs, surprised by her surliness. Maybe she'd missed me as much as I'd missed her.

Dahlia turned, and my breath froze in my chest. She was beautiful even with damp hair. She wore glasses with streamlined green frames that I wanted to pull off while I kissed my way along her jaw. The swelling of her cheek was gone now, and her face was once again symmetrical.

Dahlia's beauty was quieter than Jessica's compact vivaciousness. My stomach twisted when I realized how much I yearned for a future with Dahlia, Abbi, and Mason.

"So we're going, right? Luke'll love it."

"I don't know. I mean, I can't presume Asher wants us there… .

And I have a book to finish."

"Which you worked on until the early morning hours," Abbi said.

She had? Must have been after I went to bed.

"Then there's the miniseries to help produce. And the sound track to collaborate on."

"Pfft. You'll get all that done in, like, a week, the way you're going. You've been amazing, Mom. Though you really should sleep sometime. What did you say? You wrote, like, over a hundred pages this week. More last night. Bev's texting you for additional pages already this morning. So you know they're good. I can book a couple of hotel rooms right now."

"Abigail. You have me at a disadvantage. I haven't had any coffee."

Abbi laughed. She saw me standing near the kitchen archway. "Be sure to pour Asher a cup." Abbi bounced over and kissed my cheek. She leaned in and said, "Mom's having a mini freak-out."

"Why?"

"Lots of reasons, but mainly because of you." With a sly glance at Dahlia, who was pulling a mug from a cabinet, she said louder, "She always gets like this when the ideas are flowing, but it'll pass."

"I'll keep that in mind. Thanks," I whispered back.

Dahlia's expression finally settled somewhere between longing and happiness. Her need to observe, to think hard about a situation before she reacted, was polar opposite to my performer personality. But I'd take her angst as long as I continued to spend time with her. As far as addictions went, Dahlia was my best one ever. And I planned to keep it that way.

"Should we give her some time to calm down?"

Abbi scrunched her nose. "Nah. Maybe let her jot some thoughts in her notebook while she drinks her coffee."

Dahlia hadn't mentioned her books since our last text message exchange. Maybe Mason and me coming here had added too much stress, cutting into her workflow. "Has she let you read her work in progress?"

Abbi leaned in closer, an impish smile on her lips as she looked back at her mom. "Bits and pieces. The hero is ah-mazing. I'm waiting to meet him in real life," she said, rolling her eyes.

I liked talking to Abbi. Still filled with the optimism and naive belief everything would work out, she was a bubblier version of Dahlia. I'd do a lot to make sure that everything *did* work out for her. Abbi could never replace Olivia, nor the deep scar my daughter left, but she could add something special to my life.

"Play nice, Mom. I wanna go to Seattle."

"Abigail."

Dahlia sipped from the coffee in her mug and handed me a freshly filled cup. Our fingers met and tingled with heat from our attraction. I leaned in and wrapped my arm around her shoulders in a friendly embrace. She huffed into my chest and then wrapped her arms around me, fitting her head just right on my shoulder.

Abbi looked sad for a moment before she realized I was watching her. She smiled at me, gave me a double thumbs-up, and strode up the steps.

"She likes you," Dahlia said.

She sipped more of her coffee but didn't step back. I pulled her tighter to my chest, reveling in the moment.

"I like her, too. She's a great kid."

"I didn't realize how much she'd missed a father figure. Abbi hasn't had a dad since she was eight, regardless of what the death certificate says."

I pulled back and looked into her deep gray eyes. "I'm sorry."

Dahlia smiled at me. "I know you are." She paused, doing some kind of internal check. She blew out a breath. "I am, too, for Abbi's sake. She deserves more. Mind if I jot down some notes?"

"Not at all. I'll grab my guitar and my notebook from upstairs. Unless that's going to distract you?"

Dahlia shook her head. "I'm pretty sure whatever you do will help, actually. I like having you here, Asher."

I pressed a kiss to her temple and eased back. I'd dumped a lot on her last night. We both needed time to process that.

In the past, I'd worked hard to ground myself, to be the father my son deserved. As soon as I managed to extract myself from my mistakes, I knew what direction I wanted to go. I just hoped like hell Dahlia could see the difference in me.

"Be right back," I said.

———◆———

We spent an hour working on our separate projects, Dahlia on her book, me on the new Supernaturals album. I'd thrown out half the songs I'd worked on during our tour last year. After reconnecting with Dahlia, I'd written a stack of new songs, but I wasn't sure the guys were going to go for any of them.

They were more atavistic than our normal high-energy anthems. Like "Sweet Solace" or "Moonshine Eyes," these songs dealt with loss and grief and second chances. These songs felt right. I reread the top one, hoping Bill would get back to me with his take. I'd sent this one and a few others to him last week. I hadn't heard from him since our talk about Jessica the other night. Bill was flying into

Seattle tonight and we'd talked then. Carl and Johnny were arriving tomorrow morning and planned to meet us at the studio. We were all looking forward to getting back to recording.

Dahlia came over to sit on the opposite end of the couch, another cup of coffee cradled in her hands. Her eyes were alight with excitement as she watched me pick out chords and make notes in my notebook.

"I've always wondered how you created a song," she said when I took a break.

"The same way you write a book, I bet. It starts with a seed, either a bit of the tune or a phrase that keeps repeating in my head until I figure out how it fits in the bigger piece."

Dahlia nodded. "Play that for me, that last bit. I really liked it."

I smirked at her. "You should. It's the start of the theme song for your Gardiner series."

She beamed. "Really?"

I played it and sang the words we'd jotted down together yesterday, plus another few lines that seemed to fit. Dahlia's eyes darkened, and her cheeks flushed. She snatched up my notebook and wrote with quick, efficient strokes of her pen.

She handed it back to me, and I read her chorus, my head bobbing. A cello would add a richness, fill out the melody.

"That's fantastic," I said, smiling. "You're good at this."

Mason slammed onto the couch, almost oversetting Dahlia's coffee cup she'd just picked back up. I closed my eyes, waiting for Dahlia's pissed response. Mason acted like an animal half the time, but I was pretty sure he'd outgrow it with time. I had as a boy. Mostly.

"Wow, Mason. You jumped at least ten feet. Next time let me set my coffee down first. Maybe I can catch you."

My eyes popped open, and I think I was gaping like an idiot as I stared at Dahlia. Mason beamed up at her, pressed into her side.

"'Kay. Morning. Did the Easter Bunny come?" he asked, eyes alight. I wasn't sure if he still believed in such silliness, but he was burning with hope at the idea of presents. I hadn't even considered this part of the weekend until now, and I was a total douche for putting Dahlia in such an awkward position.

Her eyes were open wide as she stared down at my son. My heart raced as I tried to figure out what I could say to smooth over the situation.

"Hey, Mason. Why don't we go upstairs and get dressed?"

"Dad! I gotta get my Easter basket first," he said, his jaw jutting in that stubborn way mine did when I'd set my mind on something. Shit. I was so screwed. Mason was going to be in a bad mood the whole rest of the day.

"Mason," Abbi called from the dining room on the other side of the kitchen, nearest the porch. "Can you come here?"

He hopped off the couch and sprinted toward Abbi's voice. I sat my guitar down and let my head fall into my hands. "I'm sorry, Dahlia. I didn't think about it being Easter this weekend. I just thought it'd be good because we'd have more time here."

She smiled, her eyes sparkling as Mason squealed. She stood and held out her hand to me. I took it, my confusion spiking.

"Look what the Easter Bunny brought me!" Mason shot into the room, a blur of little-boy excitement, shaking a video-game box in the air. "It's got new buildings and swords and stuff. And there's a whole basket of chocolates, and you and Dahlia and Abbi all have baskets, too."

He shivered with delight as he clutched the game. I looked at Dahlia, overcome with gratitude and pleasure as Mason ran back into the dining room. I could hear Abbi laughing at whatever Mason was squealing about.

"How'd you do that?"

"I talked to Ella about what Jeremiah liked. Then I used two-day shipping," Dahlia said, a smirk forming on those petal-soft lips.

I wrapped my arm around her so I could kiss her. This was a thank-you, and I hoped she understood what I was trying to say. "You're fucking amazing."

She grinned against my mouth before she pulled away, laughing. "Let's see what the Easter Bunny brought you."

CHAPTER TWENTY-FIVE
Dahlia

I'd made an Easter basket for Abbi every year until she was nine. That year, Doug was in the hospital for some complications. The following year, because of how surly Doug had become, I hadn't had the energy for anything more than my obligatory writing time. I'd become the sole earner for our family by then, which just added to Doug's antagonism.

Somehow, I'd fallen out of the habit of celebrating these little occasions, and now I realized just how important they were, not just for Abbi, but for me, too.

"Man, the Easter Bunny even knows what guitar pick I like best." He flashed me a smile before muttering, "That's pretty good stalking."

I beamed, pleased I'd found something he'd use. I'd also packed guitar strings and some of my favorite coffee. He lingered over the last item in his basket, which I'd added on a whim this morning while he was working. It was the poem I'd written about our night on the beach. It was only ten lines but was the catalyst for my current story, the first lines I'd felt good about in years.

He cleared his throat twice as he tapped out a rhythm on his thigh. "This is about us?"

"Yes."

"From our walk?" He read the words again, his face softening. He had to wipe the corner of his eye.

"I thought you'd like it."

He pulled me into his arms, his breath soft against my hairline. "I love it. Thank you." He pressed a kiss to my temple, and I melted into his embrace. Much as I wanted to snuggle against him and watch the kids' enjoyment, I eased back, tugging my hair away from my face. We weren't a couple. We were… complicated.

His hands splayed on my back, and I paused. Bracing myself, I met his hazel eyes. His lashes brushed his thick brows.

"Promise me something." His voice was pitched low, a caress. I shivered and he rubbed my arms.

"What?"

"The poem—can it be just mine?"

I nodded.

"I'm serious, Dahlia. I want to carry it around with me and know we're the only two who've read it."

The idea of him carrying my words, words I'd written for him, was surprisingly intimate. I couldn't deny him, not with his eyes so bright with need.

There it was again: that fear of wanting Asher, wanting him forever, so very much.

I knew musicians. I knew all too well the temptations thrown at them with such consistency. Doug hadn't cared for me enough to resist. The thought of Asher cheating…

An ache settled deep in my chest. "It's the seed for my newest book."

"These words." His fingers caressed the paper, and I bit my lip. I wanted him to touch me like that. "When I read your book, I'll know why you told that story. Our story."

"Ours," I agreed. Fear and pleasure bubbled through me.

He smiled as he tucked my hair behind my ear, his fingers lingering on the sensitive skin there at my jawline. "Thank you."

I nodded, unable to speak. He slid the piece of paper into his wallet, and I drew a deep, shuddering breath. He pulled out another couple pieces of paper. Catching my gaze, he winked.

"Come see this!" Mason said. He showed me the dragon he'd built with the pack of Legos I'd gotten him. Chocolate coated his mouth as he lay on his stomach, making robot noises as he walked his Lego creation across the plastic grass he'd taken out of his basket. Abbi and I laughed.

Abbi nibbled on a chocolate-covered peanut butter bunny and doodled with her phone.

Asher helped me to my feet. "What's in your basket?" Asher asked.

"A notebook that fits in my purse and a gift card to the wine shop," I said, shrugging.

"No chocolate?" Asher teased.

"I don't eat it much."

"Mom says it's too sweet. Maybe you can get her to see reason," Abbi said without glancing up.

"I'm pretty sure there's something else in there," Asher said, flicking at the fake grass so it crinkled. I played along, digging around inside. I pulled out a business-card-size piece of paper.

I pulled it out and read it. My mouth fell open. "Really?"

He smirked and nodded. "You have one, too, Abbi."

"VIP?" Abbi breathed as she pulled a matching card from her basket.

"Absolutely. Keep 'em on you, and they're good for any of our shows. See, I signed the back with the code Reggie needs to know these are legit. He's our right-hand guy. He'll remember you after the first show. You won't really need 'em after that."

Abbi squealed and hugged him hard. "That's so awesome. Thanks, Asher."

Mason looked up. "It's no biggie. You just flash your card to Reggie, and he lets you sit in the green room or the front row."

"Front row?" Abbi gasped. She fanned her face. "I'm so excited."

"I couldn't tell," Asher chuckled. "I heard you tell your mom you want to come to Seattle." His gaze was uncertain. "Whenever you're in the city and we have a gig, I'd like you to come. You'll always have all-access to our shows."

"Thank you so much," I said.

I settled back in his arms, and he dipped his knees. I rested my head against the hollow between shoulder and chest. My spot. My heartbeat escalated. I shouldn't feel like I knew Asher well enough to claim a spot on his body. But I did.

"I'd planned to give them to you later as a thank-you for the weekend, but this seemed like a better time."

"Perfect timing," I smiled.

"So you'll come to Seattle?"

I nodded, my lips mashed together in an effort to keep my emotions controlled. "Of course. Thank you."

"Omigod, Luke's gonna freak out," Abbi squealed. She bounded up from her chair, eyes wide. "I need to call him. Can I go call him?" she asked.

I nodded. She ran up the stairs to her room.

"That was really sweet," I said.

"So was all this," Asher responded. He spread his arms to encompass the Easter baskets and the house. "I think you'd make a great songwriter. Those words—I'm getting chills thinking about them."

"Which ones?"

"All of them."

I shook my head, but happiness bubbled up in my chest. "I

needed to give you something important because you gave me back my life. My ability to hope."

He tucked my hair behind my ear as he leaned in to murmur, "Same goes, Dahlia."

———◆———

I made a huge brunch because Asher and Mason were leaving late in the afternoon. Asher insisted on helping me with the dishes. I enjoyed the coziness of working together in the kitchen while the kids played the building game on the neglected Wii I'd bought Abbi a few years before.

"No fair, Mason," Abbi moaned. "You've had more practice at this."

"You're older and should understand physics better than I do," Mason responded.

My phone rang. "Hey, Bri. Happy Easter."

"You need to sit down."

"You left The Asshole?"

She snorted. "I'm not that brave. Don't freak."

"Too late. Did something happen to Mom?" The blood drained from my face. "Did The Asshole get you pregnant?"

"No, thank God. Which says something about my relationship. Now, will you listen? Someone must have followed him."

"Followed him?" I asked. "Who?"

"What are you talking about?" Asher asked. He hung the dish-towel on its hook, concern building in his eyes.

Briar huffed. "There's no way to feed this to you gently. There are pictures of you together. That first night you and Asher met. It looks… sordid. What they did with the pictures."

My lips felt numb. The feeling, blessedly, traveled downward. I turned toward Asher. "Jessica knew you were coming here?" I asked him.

Asher nodded, a scowl forming.

Briar said, "The pictures are in today's Seattle paper, but other sites have picked up the story,"

"What does it say?"

"Nothing nice."

I stuck my hand out and asked Asher for his phone. He opened the web browser app and handed it over. "What site?" I asked. Briar named one of those news aggregator sites. If the link wasn't to all the news outlets, it would be soon.

Supernaturals Lead Singer's Wife Claims Affair is Last Straw.

I blinked my way through the next couple of paragraphs, my chest tightening.

The article talked about how I was a lonely, sexually deviant writer who liked musicians. The writer suggested I put up dating profiles so I could take men to my bed to gather new fodder for my books. My date with Dale was detailed down to the type of coffee I drank and how I lapped up the attention from one of my fans.

Dale had messed with his phone. God, he'd probably recorded the whole conversation.

Black spots formed in front of my eyes. Asher wanted a normal relationship. He wanted poems and Easter baskets, and this… this is what the world thought of me.

"Oh," I wheezed.

Asher moved behind me, peering over my shoulder. He snatched his phone from my hand. I tried to breathe through the rising panic. I could handle this. It was just my reputation. No problem.

"Jessica?" he asked. His voice vibrated with anger.

I shrugged. I wasn't sure it mattered who'd sent the pictures. Jessica and Dale had already talked to the media. Anything I said now was a rebuttal.

The pictures looked bad. While I knew I was having a panic attack in one, to the outside world, Asher was holding me in a tight clinch, his head bent toward mine. He hadn't kissed me, but it looked like he was about to screw me against the side of a building in a busy part of Seattle. Another showed us holding hands on the pier, us laughing in the surf.

"Fuck. Dale's one of her boyfriends. They set you up," he said after reading the full article himself. His voice was clipped, anger dripping from each sentence. "I'll call the record's PR head. It'll be okay, Dahlia. We'll work this out."

I wheezed out a laugh. Sure. Once I was trashed all over social media.

"Don't panic," Briar shouted.

"I'm not," I said, the response automatic. "Everything's fine." Then the phone slid from my hand. The anxiety burst through my chest. My lungs labored, failed to draw enough oxygen. I struggled against the overwhelming sensation, but the waves of anxiety were too big. Soon they'd be over my head.

Asher's arms slid around me. He was warm and smelled of safety.

"You need to stop dropping your phone," he murmured into my hair. "I'm getting you one of those heavy-duty cases. Listen to me, Dahlia, I know you're panicking. I know it's scary. I've got you. You'll be okay. This is fixable."

He repeated the words. How did he know what I needed to hear?

He understood I couldn't control these emotions. That, more than anything, helped the panic recede.

I dragged air into my lungs as I pressed my wet cheek into his shoulder.

"My phone's not important," I huffed against his chest. "Did I break it?"

Asher shook his head.

"Is Briar still on the phone?" I asked.

"Abbi's talking to her."

He nodded toward the other side of the kitchen. Abbi had my phone pressed to her ear, the other arm wrapped around her waist as she listened to my sister. Mason was still engrossed in his game. I was thankful he hadn't seen me fall apart, hadn't been scared.

"He does seem good for her. Totally calms her down," Abbi said. She was right. Asher did. Instead of pulling away, I pressed against him, but I had to say the words to him. "I-I'm so sorry I've complicated your divorce, Asher."

"You didn't. Jessica did. She told me she had insurance. I didn't get that it was you. Us."

I clung to him, hating what I had to do. I'd pushed aside my concerns about dating another musician. I'd gone so far as to build a fantasy of us, together. But life wasn't that easy. Or that perfect.

"I'm not ready to push what's between us," I whispered. "I like saying we're friends collaborating on a project. That we worked together this weekend."

I looked up and caught the pain in Asher's face. He sucked in his bottom lip but nodded. "Probably smart. I hate that Jessica's upset you," he said. He cupped my cheek. "I'll call my PR team now that you're okay. We'll let everyone know that she served *me* the papers almost a year ago. Ask your sister for those pictures of her and Dale from the cabin, will you?"

He sighed, a heavy sound weighted down with defeat and guilt. I gripped his forearm, my nails digging in when he tried to step back. He inhaled but met my eyes. The sadness there.... My lungs compressed again, but for a different reason. I'd hurt him.

"I don't want you to do that for me. I don't want to create a bigger media storm for you and Mason."

"I'm doing it for me," Asher said. "For my band."

I searched his eyes, but I didn't see anything in there to give me pause. "You're sure?"

"Absolutely." He glanced over at Abbi, who was watching us. "I meet the guys tomorrow, and we're practicing all this week on the songs I sent them and maybe the ones you and I worked on. We go into the studio the following Thursday."

I frowned. "That's good, right?"

"Sure. But I won't be around much, probably until that gig in Seattle."

Ah. He was pulling back, too. I wondered if it was because of what I'd just said.

"I want to talk to you, Dahlia even if I can't get out here to see you. Don't shut me out. I can see you want to."

The panic beat against my breastbone again. He cupped the back of my head. I shuddered as the calm he brought washed over me.

"I wouldn't do that to you, Asher."

"Yes, you would. Because you think it's best for me. And Mason. Don't. Please. I need to talk to you. For me, but for you, too."

The words I'd written him were there between us. *I crave your touch more for its kindness.*

"Yes to the talking."

Asher pressed the pad of his thumb to my bottom lip, and I could feel the longing in his gaze. "And Seattle?"

Avoiding his question, I said, "Let me ask Briar for the pictures. If I don't talk to her now, she'll worry."

CHAPTER TWENTY-SIX
Asher

Taking Mason back to Mount Vernon was hard. He was quiet the whole flight, gripping his new video game so tight his fingers turned white.

On our drive home, he asked, "Why can't I live with Abbi? I like her. They have schools in Idaho."

"But your mom's in Mount Vernon. You wouldn't get to see her often if you lived at Dahlia's."

Mason slouched in his seat and stuck out his lower lip. "I like Dahlia."

"But you love your mom." Mason was young. He needed Jessica. He needed stability.

"I guess. But Dahlia pays attention to what I say. And Abbi's fun."

I'd really let my marriage, and Jessica's behavior, spiral out of control. Already the divorce was impacting Mason.

I'd made my first public statement confirming Jessica and I had been separated for nearly a year. I'd learned to put Mason first, and it was effortless now, but I was also more worried about Dahlia's feelings and needs than my own. Maybe I was finally growing up.

Mrs. Knowles opened the back door when I pulled up to the house, which surprised me. Mason greeted her, still appearing sad.

I set his bag down by the back stairs. I'd left my stuff in the car, planning to crash in my apartment. Not just because I didn't want to be in the same house as Jessica, but also because I didn't want Dahlia to feel like there was anything still between us.

"Jessica isn't here," Mrs. Knowles said.

"Will she be back tonight?" I asked.

Mrs. Knowles shrugged, the smile sliding off her face. "She didn't say. She called me a couple of hours ago and asked me to be here when Mason came home." She wrapped Mason in a hug, but he pulled away.

"Can I play my new game?" he asked with a little sniffle.

"Sure," I said. "But just for a little bit. It's almost bedtime."

He dragged himself over to the game console and shoved the disk into the slot.

I turned back to Mrs. Knowles. "I'm worried about him." I tipped my head toward the couch where Mason was slumped, eyes glued to the television.

Mrs. Knowles pursed her lips. I knew she was trying to decide whether or not to say something.

"You should be," she finally said.

I rubbed my hands through my hair and over my eyes. "You know about the divorce?"

"The whole country knows, dear. Along with your friendship with that pretty author."

"I need Mason with me," I said. "That's going to be hard with my crazy schedule, but I'm hoping you'll come along, help me with the transition. Jessica's going to fight me."

Mrs. Knowles's chin quivered. "If I can help, I will. In a heartbeat. He's much happier when you're around."

I cleared my throat and shifted my feet. "So you haven't seen anything that could help build a case for me to get custody? Any drugs? Men in the house?"

"She calls me before she leaves if I'm not here. The time Mason was here by himself is the only I know of. I haven't seen anything more than wine or beer in the house."

"Her boyfriends?"

"She meets them elsewhere. They don't call the house phone."

"Dammit." I pressed my thumbs to my eyes.

"Do you want me to stay or are you going to?" Mrs. Knowles asked.

I was supposed to be in Seattle early in the morning for our practice session. I looked over at Mason and noticed the white of dried tear tracks down his face. "I'm staying here."

Mrs. Knowles laid her hand on my arm. "You're good with him. For him."

"Tell that to the judge."

Her eyes were serious, sad when she said, "I will, dear. Whether one asks or not."

———◆———

"Mason, get your butt down here, now," I shouted up the stairs from the kitchen.

"Isn't this domestic," Jessica said from the back door. Her hair was wild, her clothes rumpled. "Came crawling home, huh?"

"Fuck off," I said.

"That's no way to talk to your wife."

"We're separated. Papers signed and filed at the courthouse. You forced the issue, and I couldn't be happier."

Jessica's eyes narrowed. "It's that smut writer you're screwing. She's the reason you're happy about the divorce."

"No, I'm happy because we're over. Have been for years. Since Olivia died. Who'd you fuck last night? The lawyer or Car Wash Dale?"

"Like you can talk. You flew my son out to meet your bed buddy."

Dahlia had been right. I took too much delight when I said, "We're not sleeping together. She's a friend. End of story."

"I have the pictures of you two. I have the proof."

"That we talked on a beach. Sure did. Best conversation of my life."

Jessica's blue eyes narrowed further and her lips peeled back. I wondered if she'd start growling. "Dale met her for a date. Said she's pretty in a wallflower kind of way." Jessica sauntered forward so her body was pressed against mine. "Seems like a step down from me, and we both know she won't compare to me in bed. Or out."

I refused to look down and check out her cleavage. I kept my eyes on her face, noting the faint twist of her mouth as she realized her ploy failed. "You have no say in my love life."

"You don't know what love means."

"I know we never had it."

I finished throwing Mason's lunch into his lunch box. I grabbed his breakfast sandwich from the microwave, burning my finger on the melted cheese.

"Mason," I bellowed. "We gotta go now."

"Why are you in such a hurry?"

"I need to get out of here before I say something I'm going to regret. Let my lawyer know when you want Mason, but I intend to be around a lot this next month."

Mason's feet pounded down the steps. His sneakers weren't tied. I bent and tied them double-quick, snagged his backpack from its hook, and handed him his sandwich.

"Brushed your teeth?" I asked.

He nodded as he bit into his sandwich.

"Come give me a hug, honey."

Mason let her wrap her arms around him for a second before he darted out the door.

"Mrs. Knowles'll pick you up from school," she called.

I glowered at her. "No. I will. One of us is going to parent, Jessica. If you don't want to do it, that's fine. But our son is going to know I love him."

She waved me off. "Enjoy playing daddy."

I grabbed my car keys from the counter and slammed the door.

I took a minute to calm down before I got into the car.

"Are you getting divorced because you met Dahlia?" Mason asked.

I started the car, wishing Jessica would've waited ten more minutes to come home.

"You heard that, did you? No. Dahlia's my friend. I'm not marrying her."

"Too bad."

I braked harder than I expected. I peered back into the rearview mirror. "What?"

"I like Dahlia. Abbi, too. I liked Darlin'. If we lived with them, I could ride that horse every day and we could eat buffalo burgers and I'd get to play baseball with you."

"That does sound nice." Warmth filled my chest with the fantasy Mason evoked. It sounded like paradise.

"Are you really going to pick me up?"

"Of course, buddy. I want to spend as much time with you as I can."

"These new songs are awesome, Ash. Some of the best you've ever written," Bill said when I walked into the studio. He had the pages spread out in front of him. He strummed out a few chords, smiling. "I can feel the clicking, and I haven't even heard you sing the lyrics yet."

I bit my tongue. My relationship with Bill had changed. I didn't know if he was being effusive because he liked the tunes or because he was trying to make up for his mistakes with Jessica. We'd never been here before. I'd never questioned his honesty or his integrity. Now, I wasn't sure I could trust either.

"Grab your guitar. Let's work through this bridge before practice. The guys want to grab a bite and a beer after."

"Can't do the dinner. I need to pick up Mason. He's seems to be taking the divorce well, but he's just a little kid."

Bill scratched the side of his head. "Okay, man. Let's do this now. You got time?"

Professionally, we clicked. Better than we had in years. We'd made great use of our time, getting Simon's song worked out with some quick fret work by Bill. Simon offered another for the sound track, and I'd jumped on it, loving the slow, smooth chord progression. Over the past ten days, I'd compiled six more songs from other indie rock bands and one female electric viola player. As cool as her playing was, it was her voice that absolutely blew me away. I looked forward to working with her again soon. A duet, maybe.

Later that day, I dropped Mason off at Bryan's house for a sleepover and drove back to Seattle, exhausted. I'd talked to Dahlia, as I did every day, but she'd been distracted by her deadlines.

When I rolled into the apartment, Bill was already there, sitting on the beat-up leather couch in the living room. I told him he and Cammie could stay with my while they were in town for the show and recording the new racks. He watched me walk into the room, his eyes never straying back to the baseball game blaring from the big, flat-screen TV. He picked up the remote and clicked off the game.

I raised my eyebrow. Bill was a baseball fanatic. He hated to miss any play of any game.

"I should've told you about Jessica's breakdown sooner. I'm really sorry, man."

"Yeah." I raised my hand. "Look, I'm not pissed. Not anymore, anyway. I don't want it eating away at any more of my life. You and me, we go back further than Jessica."

"I talked to your lawyer after you left to pick up Mason. It's been bugging me this whole time I've been up here, what you're going through. I told him about Jessica coming to my room. Cammie wasn't happy I never told her about that night, thinks I didn't say anything because more had happened. But I swear, Asher, I never screwed your wife."

"Pete told me." I clapped him on the shoulder, ending with a squeeze. "Thanks." I met his eyes. "Means a lot, you doing that for me." I kept my hand on his shoulder as I leaned in closer. "I'll beat the shit out of you if you ever touch Dahlia, twenty years of friendship or not."

Bill nodded. "Fair enough. I always liked her. For you, I mean." He paused. "I miss hanging out."

"Me, too," I said. "Things good with Cammie?"

He clasped his hand over my forearm. "They will be. I'm going to make sure of it."

"Good. Come on. I'll buy you a beer."

Bill smiled, his eyes alight with pleasure. "I'd like that."

The problem with an hour-long commute was I spent a lot of time driving. Once again, I was on the road between Mount Vernon and Seattle. At least I'd seen Mrs. Knowles this morning when I picked up Mason for school. She'd told me she'd started a notebook cataloguing Jessica's activities and careless comments. I would've felt worse about spying if Jessica hadn't sicced Car Wash Dale on Dahlia.

I couldn't believe Dale went along with such manipulation. He'd seemed like a decent, if boring, guy the few times we'd met at school-related events.

I'd turned over the pictures from Briar, which Pete said helped my case because it showed that Dale's relationship with Jessica started while we were still married. Bill's affidavit was on file now, too. I was waiting for the media to report that information, struggling with what I'd tell Mason.

Saturday night was our Seattle gig. I still didn't know if Dahlia was coming, and it was already Thursday. I pressed her number on my phone.

"Hey," she said, picking up after the first ring. "Field trip day, right?"

She always asked about my day first.

"The kids are going to the aquarium. Mason's going to come home wanting a shark or something equally impossible. Tell me about your writing."

"Bev said she loved the story. She sent it to my publisher yesterday and also to Garcia and Paul."

"When do I get to read it?"

She was quiet. The muscles in my neck tensed as I waited.

"I e-mailed you the file."

"Excellent," I said, smiling. The sky was overcast and the roads were snarled with traffic, but my day was fucking fantastic.

"Lie if you hate it."

"I'm not going to lie to you, Dahlia. About anything. And I already know I won't hate it. I read the genesis and it was amazing."

She made a noncommittal sound, but I'd bet money she was blushing with pleasure.

"Any news on the miniseries?"

Dahlia's smile slid through the phone, wrapping me in sunshine. "Casting's started. Garcia and Paul asked me to come for the first day of filming. That's in August."

"Sounds cool."

"I'm going to bring Abbi. She'll be out of school, so we may make a week of it or something."

I sucked my lip, considering my schedule. "Let me know when. Mason wants to see you both. Are you coming to the show Saturday?" I couldn't wait any longer. I needed to know.

"I want to," she said, her voice hesitant. "Abbi's campaigning hard."

"But?" I asked. I clutched the steering wheel. Shit, I really wanted her there.

"I don't want our relationship to mess up your chances to get custody of Mason."

"You can't. You won't. Please come. I told Simon to bring Jeremiah. Mason will be there."

She was quiet. "I'm still so scared," she said.

"Of what?"

"You're building something with me but also with Abbi. What happens when you move on? This is my daughter's heart, too."

I exhaled slow and steady. This I could handle. Fix even. "I won't hurt you, Dahlia. And I swear on Olivia's grave I'll never lie to you."

The line was quiet for so long I wondered if I'd lost the connection.

"We'll leave after Abbi gets out of school on Friday. I'll call you when we're on the road."

"And when you get to Simon's."

"It'll be late," she said. Why she sounded startled I couldn't begin to guess.

"All the more reason. I'll worry about you. I've only ever worried about my kids. With you, it's not a choice."

She chuckled but it was watery. "Then I'll call."

"And be ready for an event."

"Oh, I am." Her voice was warm. "I expect a rocking performance."

"No, earlier. I'm bringing Mason to Simon's in the morning to hang out. He wants your waffles."

I hung up to her laughter.

CHAPTER TWENTY-SEVEN
Dahlia

I'd texted Abbi during her lunch break to let her know the plan. She'd sent me back a message with more exclamation points than words.

So I was surprised when Abbi was quieter than usual when I picked her up Friday afternoon. She'd been quiet the night before, too. I'd expected her normal high-energy response and a fight when I told her Luke wasn't invited because we were staying with Simon and Ella. She hadn't argued over anything, just nodded. When I'd tried to get more out of her, she'd said she was tired and went to her room.

"Thanks for taking me to Seattle," she said.

"What's wrong?"

She leaned forward and flipped on the radio. A happy beat slammed around the car, followed by peppy voices talking about how some girl didn't realize she was beautiful.

"Change the channel now, Abigail. You know how I feel about manufactured music. That's for your ears alone."

"Pfft. I've matured way beyond cute boy bands."

"Since when?"

She propped her chin in her hands. "Since I understood heartache. Luke broke up with me yesterday."

"Oh, honey. I'm sorry. Why didn't you tell me earlier? Did he give you a reason?"

"Yeah, he's going off to college and didn't want to be tied down to a high schooler. Better to break up now than at the end of the summer when I cared about him even more."

243

I patted her leg, my heart aching for my daughter. "He hurt you."

"So I'm glad you decided we could go to Seattle. I totally need to get out of town. You know, to mend my broken heart. And because I don't want to run into Luke. I might punch him. He broke up with me by changing his status on Facebook." Her pretty, peaches-and-cream complexion mottled red as she frowned.

"That's low."

"Yeah. Sucks."

I squeezed her hand. "I know, sweetie."

"Do you think I can take lots of pictures with me hanging out with Asher and the band and plaster them all over my page? That'd make me feel a little better."

"We'll do what we can but remember we have to be careful about what we post. And Asher and I are just friends. We'll definitely do some shopping before we come home. Retail therapy so that you look extra cute next time you see Luke. Maybe it'd help to talk to someone else. You want to call Asher?" I asked, my voice hesitant.

I knew Abbi talked to Asher regularly, mostly via text. She'd initiated the relationship, a painful reminder of how much she craved a father. I wasn't sure how close they'd become. I hadn't asked too many questions, fearful of the answer.

If Asher and I didn't work out romantically, he'd feel weird about continuing a relationship with my daughter. But if we stayed friends, then Asher and Abbi could build the relationship she needed. Even if the thought of losing him romantically destroyed my ability to focus.

"I will in a minute," she said. "I wanted to tell you first. Just think about how much worse Luke would feel if he saw me driving around town in a cute little convertible."

"Not happening, daughter of mine."

"Worth a try." Abbi dialed. "Hey, Asher. Luke broke up with me yesterday. Mom seems to think you'll make me feel better."

My stomach quivered as I listened to Abbi talking to the man we'd come to depend on. In less than a minute, Abbi was laughing. From her next response, Asher must have asked if she was excited about her birthday. My throat felt tight. He'd remembered my daughter's birthday with no prompting.

I was in so much trouble. I didn't want to be friends. I wanted to rely on him as much as Abbi did. I tugged at the ends of my hair, wishing I'd been smart enough to back out while I had the chance. Before our walk. Because once I'd talked to him, really talked, I was in deep.

Abbi hung up the phone looking happier. "He's the best, Mom."

I sucked my bottom lip to keep the panic from bubbling out.

She turned to look at me. "Don't you think?"

"Yeah, he is," I said.

Asher arrived at eight the next morning. He hugged me, pressing a kiss to my temple before spinning Abbi into his arms. Dipping her with a dramatic flourish, he sang her happy birthday. Abbi laughed, her cheeks pink with excitement.

Simon and Ella joined us while Asher was singing. Mason and Jeremiah already had their heads bent over a book Mason had brought. Jeremiah's dark hair was shorn short while Mason's lighter brown was shaggier. The two boys were about the same height, but Jeremiah had his mother's pale English skin that reddened in the sun. He was also missing one of his front teeth, which made me melt every time he smiled.

Asher spun Abbi one more time. Clearing his throat, he turned to Simon, who dipped his head. What was that about? Pulling a slim box from his back pocket, Asher's eyes darted to mine before settling back on Abbi's excited face.

"I hear ladies like jewelry," he said. His eyes sought mine. "Since your dad isn't here to be the one to do this, I figured I'd step in."

He looked so uncertain, my heart melted. Ella's whimper drowned out the sound of my crumbling resistance.

Abbi grasped the box, her eyes bright. "Omigod, Asher, that was so freaking nice of you."

"I don't wrap well." He shrugged. I mashed my lips together and locked my knees so I didn't collapse at his feet. Who cared about the wrapping? He'd bought my daughter a gift.

Abbi opened the lid, flashing the silver Tiffany logo embossed on the cover. Sucking in a quick, sharp breath, Abbi hugged him. He patted her back with a gentle hand.

"Thank you." Abbi's voice was muffled against his chest. "You really are the best, and I love it."

Asher smiled into her upturned face. My feet led me forward, and I pressed into his side. He curled his arm around my waist. I let the warmth from his skin saturate mine as I kissed the bottom of his jaw, the highest point I could reach.

"Thank you," I said, my voice catching. I cleared my throat. "Let me see."

With slow, careful movements, Abbi pulled out a delicate silver chain. A silver heart dangled from the end, bright blue gems flashing as it spun in a slow circle.

"Gorgeous," Ella gasped.

I nodded as I cupped the pendant, bending forward for a better look. Asher's cheeks built to a dull red as we crowded around Abbi's present.

"I know sapphires aren't your birthstone, but they remind me of your eyes."

"Holy God, it's a good thing you're into Lia," Ella said in a choked voice. "Otherwise I'd throw myself at you."

Simon and I turned to frown at her, but Ella raised her hand, eyes wide. "He bought her real jewels, Simon. That's knickers-dropping good."

Abbi laughed, breaking the tension. "I'm not dropping my knickers, but I love it, Asher."

Ella helped her put it on while Simon grumbled, his lips turning up in amusement.

I tipped my head toward Abbi, who was stroking the necklace. "Thank you for remembering her birthday," I said to Asher. "Thank you for making it special."

He pulled me close so that my chest was pressed tight against his. He dipped his knees a little so his lips were against my ear. "I care about your daughter, Dahlia. I love Abbi's sparkle and how fiercely protective she is of you. But mainly I love her because she's part of you."

I gripped his forearms to keep my world steady. We'd kept our conversations relatively light, only delving in deep late at night when we were both tired. But here he was, making declarations I didn't have the willpower to withstand.

He pressed a kiss to my ear before his teeth nipped my lobe, chuckling when my legs crumpled. "Good to know you're not much of a stander when you're being seduced."

I met his gaze, loving the flecks of brown mixed with the green. "Are you seducing me?"

His grin was full of mischief. "Of course. That's why I'm buying other women jewelry."

I wrinkled my nose, desperate to keep the smile from my lips. "I'm not sure that's how it works."

"Seems to be working on you," Asher said.

"You're right."

Mason tugged my hands. "Can you hug my dad later? I'm really hungry."

I tousled his hair. "How about those waffles?"

"Sweet," Mason hooted, running toward the kitchen, Jeremiah on his heels. "I'm eating at least ten."

"I'm gonna eat more," Jeremiah declared as his butt hit his seat. He gripped his knife and fork and turned his bright gaze toward me. "Come on, Aunt Lia. We got a contest."

Asher chuckled. "Duty calls."

"Should I seduce you with my culinary skills?" I asked.

He dropped his arm to my waist, giving me a friendly squeeze. "You could. But I don't need any seduction. I see you, hear your voice, even smell your shampoo, and I'm more than ready to—"

"Waffles coming up," I said in a loud voice, clapping my hands.

Asher laughed, and an answering smile tugged at my lips as I headed into the kitchen.

Ella and Asher cleaned up the dishes, bickering about the best way to wash a waffle iron. Simon shook his head, his eyes drifting from Asher to me. I waited, eyebrows up.

Simon scooted closer to me. "You seem happy."

"I am."

"Think it'll last?"

"Why wouldn't it?" I asked, but Simon had just voiced the question I was too scared to ask aloud.

"Because we know how hard the music world is on a relationship."

"Are you and El having problems?"

Simon shook his head, causing his dark hair to fall across his forehead. "I'm not famous."

"Yet." I stood, brushing off my jeans.

Simon leaned his elbows on his knees, hands clasped loosely.

"I've gotta go meet up with the guys to practice for a couple hours and go over our set list," Asher said after he finished wiping the counter. "Mason, you about ready to hit it?"

"Aw, Dad! I want to stay here with Jeremiah and Abbi. Your practices are always so boring."

He was going to force Mason to leave. I gripped Asher's hand and tilted my head. He followed me to the other side of the living room.

"Why don't you let him stay? Ella already said she'd be happy to have him for the night. Briar's going to stay here with Jeremiah."

Asher's eyes held indecision, which I understood. He didn't get to spend a lot of time with Mason, and he'd miss tucking his son into bed tonight. Again.

"You don't have to. I just thought it might let you focus on your work. And the show will run late. The boys will be happy here with Briar."

I frowned. My sister was talking with Abbi on the couch. Even from here, dark circles were visible under Briar's eyes.

Asher sucked in his lips. His eyes wandered to the two boys ramming Lego trucks together, laughing. "He really likes Jeremiah."

"It's clearly mutual," I said.

———————◆———————

"You sure?" I asked again. Briar looked wistful, shadows filling her eyes.

"I'm not in the mood for fun tonight, Lia," Briar said. "Thanks, though. I appreciate it. The boys and I are going to pig out on some pizza, popcorn, and soda. I'll blow the boys' bed time, and I'll be the supercool aunt I always wanted to be."

I hugged her, feeling how stiff her shoulders were. "You've been that for years, Bri. You'll tell me what's bothering you? Please."

Her lip trembled but she nodded. "I left him."

I stilled. "There's something you need to tell me. More to this story."

"I'm not ruining tonight for you." At my steady look, she dropped her gaze. "We'll talk soon. I'm okay. Really. This is a good thing."

"Mom! We have to go. Like, now." Abbi popped her head into the room. She looked lovely with her dark shadow and bright pink lips.

Briar shooed me toward the door. "You both look great."

Abbi wore her cutoff denim skirt and wedge sandals. Her tank was trimmed with sequins. She'd curled her hair so it rippled down her back in thick waves.

Abbi gave me a long once-over before nodding. "You're hot, Mom. Asher's going to love the skirt."

The flirty blue cotton ended above my knee, showing way less leg than Abbi's outfit. My top was more sedate as well, a cap sleeve blue-and-cream silk-and-lace blouse with a cute bow offset on the right shoulder.

"You sure it's okay?" I asked again. Abbi had picked this out for me, and while I liked it, it was a far cry from my normal jeans-and-tee attire.

Briar laughed. "You're gorgeous. Have fun."

I hugged Briar hard. "I want to talk to you. Tomorrow."

She nodded then walked toward the living room where Jeremiah and Mason were sprawled on the rug, building monsters out of Legos.

———•———

The excitement of being backstage and hanging out with the band before the show, seeing the envious looks cast our way when we were led to the VIP section in the front row by one of the three people the Supernaturals employed on staff, made me giddy. Abbi bounced in her seat, screaming louder than even I was. Ella's hands were clasped under her elfin chin, her bright eyes glowing like cut emeralds.

"So, I have someone special here in the audience tonight," Asher said.

He swiped a towel across his forehead and the back of his neck. His hair was darker, nearly black, and plastered to his head. I licked my lips, turned on by his sweat. Wanting to please his fans, he put such effort into these shows.

"She's a special young lady, and tonight's her seventeenth birthday. The guys and I would like Abbi Dorsey to come on up here. We have a song for you."

Abbi's eyes and mouth were wide. I smiled and shooed her on-stage. Asher went to the steps and helped her up while the crowd hooted and hollered, the noise reaching deafening proportions.

Bill and Johnny shook Abbi's hand while Carl bent over his drum set to kiss her on the cheek. He grabbed Asher's mic and turned to the crowd.

"She's a sweet girl, this one, and she's currently available, or she was until my son met her backstage." Carl winked.

She laughed and replied. I couldn't hear her over the crowd, but whatever she said made Carl cackle in glee.

"So, the song. We've been working on it with your very talented uncle, Simon Dorsey. C'mon up here, Simon." Simon leapt to the stage, accepting the guitar one of the roadies handed him. Pride puffed out my chest. My face was going to hurt from smiling so much. Ella vibrated in her chair.

"This is the first track from the album we're recording now. What better gift than your very own song?" Asher winked at me, and I beamed back. I knew he was referring to "Moonshine Eyes." He'd told me he wasn't going to include it in his set because he wanted to whisper it in my ear some night as we lay tangled together under the stars. Keep it just between the two of us, like my poem.

My stomach quivered at the thought.

Asher conferred with Carl, who knocked out the beat on his sticks. The melody was soft and lovely, just like Abbi. She was too excited to hear the lyrics properly, I decided, because if she had, she would have been teary-eyed like all the rest of the women in the audience.

"Summer days drift past
Those half-loves never last.
They're memories left, hell-bent on survival
As I wait for her arrival."

I put my hands to my mouth. Asher's eyes were warm and steady when he met mine, and he continued to sing about heartache turning into lasting love.

I'd been fighting my feelings for Asher because they seemed so intense, seemed so sudden. I didn't have the fight left in me.

I wanted to be part of a relationship, not defined by it. Asher did, too. More, he needed love. He'd not gotten that from Jessica or from the other women who'd come before her.

We might not last forever, but I was sure I loved the man Asher was now. I couldn't protect myself from feeling that, no matter how scary. What was it Ella and Simon had said in their kitchen a few weeks ago? Love was worth the risk.

Living this time, each of the moments we created together, would have to be enough.

The song ended, and Ella leaned toward me. "That was scorching," she moaned. "Simon will get a proper thank-you later."

Asher was still looking at me so I smiled and blew him a kiss. He winked, and my blood revved, my skin warming, even as my heart burst with emotion. Yes, a proper thank-you was in the near future.

CHAPTER TWENTY-EIGHT
Asher

I was on that after-a-great-performance high. The crowd dispersed outside, the energy slow to ebb from the theater. Carl banged his drumsticks against the wall and the couch, screaming "woo!" over and over.

"Let's party," Carl said, throwing his arm over my shoulder. He was as sweaty as I was, but hopefully I smelled better.

"Shit, man, you need a shower before you go anywhere," I said.

"You coming out for drinks?" Bill asked. "I need one, but first I need to find Cammie. She's with Seth and Laura. Right, Carl?"

"Should be."

Dahlia, Ella, and Abbi came around the corner. Ella walked straight to Simon and kissed him long and hard enough to make me smirk. Simon was going to enjoy the rest of his night.

Abbi bounded over, her normal effervescent self, her long hair swaying across her back. Dahlia was quieter, but my eyes were drawn to her immediately. Just like they were every other time we'd been in the same room.

"Nah, I got some ladies to celebrate with," I said.

"Oooh, are you going clubbing?" Abbi asked.

"You're not," Dahlia said, her tone final.

"Mom," Abbi said.

"You're seventeen. That is not eighteen."

"We don't club anymore," Carl said. He stretched, his back cracking. He winced. "An hour and a half on a stage is enough of a workout." Carl was the oldest member of the band at forty-seven. His hair had turned all gray over the past year. "We were thinking about

254

a beer and maybe something to eat. I hate eating before a show."

"I thought you wanted to party," I said. Carl rolled his eyes. We'd all toned it way down the last few years, and we were playing better music for it. We'd been surprised how much more focused we were off the sauce-and-pill mix to the point we'd had a long discussion about sobriety and what it meant to us as individuals as well as a band.

"Sounds fun," Dahlia said. "We just wanted to tell you all thank you for a fabulous show. That was the most fun I've had in years." She smiled at Carl, Johnny, and Bill, who turned into bumbling asses. "You finished up the sound track?"

"Our part," Carl said, twirling his drumstick. "Got two more songs to lay down for our record. Some mixing. We're in the studio all next week. Maybe the following, depends on how it goes."

"How about I buy a round to celebrate that, too?" Dahlia asked.

"They'd like that," I said, shooting them a look that said *don't fuck this up for me*. The guys grinned.

"Come out with us," Carl offered. "It's Abbi's birthday, right? My son turned nineteen last week. We'll grab an ice-cream cake. Take it down to the beach, light a bonfire. Seth's hanging out around here somewhere with his mom. I'm sure he'd like to come along. So will Laura."

I'd introduced Dahlia and Abbi to my bandmates' wives—well, Carl's ex-wife, earlier, and I'd been pleased to see them bond over Dahlia's books.

"Laura and Cammie were talking to someone they knew at the entrance when we came back," Dahlia said.

"Let's grab 'em and hit the beach," Bill suggested.

"You like that kinda shit, er, stuff—right, Abbi?" Carl asked.

She was smart enough to look at her mom, who turned to me. I smiled and dipped my head. If they wanted to go, I was happy to take them.

"That's a great idea. We can shove Carl in the sound," Bill said.

"Funny as ever, my man," Carl muttered.

"I'll go find our crew," Bill laughed.

"As long as I buy the cake and the beer," Dahlia said.

"I'm always up for a swim with a pretty lady," Carl told Dahlia with a wink. "Especially one as generous as you."

"Back off," I growled as I threw my arm over Dahlia's shoulder. She didn't seem concerned at all by my sweat-stained shirt. She smiled up at me, and I turned into a complete idiot, grinning back. The woman had a beautiful smile. I wasn't even sure I understood what she was doing to me, but I liked it. A lot.

"You good with Simon and Ella joining us?" she asked.

"Course," Carl said, leaning over to slap Simon's shoulder. "Simon's a great dude."

I pulled Dahlia to her feet. "We're going to walk off that ice cream," I said.

She looked at Abbi. "You okay here?"

"Fine, Mom," she said. She was seated next to Seth, who was leaning back on his elbows in the sand. The rest of the guys, Simon, Ella, Johnny's girlfriend, Susie, and a couple of Susie's friends sat around the bonfire, talking and laughing. Carl still floated in the surf though Laura held a couple of towels, yelling at him to get out. I shuddered at the thought of how cold that water must be.

"I'll take Abbi home," Simon said. Dahlia bit her lip, her gaze sliding toward mine. She didn't want to make a scene, but Simon had consumed a couple of drinks, as had most of the group. Only Dahlia, Seth, Abbi, and I hadn't imbibed more than soda.

"I'm the designated driver tonight, so no worries, Lia," Seth called. "I'll get everyone back to Simon's place. Enjoy your walk."

He winked at Dahlia, and I stifled a growl. I was like a stallion around this woman—anyone who got too close was likely to get trampled.

"Abbi's enjoying flirting with Seth," I whispered in her ear, putting Seth's forwardness from my mind. "And I want to do some flirting with you."

Dahlia laughed and waved. She snuggled tighter to my side, and I clasped her hand as we walked for a while in silence.

"Thank you for tonight," Dahlia said. "Abbi had a great birthday. I'm not sure we'll ever be able to top it."

"We have a year to figure something out," I said.

Dahlia stopped walking. She turned to face me. The water lapped over our feet. Shit. It was freezing. "You sure you want that?"

"Us, together? Yeah," I said.

"Asher, I'm not asking for more than you can give me."

I tugged her into my arms. Her skin was cool but the underlying heat was there. Dahlia burned hot but she kept it bottled up tight. I planned to uncork that desire and drown in her passion. "My life's so much better now that you're in it again. Remember when I told you I wrote 'Moonshine Eyes' after I met you? It was that first time in that shitty garage."

"Mmm."

"I've thought of you every time I sing that song, Dahlia. I didn't do ballads and romantic shit. Until you."

She blinked up at me, her eyes luminous. "I've been in love with your lyrics since I was seventeen."

"Just my lyrics?" I asked, my heart slamming into my chest.

"No." Her mouth formed the word but I couldn't hear it over the thrumming of my heart in my ears. She held my gaze, her eyes bright, molten silver. "I've been in love with you since our walk. Maybe before."

I needed to connect with her, touch her. "That's really good because I wanted to put my fist through Doug's face and claim you as my own. I think I fell in love with you then. I just wasn't smart enough to understand it."

Amusement softened her features. Her fingers played with the buttons on my shirt. "That would've been one hell of a show. I'm glad you didn't."

"Why?"

"I wouldn't have pined for you if you had."

"I don't want you to pine, Dahlia. I'm here. I want you. Fuck, I want you." I splayed my hand across her spine, pulling her snug against me. "However and whatever you want from me. I'll give it."

She slid her hand up my chest to cup my cheek. "You're the least selfish man I know, Asher."

I brushed her hair behind her ear. "With you, for you. Yeah. You bring out the best in me."

She stilled, her eyes roving the area. "We probably shouldn't do this here." Her voice was filled with regret. "Not if Jessica had us followed the last time."

My hands slid to her hips, gripping her tighter to me. "People already saw those pictures. I don't care if people know we're together.

In fact, I want them to know you're mine."

"I am. I will always be." She stepped on my feet and pulled my head down so she could kiss me. It wasn't a tentative kiss, so I pulled her tighter to my body, shoving my thigh between hers. Her tongue wrapped around mine, sucking. I groaned at how good she felt. She tugged my hair as she nipped at my lip.

Blood rushed to my dick, and I wanted to drop her to the sand, kissing and licking every inch of her. I resisted the urge. Barely.

"I want you, Asher. I have since you walked up to me in that bar."

"You want to come back to my hotel room tonight?" I asked.

Her eyes glinted with humor and sensual promise.

"If you want that I will. But I want you to make love to me, here, on this beach. Will you do that, Asher? Make love to me in the sand and water?"

I swallowed hard. The woman had a direct line to my dick, which raged out of control.

"No."

CHAPTER TWENTY-NINE
Dahlia

I blinked at him three times in rapid succession. "No?"

He pulled me even closer. His erection pressed hard, insistent against my stomach. "You have no idea how much I want to make love to you." We were about a half-mile from the group. The yellow glow of the bonfire was visible. "You told me you made love to Doug in the water. That's your memory with him. I want our first time together to be different from all your other experiences."

I cupped his cheeks and brought his lips to mine. They were warm and soft as they brushed across my mouth. "You're right." I smiled at his thoughtfulness, at him remembering every detail I'd told him.

"So, I'd rather it be at my hotel room," he said, eagerness growing in his eyes. "But then again, I'm not sure I can wait."

I gasped at the feeling of him pressed against me. Battling my need, I managed to ask, "Why a hotel room? What about your apartment?"

"Bill and Cammie are staying at my place while in they're town. I got a hotel room tonight, hoping you'd maybe want to spend the night with me."

I nodded, hesitant. "I haven't had sex in a hotel room," I said. Shock flooded my system at that realization. How was that possible?

"Really?" He seemed pleased. "We can fix that. Soon. After I kiss you again." And he did, his tongue in my mouth, demanding a response that was hotter than the bonfire down the beach. Heat licked over my skin, pooling deep in my belly, sizzling across my breasts.

He ripped his lips from mine, his eyes wide and wild. "Terrace," he panted.

"What?"

"Have you ever made love on a terrace?"

I shook my head, desire clogging my ability to think.

He grabbed my hand, our palms meeting in just that way—heat and trust and the promise of more—and led me toward the marina. "My hotel room has a terrace with a heater. It's private. I'm going to make love to you there while you look up at the stars. It'll be warmer, and you still get your thrill of making love outside. And it'll be a first for me, too."

I cupped his cheeks, loving that he'd thought of a way to make this even more special for both of us. He kissed the corner of my lips, which heated my blood further, and I gripped his shirt, trying to pull him closer.

"In such a hurry, Dahlia."

"You've no idea," I gasped. "How far?"

"A quick drive."

I moaned. Now that I'd committed to this, to him, I didn't want to wait. Never again.

He stopped and bent down, shoving my feet into my sandals. Sand clung to my toes, and his warm, callused palm slid up over my calf, fingers skating over my thigh, to my panties. He rubbed his thumb across the material. I moaned at the friction he created against my swollen, desire-slicked folds.

"Can you wait?"

"We have to. This is too public. I shouldn't have kissed you here. God. Stop that." My inner thighs quivered. "Asher. Please."

My legs shuddered as he pressed firm and hard against my clitoris. The idea of him making me come here excited me, and my inner muscles quivered in anticipation.

"You seem really hot and bothered."

"I am," I moaned. "It's been seven years."

He leaned back, his eyes shooting to mine. "You're shitting me."

I bit my lip, shook my head. My inner muscles clenched tight. Oh, I'd missed this. "But I would've waited longer. For you."

His smile was slow and devious as he pushed up my skirt. I gripped his shoulders for balance as he dipped his head and pressed an open-mouthed kiss to my bare thigh. He rubbed his nose against my damp panties. "You smell good."

"Asher. Let's go. Now."

I tried to push him back but he pressed his thumb against my clit again and my muscles tensed once more. "It's dark here."

I whimpered as the last threads of my self-control unraveled.

He rubbed in a slow, easy circle, a little harder each time. His other hand slid under my skirt to knead the supple flesh of my thigh. He kissed my stomach, his breath warm even through the material of my shirt.

He tipped his head back and met my eyes. "Come for me, Dahlia. You're not waiting longer."

He wasn't just talking about release. He wanted this, me. The orgasm rippled through my stomach as my thighs quivered and my knees gave out. Asher held me up, palming my bottom cheek, his other hand still between my spread legs, soothing now to bring me down from the pleasure still blooming through my body.

He stood and kissed me, his teeth and tongue urgent. I floated against him, open and willing.

"My hotel room," he growled. "Now."

CHAPTER THIRTY
Asher

Finally. Dahlia was mine. In the parking lot of the hotel, I held her close to my side, loving the way she fit against me. She smelled of smoke and salt and desire. I ran my hand down her back to the dip in her spine, pulling her even tighter against me. Her taste lingered on my lips. I quickened my pace, needing her sooner than now, cursing the distance to my room where I'd finally get her completely naked.

The elevator ride up was quiet. I held her hand, rubbing my thumb against the thrumming pulse in her wrist. Two floors from mine, she stepped in front of me. "I can't wait."

She leaned forward so her mouth touched mine. Her tongue slid across my bottom lip and then she moved down and nipped the cleft in my chin.

My muscles coiled tight as I struggled against the urge to shove her against the back of the elevator and take her now. The elevator dinged, and the doors slid open. She walked out into the hallway, her skirt showing off those toned legs. I couldn't follow fast enough.

She stopped at the door to my room.

"Where's the key?"

"Back pocket."

Her eyes traveled down to the bulge in my jeans. Her nostrils flared as she reached out, cupping my aching dick in one of her delicate hands as she pulled the key card from my pocket. I braced my hands on the doorframe, biting back a moan.

She turned her body to slide the card into the slot, and I trailed kisses from her ear down her neck. She arched back, her breathing ragged. She opened the door and I grabbed her waist and spun her to face me, pulling her flush against my body.

Stepping into the room, I slammed the door shut with the heel of my boot.

I grabbed the hem of her skirt and whipped it down her legs. My hands moved to her top. Dahlia raised her arms.

Her skin gleamed in the soft moonlight, and I couldn't help but run my thumb across the swell of her breast, just above her bra. I bent down and kissed the hollow between her neck and her collarbone.

"Asher."

"Right here."

I stepped back and nearly ripped the buttons of my shirt as I kicked off my boots. I tossed my shirt and jeans onto the growing pile of clothes. Once I was in my boxers, I picked Dahlia up. I grabbed the comforter from the bed and carried her to the terrace. I pulled my hand from behind her knees, letting her slide down my body.

She wrapped her long leg around my waist to nestle against my erection. I pressed my lips to her throat, using my teeth to make my way back to her breasts, which rose and fell in a ragged rhythm.

"I'm on the pill," she said.

"I'm clean," I replied.

She raised an eyebrow. "You damn well better be."

I laughed. I trailed my fingers down her stomach.

"You singing tonight… I felt like you were singing just to me, and it was so sexy."

"I was singing to you," I said. "And just so you know, it's not the first time."

I brought my hand back to her breast, rubbing and rolling the soft flesh in my palm. Her tits were just big enough to fill my palm, her cleavage slight. I loved her spare build. She was delicate and light. Soft and hot. I loved that she was mine.

She brought my head down and kissed me again. We tangled lips, tongues, and even teeth. My hands were in her long hair, my thumbs against her temples, cradling her head like I'd dreamed for months. No, years.

"I want to take you here. I want to see the moon caressing your skin while I slide in and out of your body."

"Yes."

"Next time I'm going to lick across your stomach until you scream for me to be inside you."

"Yes," she panted.

"And after that I'm taking you in the shower, from behind."

"Oh, God."

"Then in the bed, slow and sweet as we wake from sleep, hands clasped as our bodies fit together, finding our rhythm."

"Asher," she mewled.

"Just wanted you to know the plan." I stepped around her and dropped the comforter onto the lounge chair. I pushed her down onto the thick blanket, dropped my boxers, and slid on top of her.

"Okay?" I asked. My tongue traced her jaw. Her fingers were in my hair, her hips tilted forward to cuddle me right where I needed to be touched.

I shoved her panties to the side, too needy to take them off. Her flesh was plump, her clit still swollen. She leaned forward and bit my shoulder when I rubbed my fingers against her.

"Hard and fast. Now." I slid the tip of my cock into her. "Taking you like this, it's about us now, Dahlia. I mean that."

She shifted her hips, pressing herself up onto my dick. I groaned as her warm flesh clung to mine.

"Don't you dare stop," she said.

I splayed my hands over her hips and slid into her. She arched upward, an inarticulate sound tearing from her throat. I pulled in and out of her wet heat. She held onto my neck, her lips just touching mine as we both breathed in time with my thrusts.

I pulled back, looking down at our joined bodies. Moonlight danced over her skin and I licked the brightest line across her breast, pulling her taut nipple into my mouth. She hooked a knee over my hip and slammed her body up against mine. I hissed as my cock slid deep into her warmth. She held me there, making small needy sounds.

"More, Asher. I need more."

I slid out and thrust back in hard. I needed to come. I moved one hand between her splayed legs and pressed against her clitoris as I pumped into her. She clenched around me, her whole body tight.

"Harder," she whispered.

I pushed my hips against hers, my cock as deep as she could take me. She unwound just like she had on the beach, making breathy sounds against my lips. I thrust again and my balls tightened high and hard against my body. And I was coming into Dahlia's welcoming heat.

We lay there, breath ragged, as the moonlight kissed our sweat-slicked skin.

"That was so good," she said.

"You damn near killed me." I pulled out of her and smoothed

her panties over her vulva. I couldn't help but caress her there one more time. She shuddered against me.

I kissed the top of her head, the moonlight reflecting off the thick strands of her hair. This was one of those perfect moments.

I should've known it would be tainted somehow.

CHAPTER THIRTY-ONE
Dahlia

I clasped Asher's hand, and he rolled onto his side, making sure I didn't fall off the lounger. He settled his head on his palm and looked down at me, trailing his fingers over my collarbone then down to my breast.

I hoped I measured up to his former lovers. Asher was much more experienced in love-play than I was, and I didn't like the shyness or inadequacy creeping over me.

"I don't know how we're going to make this work, but I need to see you more than once a month. I want to wake up next to you, Dahlia. I haven't wanted that in a long time."

Warmth filled my chest, pushing away the needle-sharp pricks of fear. I slid closer and wound my arms around his neck. "Just what are you proposing?"

"A relationship. Monogamous, mutually satisfying. If all our lovemaking is like that, I'm going to die a very happy man."

Apprehension prickled again, so I forced myself to ask, "Is that enough for you?"

His large palm cupped my cheek, and he tilted my face to his. The silence grew as he studied me. "I know you can't tour with me all the time, but I want you there, as much as possible. I want you to tell me about your writing while we cuddle in bed."

"Cuddle? You like to cuddle?" I giggled.

He licked his way across my collarbone before pressing a kiss to the pulse at the base of my throat.

"With you."

I inhaled, trying to stave off tears. This man. "Just when I think

I know you…"

"I want you happy," he said. "I want to make sure you don't have a reason to panic again."

"This right here is me blissed out."

He smiled, his teeth flashing white in the moonlight. "I'm glad. I want to keep you that way." His face settled into a serious line. "I talked to Pete after I left Simon's earlier. On the way to the venue. They pushed up the hearing to Monday. I have a final meeting with my law team tomorrow."

The prickles of apprehension condensed into a hard knot next to my heart. "What about Mason?" I kept still, waiting.

"The pictures weren't enough. She has her own—of us. Plus the story in the paper. One of her friends said she stayed with Mason at that cabin. I can keep fighting this, but it'll drag out for months. I decided to give in to her demands. We'll sign the documents on Monday, Tuesday at the latest. Then I'm done with that part of my life."

I searched his face. "Are you sure?"

He shifted so his cheek was against his bicep. "As long as I get Mason, I can live with the agreement." He was quiet as his finger slid along the slope of my breast. "I want to build a life with you. The kids get along well. I think we can make this work." He met my gaze, his eyes clear. "I need us to work."

"I know it's your decision, but I hate that she's taking so much from you."

Asher's fingers plucked at my nipples. "You're thinking too hard right now." He tugged at my panties, and I helped him slide them down my legs.

I rolled over so I straddled him. My hair fell over both of us and he smiled as he brushed it back. His hands slid down my cheeks and back to my breasts.

"You are gorgeous, Dahlia. Better than I imagined."

"How about you focus on your favorite parts of me for a few minutes then?"

"Just a few?" he laughed.

I giggled. "As long as you can last."

He groaned as I wrapped my fingers around his growing erection. "Not long if you keep doing that."

He pulled my head down and kissed me as I positioned my body to take him inside. He pulled me back up his chest and ran his tongue across my stomach before his teeth nibbled at my hip bone.

He kissed and licked his way to my other hip.

"I want you inside me again," I moaned.

"Once you scream my name."

His tongue delved into my belly button, making me giggle. I tugged at his hair, wanting to kiss him. He ignored my efforts and traced each of my ribs, his hands sliding up and down on my hips.

"Asher," I moaned.

He lifted his head, eyes glittering. "Not good enough. I said scream."

I ran my hands over his shoulders, down the smooth muscles of his back. He chuckled against my stomach. "Scream first. Then your reward."

I dug my short nails into his back, and he grunted as he feathered kisses over my pubic bone.

"Asher!"

"Close enough," he said as he slid me down, guiding his erection into me.

I clasped his hands in mine and stared down at him, arching back against his raised knees.

"I love you," he whispered before his lips took mine in a deep kiss.

I rocked my hips, reaching my lips toward his.

We lost ourselves in the moment, and it was beautiful.

———◆———

I didn't leave the hotel until we'd fulfilled Asher's other requests. The shower. The bed. I was still smiling as I let myself into Ella's house, hair damp, body sore and well loved.

"Good night, darling?" Ella asked, eyes dancing.

"Very," I purred. "Everything fine here?"

"Mmm. The kids are outside." She passed me a cup of coffee. "Didn't expect you for a while. If at all."

"Asher has a meeting with his lawyer in about an hour."

My phone beeped. I set my coffee cup on the counter and pulled it out.

"Holy mother of God," I whispered.

"What?"

I blinked, shook my head. "Jessica sent me a text. How did she get my number…"

I could feel the tension building in my chest, forcing the air from my lungs. Ella plucked the phone from my hand.

"That bloody stupid cow. I'm going to rip her hair out. It's probably the only part of her that's still real."

I sucked in a deep breath, trying to get enough air so my brain could function. "Why would she send me a text and say that to me?"

Meet me in the lobby of the Fairmont. Unless you want the rest of the pictures released.

The picture below was from last night on the beach. Asher was on his knees, looking up at me with so much love tears filled my eyes. That was supposed to be private—ours. Jessica had stolen that and was more than willing to leverage it for her own purposes.

"And we watched her son for her," Ella snarled. "How selfish can the bitch be?"

"Where's Briar?" I asked.

"On the deck with the kids."

I raced out there, barely fitting through the sliding door in my haste. "I need your help," I panted.

Briar looked up, her face screwed up in a frown.

"Get inside and change into real clothes. Hurry up!"

"What the hell, Lia? You're wound up so tight. I'm coming."

I practically shoved Briar into the bedroom we were sharing.

Anxiety reared back up, trying to roll over me. Should I call Asher and tell him Jessica was trying to blackmail me?

No time. I'd figure that out later. I ripped off my skirt and top. Running to my suitcase, I pulled out a pair of nice jeans and a spring sweater.

"I need you to be sneaky like you used to be. I need you to film something for me."

"What? Are you crazy?"

I showed her the text and explained my plan. She scratched her head, considering me. "It may work."

"It has to. Please, Bri. I need you to help me. I can't let Asher lose Mason because of public opinion. I'm the other woman in these pictures. He told me he was going to sign over most of his money to her. And that's still not enough. She's still going to try to keep

Mason. Just to hurt him." My eyes filled with tears. "Think about if it was Abbi. I couldn't stand not seeing her every day."

"I'm coming, too," Ella said from the doorway.

Abbi peeked out from behind her. "Me, too," she said, her jaw set in stubbornness.

"No, Abbi. This is sordid. Nasty." I swallowed hard. "And very personal. I don't want you to see or hear about this."

Abbi moved into the room and wrapped her arm around my shoulder. "Mom, I've waited a long time to see you happy. I'm seventeen. I don't need you to protect me from everything. I can help deal with that lying b— er, witch's butt."

"Damn straight," Briar said. She pulled on her jeans and slid her feet into a pair of strappy sandals. "We'll need Abs to make sure we get the whole thing covered."

"Simon will stay here with the boys," Ella said.

I nodded my thanks. "Time to move out, ladies. We'll lay out the strategy while Ella drives."

———◆———

My girls were all in their places. I'd forwarded each of them Jessica's text, so they had the evidence in case something happened to my phone. I sucked in a breath, trying to calm my racing pulse. I really hoped Briar's plan would work.

Jessica strolled into the lobby in a halter-top sundress. Her makeup was as perfect as her hair. She wore an expensive watch—I wasn't good with brand names—and a large diamond pendant. A man walked behind her, his eyes never leaving her swaying hips.

He was somewhere between a lapdog and a rutting stag. His

273

hair was thinning and light brown. I had no idea what color his eyes were because they were glued to Jessica's rear. He had that middle-aged stomach fluff going on, but he was dressed in an expensive pair of slacks and a blue button-down. He looked familiar. Ah. Dale.

I waited, hands clasped on opposite elbows, trying to look even more pathetic and panicky. Not hard when my hair had dried naturally and I wasn't wearing any makeup.

"So you're Asher's latest fling," Jessica said, tossing her hair over her shoulder. I knew what she was thinking. Her eyes cleared when she decided I wouldn't keep Asher's interest.

"You must be Jessica," I said. "Mason's mentioned you."

"I bet he has. Loves his mama, that sweet little boy."

She smiled, her eyes lit with pleasure. Did she actually want Mason?

My anxiety spiked. Maybe I'd demonized her because on some level I considered her my enemy. I couldn't be the reason a mom and son lost a connection, but neither could I let Asher lose custody of Mason. My chest clenched as the waves of panic rose.

"What's wrong with you?" Jessica asked stepping back.

"Panic attack. Stress and anxiety bring it on."

"You need to sit down?" Dale asked. He slid around Jessica to grip my elbow. I yanked from his grasp, shooting him a glare I hoped showcased my loathing. I headed in the opposite direction where Abbi was slouched in a chair, playing on her phone and smacking her gum. I sat down in a chair kitty-corner from Abbi.

"Can't we talk somewhere more private?" Jessica asked.

"She has on earphones," I said, pointing to Abbi. "I doubt she can hear anything, and I need to be under a vent. The stream of air helps. I wasn't expecting Dale to be here. He asked me for a date just weeks ago, and his messages afterward were disturbing."

Why hadn't I thought to send those messages to Asher? I would, as soon as this conversation was over.

Dale had the decency to look chagrined. Jessica's eyes narrowed as she considered me. Her lips curled as she settled into the chair opposite me. Dale sat next to her.

Abbi glanced at us before ducking her head back down over her phone.

"Just a girl waiting for someone," Dale said, patting Jessica's hand. "No need to worry."

"Did you see the paper this morning?" Jessica asked.

"I don't read the paper," I said, keeping my eyes round. "I helped Mason and Jeremiah make a fort." I hadn't. Briar had. But I wanted to see her reaction to her son's name.

Jessica frowned. "So Asher is sleeping with you and has my son there?" She smirked, tossing that hair over her shoulder.

"No, not at all. Jeremiah's my nephew. I'm staying with my family," I said. "Mason and Jeremiah have become friends. They met because my brother-in-law is recording a few songs with the Supernaturals. Mason spent the night last night." I frowned. "I thought you knew that."

She snorted. "Like I care where Mason is when it's Asher's night."

"Oh, I'm glad you were okay with him spending the night, then. Because Asher gave me his cell number, your cell number, and the number at the hotel in case something happened to Mason. Asher wanted to make sure we had an emergency covered. Since he was at the venue, you know."

Jessica waved her hand. "So Asher stuck you with his kid while he did, what? Screwed some groupie in his hotel room?" She sat back, her mouth twisted in an ugly line. "Wouldn't be the first time."

Abbi shifted in her seat, the frown on her face fierce.

"He's cheated on you?" I asked.

"Of course he did. Asher likes sex. What man doesn't? He writes about his hookups." Jessica crossed her arms across her chest. She had cleavage, all plump and perfect. I wanted to cross my arms now to cover up my failings. Why would Asher want me when he was used to someone who looked like Jessica?

"So you proved his infidelity?" I asked. "Besides pictures with me. There are others? You do this often?"

"I'm the one who suggested Jessica have Asher followed," Dale said. "Unfortunately, you're the only woman he's been with."

I blinked, forcing my gaze toward his face. "Why would you do that?"

"I was in the process of going through a rather messy divorce myself. My wife—"

"Ex-wife," Jessica snapped. She softened the blow by taking his hand and placing it high on her thigh.

Dale cleared his throat. "My ex-wife was much more amenable to the settlement once she knew I was having her tailed."

I raised my eyebrow, eyes dropping to his thumb caressing her trim leg. "That's why you're cheating on him?" I asked. "To get even?"

Jessica waved her hand. "It's not like Dale and I are a secret. My marriage to Asher has been over for years. I'd've left him sooner, but I needed leverage."

"Jessica," Dale murmured.

"What's she going to do? Run to Asher's lawyer? I may not always be the best mother, but Asher promised to take care of me. He hasn't, not like he said he would. I deserve my share of the money. I've raised Mason while Asher is off fucking his way through groupies."

"I'm sure the judge will have an opinion on that," I said, trying to keep my voice neutral.

"You don't understand what it was like. He's just a new, exciting flavor for you. He'll leave to tour because that's what he loves."

"I've known him for years. Long before you ever met him," I said.

Jessica narrowed her eyes. Ah, so she wasn't good with research. I considered adding more but decided I didn't want that on Abbi's video.

"He dumped you then," she decided. "Just like he left me alone for weeks, sometimes months at a time. The worst was with the crying babies."

"He was home after you had the kids," I said. "Didn't you ask him to leave? You wanted him to tour."

She glared. Dale's pale eyes turned assessing. I might be quiet, introspective, but those traits didn't make me weak or stupid.

"When I met Asher, I thought he'd give me financial security. Growing up like I did, you learn the power of money. Not something you'd understand."

"My sister and I went hungry for weeks until my mother came to get us. I'm well versed in hunger."

"Then you should help me." Jessica sat forward, her face animated. "If you were to mention Asher's pill problem, then I'd get custody of Mason."

"I've never seen Asher take any pills," I said. "Why do you want Mason?"

She preened like a cat with a fresh-caught mouse. "I'd be in charge of Asher's visitation days."

"And that matters because?"

Jessica leaned back, her eyes shuttering. I caught Abbi's panicked eye. She didn't have a lot more video time.

"I'm sure lots of places would like those pictures I have of you two."

"You can sell them, sure." I stood, unable to banter any longer. This wasn't working. "But all this does is hurt Mason."

Jessica tossed her hair back over her shoulder. "Mason's fine. He'll continue to be fine."

"Look, this is pointless. Asher's a good man, Jessica. He's still hurt about Olivia's death. He was willing to stick it out with you, to help you get beyond that. He tried. You didn't."

Jessica stiffened, her breathing escalating. "Don't bring up my daughter."

"What happened to her is tragic," I said. "But that doesn't mean you get to rip Asher apart about it forever."

"I said don't talk about her!" Jessica shrieked. "You have no idea what it's like to have a child die in your arms."

"Calm down," Dale said, his eyes darting around. People had turned toward us. Dale waved apologetically.

"Don't tell me to calm down! Everyone thinks he's so amazing. He's always been so damn selfish. He was supposed to help me with the babies. He'd done it every night for months, but that night, he went to bed. She wouldn't stop crying."

Jessica put her face in her hands. Dale stood and wrapped his arm around Jessica's waist, but he looked just as lost as I was.

"It's his fault. He promised to make my life better. He promised."

Jessica pressed her face into Dale's neck. He and I stared at each other for a long moment, me trying to breathe through the horrible realization blooming in my mind.

"Let's go, honey," Dale said.

Briar slid next to me. She tilted my head back, and I looked into her stormy eyes. "Breathe, Dahlia," she murmured just for my ears.

"In her arms?" I rasped.

"What?"

I forced down the panic and breathed deep. Calmer, I said, "Asher told me Olivia died in bed with him, but Jessica just said she was holding her when she died."

Ella put her arm around my waist. "Babies don't suffocate while being held." Her voice was scratchy. She was trying hard to maintain her emotions, just as I was. Briar's eyes widened as she processed Ella's comment.

"Holy hell," Briar whispered.

"Did you video tape it?" I asked Abbi. My chest hurt, and I rubbed at the ache, trying to focus through the discomfort.

She nodded, her face pallid.

"I did, too," Briar said.

"Bri, find out anything you can about Olivia Smith. Call Mom. She still works in hospital records, right? Have her go in and pull the autopsy. Use your media credentials if she gets difficult. We need to send whatever they have on Olivia to Asher's lawyers before the hearing tomorrow."

"On it," Briar said. She pressed the screen on her phone and stepped away. Ella sat me down before taking the chair next to mine. She gripped my hand. Abbi sat on the other side.

"She said some horrible things," Ella said. "They don't sound like Asher at all, love. She's determined to rip him apart, deserved or not."

"It's a divorce," I said. "They don't bring out the warm fuzzies between a couple."

"She's angry and wants to hurt Asher," Abbi said, her jaw thrust out in that stubborn tilt.

"She didn't say anything I wasn't already worried about." I closed my eyes, thinking back to last night. To the night he'd told me about Olivia. To yesterday morning when he spun my daughter around, sang her happy birthday. "I'm going to trust him. That he means what he's said to me."

"He loves you, Mom. Even I can see that."

Briar walked back and settled into the same chair as me. I scooted over to make more room for her.

"We got lucky. Mom was in the office. She remembered the case. It was in the paper when it happened. Media sued for details, so she wasn't really providing anything that wasn't in the public record."

"But I never read anything about it," I said, mystified.

"Someone was willing to bury it," Briar said with a frown. "Maybe Asher had a hand in it."

The panic swelled again at the thought of Asher hiding the details of his baby's death to protect Jessica. Ella clapped the back of my head and shoved my head between my knees. "Breathe!" she yelled.

I would have laughed at her if I wasn't in such bad shape. We were making a huge scene in the middle of a five-star hotel.

I slapped Ella's hand off my head and looked at my sister. I cleared my throat, certainty settling over me. Asher didn't know. He loved Mason, and I was sure he'd loved Olivia just as much. He'd wanted to leave Jessica then, and he definitely would have if he'd known Jessica's part in this situation.

"Tell me," I demanded.

"They did an autopsy, of course. She definitely died of suffocation. There's more—time of death, a few fragments of cotton fibers from her nasal passages. That kind of thing."

———◆———

"Asher buried it." I was certain he did. "The story. I bet he buried it because he thought it would hurt Jessica more. He said she had postpartum depression." I rubbed my hands up my arms. "I bet he didn't even look at the results. I bet the police didn't push it once the idea of accidental suffocation was suggested. I mean, he's still torn up about it."

And always would be. He'd told me he wasn't sober for months afterward. He wouldn't question what the people around him told him. What his wife, who'd been awake, told him.

The four of us sat there, stunned.

I looked at my sister and sister-in-law. "You know what that means?"

They nodded, looks of revulsion on each of their faces.

"He doesn't know." I swallowed. "He doesn't know he covered for Jessica's crime."

Briar looked thoughtful. "It was easy to cover up, I bet. Babies die in the family bed all the time. Sad but fairly common."

"Don't tell him," Abbi suggested. "The truth will just hurt him."

"I have to, Abs. This is the information he needs to get custody of Mason."

"But at what cost?" Abbi whispered.

"I don't know. But he deserves the truth."

I stood, forcing my wobbly legs to accept my weight. It was after two. Asher was already in the meeting with Pete for the hearing tomorrow. I pulled out my phone, trying to ignore the anger surging through me. I didn't want to do this. I didn't want to be the one to tell him. And over the phone—that was so cold, so impersonal.

"Send the video to me and Asher," I said.

"Shouldn't you go see him?" Briar asked.

"Not yet. He'll need to process this. He's going to be angry. So hurt."

"Exactly why you should go," Ella said.

I met their eyes, each in turn. "What if he thinks I was willing to help Jessica?" I whispered. Fear clawed deep in my chest. "I didn't tell him about meeting her today. All anyone's ever done is sell him out. Lie to him." I let go of my hair once I realized I was pulling it. "This is the worst betrayal. And I-I'm part of it."

"He's going to need you," Ella said.

She was right. I wanted Asher to trust me with his pain as much as I trusted him.

"Let's drive over there while the video sends," I suggested.

It took a while for the video to come through because it was such a big file. Abbi had to use Dropbox to send a link. I had her send it to my e-mail account and Briar's as well. Just to make sure we kept copies.

"Bri, I need the date of the autopsy."

While Briar ran through the records sent to her e-mail, I typed a text to Asher.

Jessica asked to meet with her today. I know I should've told you when I got her text. I'm forwarding it now. I didn't want to tell you she knew about last night. I wanted to keep it ours. Because what we did, what I hope we have, is so special to me.

You have to know I had no idea what she'd tell me. I don't want you to miss this chance to keep Mason safe. I'll explain the rest when I get there.

A minute later, my phone rang. Asher's name flashed on the display. I stared, my chest aching.

"You have to talk to him," Ella said. My hands shook as I pressed the Accept button. I clambered in the passenger's side of the car, my chest still locked in a vise. I couldn't believe I was upright, working through the anxiety. But I had to. For Asher and Mason, I had to fight back against my own weaknesses and fears.

"What is all this?" Asher asked. He sounded out of breath.

"The information you need to make sure Jessica can't dictate the terms of the divorce," I said.

"But how did you get this?"

"Jessica asked to meet me at her hotel. She wanted me to tell people you're using drugs in exchange for not sharing photos she has of us together last night."

Asher's curse was vicious. I tightened my hand on the phone. If he was upset by that part... "I had Abbi and my sister videotape our conversation." I swallowed hard then forced the words out. "She admitted to being alone with Olivia. It's toward the end. The rest is fairly self-explanatory."

"You think she hurt Olivia?" he asked, his voice cracking at her name.

"It doesn't matter what I think," I whispered. I waited a beat. "I'm so sorry, Asher."

"She said it was me, that I must have rolled over on her or something. That's what they wrote in the paper." He sounded so lost, confused.

"You didn't do anything wrong, Asher."

"I left my kids alone with a woman who killed one of them," he rasped. The pain in his voice was so vast it flowed through the phone. Briar's hand was on my shoulder, rubbing in gentle circles.

"I have more information," I said, my voice rushed. I needed to tell him all of it. "Dale sent me nasty e-mails after our coffee date that I'll forward to you. I never answered so they switched tactics, I guess. And there's a woman in records. Her name is Lesley Jennings. She's pulled the autopsy information for you."

Asher inhaled sharply. "I can't talk to you anymore," he said, his voice strained. "I have to talk with my lawyer."

"I want to help you," I whispered.

"Not yet, Dahlia. God. I just—not yet."

I swallowed down the thick lump of emotion ripping through my throat. "Bye, Asher." The phone fell into my lap. The screen was black. He'd hung up. Shut me out.

Ella patted my fist. "He'll want to see you when he picks up Mason later," she said, and she turned the car around to drive to her house.

After we pulled up to Ella's place, Briar opened my car door, Abbi flanking her. I hated the look in my daughter's eyes. She was growing up too fast.

"Abigail. I'm so sorry you had to hear this."

"Me, too. But Asher will be okay. He's going to keep Mason."

I held my daughter tight as my insecurities swirled through my head, now in Jessica's voice. We were so different—our needs, our futures. Still, I waited for him, phone in hand.

Because this wasn't my pain. It was Asher's. And I had to comfort him when he needed me. Even though I didn't know how to walk

284

him through this. And I couldn't imagine him wanting to be with the person who'd delivered the news of such a devastating betrayal.

CHAPTER THIRTY-TWO
Asher

I played the video, wishing I could stay numb. Instead, my stomach knotted and sweat broke out along my upper lip.

Pete slapped his hand on my shoulder as a huge grin stretched his mouth. "Nailed her. Unfit. Oh, is she in for a world of hurt. I've been waiting to play hardball."

Mason. I needed to hold my son. He was safe. Dahlia and Abbi were there. They'd protect him. He needed protection from his own mother. The woman I'd married.

I lurched back from my chair, yanked my keys from my pocket.

"Where are you going? We need to get the autopsy report and discuss how we're moving forward with your assets."

"I need Mason." I walked out of the room, ignoring Pete's calls. Fuck, my chest hurt. Instead of seeing Mason's face, Olivia's wispy brown hair and big, hazel eyes filled my thoughts. She'd slept with her mouth parted, bottom high in the air, the same slight cleft in her chin I had. Sure, Olivia hated to fall asleep, but she awakened smiling and laughing.

I missed her.

Jessica smothered the life out of my baby girl. And I'd stayed with her, slept next to her in our bed, left her alone with Mason.

Bile rose fast, and I vomited at the base of a tree. Pushing off, I continued to my car, ignoring my clammy skin.

Olivia had been five months old when she died. Just five months. If I'd hired Mrs. Knowles sooner like my mom wanted, maybe... I tried to breathe through the vise clamped around my lungs. This was how Dahlia felt most of the time. The pain was unbearable.

Too big.

Dahlia. I was angry with her, too. She'd gone to see Jessica. I didn't want Dahlia near my ex-wife. I didn't want Dahlia to see me this broken. I wanted the blessed relief of Percocet and a bottle of whiskey.

But I needed Mason more.

I needed Dahlia, too. She'd calm me down, just as I did her.

I pulled into Simon's driveway and leaned my head against the steering wheel, trying to get my shit together enough to knock on the door.

A shadow fell across the window. Dahlia. She looked uncertain, her eyes filled with an agony that answered my own. She knew about betrayal. She'd lived it with her husband. But this—this was so much worse, and we both knew it.

I opened the door and stepped from the car.

She backpedaled, giving me space, but her eyes never left my mine.

"I love you, Tristan Asher Smith. No matter what the papers say about us or what your ex-wife tries to do. And I'm sorry—*so* sorry—that I had to be the one to tell you. For all you're going through now."

"Fuck," I said through gritted teeth. "I needed to hear that. So bad." I pulled her into my arms, dipping my knees so Dahlia's head nestled in her spot where my shoulder met my neck. "I feel like it's breaking me apart."

"Because it is," she whispered. Her arms tightened around my waist, her fingers digging hard into my back. "I hate that I had to tell you, Asher."

Tears spilled down my cheeks. I'd never cried for Olivia before. I'd been too shocked, then too hammered. Years of tears I hadn't known I'd had in me poured down my cheeks. The pain eased in small increments as I bawled out the poison into Dahlia's long, auburn hair. She held me, her grip firm, and her patience endless.

"Mason. I need him."

"He's in the backyard with Simon and Jeremiah. They're having a tree-climbing contest."

I scrubbed my hands over my face, up into my hair. I had to look worse than a beaten, three-legged dog.

"Come in. Wash your face, then we'll go get Mason."

"I hurt you. Now and earlier." I leaned against the car, pulling her with me. She settled against me, and the pain was manageable. Still huge, but Dahlia was in my arms. She understood. She'd help me through.

"Not intentionally."

"But I did. Simon told me you were dealing with your own shit and not to drag you into my steaming pile." I opened my gritty eyes and met her gaze, which filled with trepidation.

"You've never been selfish with me," she said. "You're in a bad situation."

I was so tired. Too many emotions in too short a time frame. From loving Dahlia last night to finding out about Jessica and Olivia… "You deserve better than this. Better than me."

She cupped my cheek. "I want you."

I shook my head, trying to clear the fuzziness there. "I don't want to fuck up your life. Or Abbi's."

Her face froze, her eyes broken shards of moonlight, as her breathing escalated. "What are you saying?"

"I need to get my shit together." I leaned back against my car and closed my eyes, trying to block out Olivia's plump, sleep-warmed cheeks.

"Okay."

I frowned, wondering at the thread of distress in Dahlia's voice. "I just need to get Mason. These next few days are going to be rocky."

Dahlia nodded, her eyes dulled. "Mason comes first."

CHAPTER THIRTY-THREE
Dahlia

As soon as Asher gathered up Mason's things, he left. He didn't come back that day. Not that any of us expected him to. But when he didn't call the next day, my anxiety spiked again.

"My boss asked me to get the scoop on you and Asher," Briar said late that afternoon. She'd stuck around the house, not mentioning Ken at all. If I wasn't so worried about Asher's mental state and Abbi missing school just before finals, I would have questioned her on her desire to stay with me.

She looked as wan and tired as I did. Simon and Ella were at work, but they'd both been pinch-faced and unhappy when they left that morning. Only Abbi was holding firm in her belief that everything would work out.

"His divorce is pretty sensational, and you're caught in the middle," Briar said. "Maybe you should head back to Rathdrum."

"I'm not leaving him," I said, setting my jaw against the need to cry. "You all said it. He needs me right now."

Abbi gripped my hand, but even her optimism dimmed a little as another day passed.

———

He called me, two days later. "We're still in divorce hell. We needed experts, and all kinds of people had to testify. Jessica's screaming you and I set her up. You're in that video, Dahlia. Her lawyers are using that. It's going to get worse."

"How's Mason?" I asked, refusing to acknowledge his other

comments.

"Mrs. Knowles has been amazing. She's stayed here at my apartment with him. Kept him from all this. But he wants to see Abbi and Jeremiah. He asked for your waffles."

"I'd make him some. How are you?" I asked.

"No, don't. The media's trying to find him and you. I don't want this to get bigger."

We were quiet. I didn't know where to steer the conversation, my anxiety ratcheting with each breath.

"I miss you," I said, needing him to know.

"Yeah. Same goes."

Another long break.

"Thank your sister for me," he said. "The fact her paper's carrying the same headlines as usual is a relief."

"She wouldn't capitalize on our relationship. Not even to sell more papers."

"She's the only one then." Bitterness crept into his voice. "Look, Dahlia. My lawyers advised me to not be seen with you for a while. The shit storm is just starting, and I'm the center. Why don't you go home?"

I dragged in a ragged breath. "That's what you want?" I asked.

"I can't come see you. So that makes the most sense. Abbi's close to finals. She needs to be there for those. You can finish your book, and I…" Asher swallowed hard. "I need to deal with my shit."

Arguments died on my lips. "If that's what you want," I managed to choke out.

"What I want and what I have to do are at odds. I've just got to clear this up. Then I can see straight again. God, I miss her."

His grief broke my resistance. Fighting with Asher wasn't going to help either of us, and it definitely wouldn't help him grieve his daughter. I couldn't stay in Seattle another night.

Abbi and Briar drove me home. I sat in the backseat, dazed and nauseous, praying Asher would call me.

He didn't.

———◆———

We got home that night after a mostly silent, painfully long car ride. The next few days were brutal for all of us. Briar still hadn't told me why she'd broken it off with Ken The Asshole yet, and I didn't push. She moped around, just as miserable as I was. Worse, her boss had given her an ultimatum: write all the dirty details of my relationship with Asher, or she was fired.

After multiple arguments where I begged her not to give up her job, she took the pink slip. "Don't you dare tell me you're sorry," Briar said, her eyes as fierce as Abbi's were whenever she said Asher would call. "I'm a big girl, and I won't be forced into putting a story before my family. You're the only one I could really count on for years, Lia. Let me do this for you."

I hugged her hard. She hugged me back. Our tears mingled.

"Thank you," I whispered.

I called Asher, needing to know he was okay. That the story I'd helped break was worth it, that he was getting to keep Mason. He didn't answer the phone, and he didn't call back.

I asked Briar to move in. She stayed in the room Asher had slept in. I hated giving it to her, but it was the bigger guest room and she'd been fired for my sake. It would be best for both of us to have her here.

———◆———

"How was school?" I asked Abbi. It was her first day back since we left Seattle.

"Shitty," she said, scowling. "There were a couple of reporters there, and all the kids swarmed me, wanting to know the details of the video. It's all over the Internet."

"I'm so sorry, Abbi. What can I do?"

She shook her head. "Nothing. In fact, it's better if you stay away. Sheriff Lindon's going to take me to school tomorrow and stay on campus. Even Luke's being all nice and keeping the reporters away from me."

"So are you getting back with Luke?"

Abbi snorted. "No. He dumped me."

"I wish I could do something for you," I said. "Make this easier."

"Much as today sucked, I think you're in worse shape. You didn't sleep last night, Mom."

"I'm worried about Asher and Mason," I admitted.

"He'll call. When he can." I no longer had my daughter's faith, but I hated saying it out loud, especially when she had her hand wrapped around the pendant Asher had given her.

The next morning, I suggested Abbi stay home. She shook her head. "I have a final today. I have to go."

I let her climb into Ralph Lindon's patrol car, feeling lost and impotent. I hadn't helped Asher, just blown up his life in the worst way, and now my daughter was dealing with the fallout.

Twenty minutes later, Briar bustled into the kitchen. "I'm borrowing your car. I have a meeting with the editor in Spokane."

"Good luck with that," I said. I smiled, hopeful that Briar's future was improving. Maybe she'd stay here and I'd get to see her more often, a silver lining in the mess I'd made of my life.

After waving Briar off, I locked myself in my office. This time, the words poured out of me. All the fantasies with Asher I would never have filled page after page.

The longing for what could have been pulled at me, ate me up until I wrote it down. In just two weeks, I'd finished the last book. The Gardiner series was complete.

I clicked send on the e-mail to Bev, trying not to think about the three weeks since I'd last seen Asher.

Abbi knocked on my door. "Phone's for you."

"I'll call whoever it is back tomorrow."

"Take the phone, Mom."

I put it to my ear with reluctance. "Hello."

"Dahlia."

My heart raced, my vision tunneled. "Asher."

"I need to see you."

"Um."

"Hey, breathe. You can. Just breathe. I'm right here."

"I'm okay." I managed to wheeze.

"I'm worried about you."

I should be worried about him. He'd just gone through one of the most traumatic periods anyone could experience, and he'd done it pretty much alone. I hated that. So much.

"I want to see you. Please." His voice was still tired.

The panic gave way to a flutter of something. Not hope, but need. I needed to see him again. I'd always need him.

"I can meet you this weekend," I said. "Just tell me where."

"I'll be there in an hour." He hung up.

What? No! I was in the same pajamas I'd been wearing for... I didn't know how long. I'd dumped coffee down my front at some point. Had I brushed my teeth recently?

I pushed up from my chair. I didn't have time to panic. I needed a shower. Asher couldn't see how bad my wallowing had been.

"What are you doing?" Abbi asked from the doorway. She sounded just like I used to when she was doing something crazy.

"Asher. An hour. I need... clean."

Abbi wrinkled her nose. "Yeah. You've smelled funky for a while."

Only when I was in the shower did I realize Abbi hadn't been surprised that Asher was coming.

I shaved my legs and washed my hair and body in record time. I got out, dried off, considering Abbi's reaction. Asher hadn't said what, exactly, he wanted to see me about.

What if Abbi wanted to go on tour with him? They'd gotten close during the time they'd spent together. How could I keep her from the closest person she had to a father?

I wriggled into my underwear and bra, my hair wrapped toga-style.

"Here, wear this," Abbi said, tossing a dress at me. I swiped it from the air and clutched it to my chest.

"You've been talking to him, haven't you?" I asked.

"Yeah."

"Oh, Abbi. I'm so sorry you had to go through this. I would do anything so you don't hurt like I do."

Abbi rolled her eyes. "First, I'm not mourning the end of a relationship. I think you're the only one doing that. Second, Asher's here. I'm going to send him up in a minute. I suggest you put that dress on and comb your hair."

I sank onto the bed, unable to get beyond my fear he was going to break up with me. "I can't see him," I whimpered.

"Yes, you can. You have to. He wants to see you. Bad. He needs it, Mom. So do I. Dress on. Hair. Now." She pulled the towel from my hair, causing me to wince when the towel caught on some of the strands.

"Where's Briar?"

"She drove to Spokane to start that freelance gig this morning. Don't you remember?"

I didn't. I'd been so spacey. "That wasn't an hour," I said, feeling hollow.

"Nope. I wouldn't let him call until he was actually here. That way you couldn't run away." She turned and opened the door. Asher stood there, in my hall, trying to peer around Abbi. With a yelp, I ran to the bathroom and slammed the door.

"She'll be out in a minute," Abbi said loud enough for me to hear through the door. The rest of what she said was too muffled for me to catch, and my heart beat too loud for me to hear anyway. I pulled the brush through my hair in quick, jerky strokes.

I forced my shaking fingers to unwrap the tie on my dress. Putting it on, I retied the bow. Anxiety pummeled my chest. The mirror reflected a pale, hollow-cheeked version of my face. Dark shadows circled my eyes.

There was a knock on the door. Soft. Just a knuckle. Asher was in my room. My knees turned to jelly.

———•———

He looked taller. No, he'd lost weight. I wanted to go to him, soothe him. I hadn't realized how much I needed to know I could calm him, too. The pain in my chest expanded, licking into my throat.

Asher's eyes slid from my mouth to meet my steady gaze.

"I was stuck in the divorce hearings. Your evidence both helped and also slowed the process. I had to finish the sound track, too, because we had the studio time all booked. Media's been a bitch."

My skin chilled, but I kept my eyes steady on his, hoping he wouldn't call my bluff.

"Social media is an amazing tool," he said. His fingers tapped his thigh. "Especially for my new hobby of cyber stalking."

I swallowed. This was it. We were over. At least he had the decency to tell me in person, unlike Luke who'd simply switched his relationship status on Facebook.

"Mmm."

"But you weren't on social media. And you haven't posted anything on your blog or updated your website. It's like you've been hibernating. You thought I was leaving you."

Thought? He had. For three weeks. Of course we were over.

"Dahlia, if I hadn't talked to Abbi—because you weren't even answering your e-mails—and found out why you thought I'd dumped you, I'd be really fucking angry."

"I turned off my Internet access after Briar left."

"Because of the media coverage?" he asked.

"In part. I didn't like seeing you so tired and alone. And I couldn't help myself—I kept going to the news sites to see what was happening."

He slid his hand up the back of my neck, cupping it in his long-fingered palm. My heart rate escalated, but not with panic. With need. I could see the image of me naked, that night, in his eyes. How I wanted this man.

I closed my eyes, trying to regain some semblance of calm.

"The pulse in your neck is going crazy. You're not having another panic attack, are you?"

Concern laced through his voice. He'd offered me the perfect out. I could lie and push off this conversation, but that wasn't fair to either of us. The one thing Asher and I had always had was honesty.

"N-no," I stuttered. I met his eyes. "Tell me the rest."

"Jessica caved. Finally. The evidence was too much. She told us Olivia wouldn't stop crying. She covered her mouth with a pillow until Olivia stopped. But by then, she'd quit breathing altogether."

He tipped my chin up, his thumb caressing the curve of my jaw. I gripped his arms, needing to offer something back, even if it was just my touch. "I'm so sorry."

"So am I. Olivia deserved better than she got. So does Mason. These past weeks have been hard on him. He's seeing a counselor." He ran his free hand through his hair, fear clouding his hazel eyes. "I thought I deserved more, too."

I stepped closer, our bodies nearly touching, drawn to him as I always was. "You do."

This might be the last time he ever looked at me. I stood up on my tiptoes and pressed my lips to his, showing him I cared about his pain. His other hand came to the far side of my waist, pulling me tight to his lean body. I'd missed this, him. My hands tangled into his too-long hair, pulling him closer as the kiss deepened.

Finally, I pushed back, my chest heaving.

"The record company contacted my agent this morning. The single we released last week—the one we did at the show with Simon—it's getting loads of airtime. Richard thinks it'll go platinum."

I grabbed his hand before I thought better of it. "You all deserve the recognition and success."

He linked our fingers together, pressing his palm tight to mine just as he had when we walked on the beach that first night in Seattle. Memories built in his eyes and longing welled up my throat, about to flood my face. I tugged my hand from his and turned away.

"I want you to be happy." I didn't like how small my voice was. I forced my gaze to his. "You've spent so long trapped in a situation you didn't create."

"Oh, I created it. Jessica was right when she called me selfish. I never loved her the way a woman deserves to be loved. She knew that, and she resented me for it. But once I found out she was pregnant with my kids, I planned to stick by her. It all came back to not wanting to be like my father. I just fucked up lots of lives in a different way."

I cupped his cheek. "You didn't fail your son or daughter, Asher. Your wife failed you when she didn't ask for help when she needed it. She failed you when she went too far and hurt your child."

He pressed his lips into my palm, and my breath caught, my chest heaving as I tried to inhale, but couldn't.

"Like Doug hurt you?"

"That's different."

"Yeah. But he hurt you. Bad."

I couldn't hold his gaze. My throat tightened. "He was something I needed. Once."

Asher dipped his head. We stood like that, our breath mingling.

"Abbi and I text throughout the day. She told me you finished the last book in the series. That's fucking amazing, Dahlia. I'm really proud of you."

"They're all about you," I said. "I couldn't stop wanting you, and it just kind of all came out."

"I'll be your muse anytime. Just as you've always been mine."

Much as I hated to, I disengaged from his embrace. My heart pounded. We stared at each other. I wet my lips and said, "You need time to grieve, to recover from your divorce."

He snorted. "That would be true if I'd done nothing but grieve since Olivia died. Sort of. I'm not saying it's going to be easy." He stepped closer. Held me like I needed. "But I *need* you. I wanted to be here sooner, but I had to stick around to finalize the settlement. Then Mason wanted to go to the camp Jeremiah's in for the next few weeks."

"Wow." Confusion and anger swirled through me. Ella hadn't said anything. Neither had Abbi.

That wasn't exactly true. They'd brought up Asher, and I'd changed the subject or walked out of the room.

"But you didn't answer your phone," I said.

"I was recording or I was in court. It was off."

"But you didn't call back."

"Abbi said you were writing. I didn't want to interrupt. Then you quit calling and I was worried. I knew I had to come here, tell you these things in person."

Asher slid his lips over mine, a gentle caress that eased the painful ache. I opened my lips so I could kiss him the way I needed to. Our tongues met, and desire exploded. I gripped his hair just like I'd always wanted, while he slanted his mouth over mine, again and again. His palm rubbed over my breast.

I'd thought for years I was better off not feeling. I'd been so wrong. Every second with Asher was worth whatever pain came after.

A knock sounded on the door, and we broke apart.

"They do have impeccable timing," I said, struggling to catch my breath.

We glanced over his shoulder at Abbi. Her eyes danced with excitement. Mason peeked under her arm, and I was pleased to see he didn't seem angry or resentful.

"They do," Asher said.

"See, Mom. Asher loves you."

Mason slid under her arm. "Yeah, heaps. He told us so. Right, Abs?" Mason grinned up at her, his eyes greener than usual. He seemed happy. Moving away from his mom and his security would cause ongoing problems. The healing from the divorce was a process with better and worse days. But we could get him through this. I wanted to help.

Asher turned to face the kids. "We're trying to work out our living arrangement."

"I liked that room I stayed in before, and there are horses. And we don't have a house anymore. Dad gave it to my mom. But that's okay because I get to stay with Dad. Most of the time, anyway. And maybe you and Abbi."

I disentangled myself from Asher and went over to kneel in front of Mason. "You're always welcome here." I brushed his brown hair off his brow. I bet Asher looked similar at his age. "I'd like to have you stay with me, with us, as much as you can."

The concern slid from his face and Mason beamed. "I brought a suitcase."

"I'll help you bring it in," I said.

"Already did." Abbi grinned. "I'm taking Mason to the diner in Asher's car. It's a freaking convertible. I hope we see Luke," she said. "He's going to be so jealous. C'mon, Mason."

"Can I get one of those buffalo burgers?" Mason asked as he skipped down the hall after her.

"Be careful," I called. I turned back to look at Asher, amusement building. "You bought a convertible?"

"I want to see your hair dancing around your head. Or better"—his voice dipped low—"you naked on the hood."

My eyes stayed on Asher's as I gripped his biceps. I pressed my lips to his and thrilled when he cupped the back of my head.

"I love you, Dahlia Moore Dorsey. I'm going to love you forever."

"Oh."

"That's it? Aren't you supposed to be good with words?"

I took a deep breath. "From the moment I met you, I wanted to know you. But I think I fell in love with you when you sang me 'Moonshine Eyes.'"

"You do have a thing for being sung to."

"By you. You speak to me. Because I love you."

He grinned, one so full of life and happiness I had to grin back. He dipped his head and pressed a tiny kiss to the corner of my mouth. Heat slid through my chest, sliding down into my belly.

He loved me. He was here. I couldn't control my hunger for him anymore than I could stop breathing.

I caught my heel behind his knee and shoved him. He cursed as he fell back onto my big bed. I followed him down, landing on his pelvis and then his chest.

His eyes gleamed bright. I tangled my fingers through his silky hair again and leaned down so that my lips were barely an inch from his.

His neck strained trying to reach my mouth, but I leaned back so I could nibble my way to his ear and that spot I'd found. He rolled over.

"I'm taking you here, right now," I muttered.

He slid his hands down my arms until our fingers were entwined. "I like the way you think."

"You'll like the way I act more," I said.

"Keep it coming. I got plenty of ever-after to work on."

ACKNOWLEDGMENTS

So many people to thank for this book! This one was fun (and steamy!) to write. LERA ladies and gentlemen, you're welcome. And thanks for being so supportive, for making me love writing again and for sharing your knowledge so freely. You are the best.

As always, thank you, Chris. Your unwavering support and love shine through in all you do. I'm me because you're you. To my family, thank you for your love and the patience to let me write.

To Nancy, thank you for your eagle-eyed editing services. I hope you're proud of where we ended up.

To Nicole, thank you for the advice on Seattle and the fantastic copy edits that make the story shine.

To Clarissa, once again the cover is gorgeous. I love working with you.

To my AuthorLab writing pals: You keep me on task and keep me motivated. I love seeing what you write. And I love how diverse our group is.

And to my readers and reviewers. Thank you for your time. It's precious and I'm so, so glad you spent some of it with me.

ABOUT THE AUTHOR

With a degree in international marketing and a varied career path as a content manager for a web firm at the height of the tech boom, marketing director for a high-profile sports agency and a two-year stint with a renowned literary agency, Alexa Padgett has returned to her first love: writing fiction. She is a card-carrying member of RWA, or would be if Romance Writers of America had cards. She's also a member of Land of Enchantment Romance Authors (LERA), and Fantasy, Futuristic, and Paranormal (FF&P) chapters, where she's met fabulous writers. She aspires to be as witty and kind as her writing family is.

Alexa spent a good part of her youth traveling. From Budapest to Belize, Calgary to Coober Pedy, Alexa soaked in the myriad smells, sounds, and feels of these gorgeous places, wishing she could live in them all—at least for a while. And she does in her books.

Alexa loves to read, especially her friends' stories. She also spends a great deal of time in her tiny kitchen, channeling her inner Barefoot Contessa.

Write her at alexa@alexapadgett.com or sign up for her newsletter to receive notifications for upcoming books and exclusive excerpts. You can also find her on Facebook or follow her on Twitter (@AlexaPadgett).

ALSO BY ALEXA PADGETT

Between Breaths, Book Two in the Seattle Sound series

She's the harmony he can't get out of his head.

Hayden Crewe took a leave of absence from his high-flying band for one reason: His dying mother summoned him. Not that they're close. He doesn't like to think about her. But he's not one to shirk his duties, no matter how much she did.

Briar Moore's summer is spinning out of control. She was fired, her boyfriend betrayed her, and her best friend's in hospice. The last thing she needs is more drama. Or to fall for Hayden Crewe.

Hayden and Briar crash into an affair as brief as it is intense. In less than a week, he's gone, back to his band tour, leaving Briar to deal with the media's speculation and a broken heart. Briar picks up the pieces and moves on. It's either that or give up altogether.

For once, Hayden's music doesn't offer the escape he craves. His band's tour stretches out for months—but all Hayden wants is to wrap Briar up in his arms. Where she belongs. And where he can never have her again. Back in his arms. Where she belongs.

The Spirit Seducer, **Book One in the Echo Series**

A god undone by prophecy. A warrior strong as the earth. And the woman who will decide their fate...

The dream comes every night: A warrior clad in leather and wielding a spear, fighting off demons with the heads of jackrabbits and pumas. Defending her.

Echo Ruiz knows it's ridiculous. There's no one in Santa Fe less likely to need defending. She's confined to her mother's house. Her Native American Studies classes are online, and she hasn't made a new friend in a decade.

Until her twenty-first birthday party, when Coyote himself shows up. An hour later, Echo is on the run from the power-hungry trickster god. Her headaches are gone. Her mother is a hostage, and she's been thrust into a mirror-world of deadly loveliness to fight or die alone.

Except for her dream warrior, who's as real as the sweat on her skin. His name is Zeke, and he remembers a lot more about Echo than she does about him.

But if Echo wants to defeat Coyote—if she wants to survive—she'll have to discover the way herself. Because that's one ending the legends have never told...